HEART OF GOLD

Robin Lee Hatcher

THOMAS NELSON
Since 1798

NASHVILLE DALLAS MEXICO CITY RIO DE JANEIRO

Published in Nashville, Tennessee, by Thomas Nelson. Thomas Nelson is a registered trademark of Thomas Nelson, Inc.

Thomas Nelson, Inc., books may be purchased in bulk for educational, business, fund-raising, or sales promotional use. For information, please e-mail SpecialMarkets@ThomasNelson.com.

Publisher's Note: This novel is a work of fiction. Names, characters, places, and incidents are either products of the author's imagination or used fictitiously. All characters are fictional, and any similarity to people living or dead is purely coincidental.

Scripture is taken from the King James Version of the Bible.

Library of Congress Cataloging-in-Publication Data

Hatcher, Robin Lee.
Heart of gold / Robin Lee Hatcher.
p. cm.
ISBN 978-1-59554-488-9 (trade paper)
I. Title.
PS3558.A73574H43 2012
813'.54--dc23
2011044566

Printed in the United States of America

12 13 14 15 16 17 QG 6 5 4 3 2 1

Fire tests the purity of silver and gold,
but the LORD *tests the heart.*

—PROVERBS 17:3 NLT

PROLOGUE

JANUARY 1864

Covington House, Virginia

"Am I doing the right thing, Adelyn? Is this truly God's will for us?"

Delaney Adair didn't believe his dearly departed wife could hear his words or read his thoughts in heaven. Nothing in Scripture led him to believe she could. But it always seemed to clear his head when he "talked" with her this way, the same way they had talked over everything—matters large and matters small—throughout their marriage. Especially matters pertaining to their daughter.

"Shannon has grown even more beautiful than you remember her. She has a good heart. She likes to help others. But she is also quick to judge, even more so since the war began. I fear her pride will be her downfall. Perhaps I've spoiled her." He shook his head. "No, I know I've spoiled her."

Would his daughter forgive him for taking her away from Covington House, away from her friends and neighbors?

We'll have a new life in Grand Coeur. Shannon will make new friends. And there won't be so many reminders of a past that is gone for good. For her . . . or for me.

Despite the number of years that had passed since Adelyn's death, Delaney felt the loss of his wife afresh. How he missed her. How blessed he'd been in his choice of helpmeet. He'd married not only the woman he loved but an heiress. Adelyn, the daughter of a wealthy planter whose family's roots went deep into the Virginia soil, could have had her pick of a hundred young men in Southern society. That she'd chosen Delaney Adair, a second-generation American of modest means with a desire to serve God, still amazed him.

He let his gaze roam the room, remembering how lively and happy their home had been. Parties and barbecues and balls and hunts. Adelyn had been a perfect hostess, and she'd loved others, no matter their status, without discrimination or hesitation. Such a charitable heart. Such a perfect minister's wife.

I wish I knew what you would say to Shannon if you were here now, Adelyn. How would you counsel and guide her? How would you help her to make better choices? How can I help her learn to trust God with her future and to follow His will in humility?

"Yes, I have spoiled her. May God make up for my shortfalls and soften her heart toward others." He drew in a breath and closed his eyes. "Tender her heart, Lord. May she not be so quick to judge. May she not be so determined to stumble over a stool in her path that isn't really there. Fill her heart with love and let her know love in return. Take us safely across this country to our new home, and help us both to make a difference for Thy kingdom. Nevertheless, may Thy will be done. In Christ's name. Amen."

May 1864

Shannon Adair leaned close to the door as the stagecoach slowed, trying to catch her first glimpse of Grand Coeur, wanting it to be more than she had any right to hope it would be. She'd said good-bye to everything and everyone she loved in order to come with her father to the Idaho Territory. She was both scared and excited now that the dirty, bone-jarring, difficult, and sometimes treacherous journey was at an end.

The coach jerked to a stop, and the driver called down, "Grand Coeur, folks."

Shannon glanced toward her father, seated across from her.

The good reverend gave her a weary smile. "We are here at last."

"So it would seem."

The door opened, and the driver offered his hand. "Let me help you down, miss."

"Thank you." Shannon placed her gloved fingers in the palm of his hand. "You are ever so kind."

The driver bent the brim of his dust-covered hat with his free hand, acknowledging her comment.

Once out of the coach, she turned a slow circle, taking in her surroundings. Her stomach plummeted. This was Grand Coeur? Merciful heavens! It was not *better* than she'd hoped. It was *worse* than she'd feared.

The street they were on was lined on both sides by unpainted wooden buildings of various shapes and sizes. The boardwalks in front of the buildings were uneven, sometimes nonexistent. And the hillsides that surrounded the valley had been stripped clean of trees, undoubtedly for the wood used to throw up this ugly, sprawling gold-mining town of more than five thousand souls.

"Oh, Father," she whispered. "Whatever shall we do here?"

"Don't look so despairing, Shannon."

She turned to find her father had disembarked from the coach and now stood nearby.

"We knew it would be different from home," he said. "And we are needed here."

More than they'd been needed in the war-torn South, where he'd ministered to his flock and she'd been able to help nurse the injured?

As if he'd heard her unspoken question, he said, "I have always tried to answer God's call, even when I don't understand it completely. Would you have me do differently now?"

"No, Father."

The lie tasted bitter on her tongue. She *would* have him do differently. She would have him decide to go back to Virginia, to recognize that God wanted him to be there to help rebuild when the war was over. When the South no longer had to fight for its existence, the Confederacy would need men like her father. He was a natural leader with a head for governing and a heart for the kingdom of heaven. He was strong in his faith and able to forgive and show others the grace of God.

What on earth made him believe the Lord wanted him in such a place as this?

"Reverend Adair?" a voice called.

Shannon and her father turned in unison to see a rotund man in a black suit hastening toward them.

"Are you Delaney Adair?"

"Yes, sir. I am."

The man stopped in front of them and thrust out his hand. When her father took it, the man gave it a hearty shake. "We've been watching for you on every stage for the past week. Welcome. Welcome. We're glad you've come. I'm Henry Rutherford."

"It's a pleasure to meet you, Mr. Rutherford. May I introduce my daughter, Miss Shannon Adair."

"How do you do, miss?" Henry bowed in her direction.

She decided a simple smile and nod of her head would need to suffice. If she opened her mouth, she was certain she would say something disparaging about Grand Coeur.

"My wife's got the parsonage all ready for you. 'Course, it probably isn't what you're used to. Kinda small and plain. But we hope you'll be comfortable there, you and your daughter."

"I'm sure we will be," her father replied.

Shannon wasn't at all sure.

"I've got some men with me to help with your luggage." Henry turned and waved his helpers forward. The three men were a rough-looking bunch, with scruffy beards and weathered faces. Their trousers, held up by suspenders, were well-worn, as were the dirt-encrusted boots on their feet. The sleeves of their loose-fitting shirts had been rolled up to their elbows, revealing dark skin on their arms. Miners, she supposed, who spent every hour of daylight panning for gold in the streams and rivers somewhere nearby. At least that's how she'd been told it was done.

Shannon's father identified their trunks and one small crate, then he took hold of her arm at the elbow and the two of them followed Henry Rutherford down a narrow side street.

She saw the church first. Built on the hillside, its steeple piercing the blue sky, the house of worship had white clapboard siding, giving it an air of elegance in comparison to the mostly unpainted buildings in the town. There was even a round stained-glass window over the entrance.

Perhaps Grand Coeur was not completely uncivilized if the citizens had taken the time to build such a church.

Her moment of hope crumbled the instant Mr. Rutherford pointed out the parsonage. It was little more than a shack. Crude, cramped, and completely unsuitable.

Oh, Father. You cannot mean for us to live here.

Matthew Dubois opened the door of the Wells, Fargo & Company express office and stepped inside. At the far end of the spacious room, William Washburn looked up from the open ledger on the desk. The instant he recognized Matthew, he grinned.

"Well, I'll be hanged. Is that you, Matt?"

"It's me, Bill."

"You're not the new agent they sent?"

"I am."

William rose and came to meet him in the center of the office, giving his hand a hearty shake. "You tellin' me you're givin' up drivin' for the company?"

"Only temporarily."

William cocked an eyebrow.

"My sister's ailing and needs a place to stay—Alice and her son—until she's back on her feet. They don't have any family but me. She lost her husband in the first year of the war."

"Sorry to hear that. Right sorry."

Matthew acknowledged William's sympathy with a nod.

"Can't say Grand Coeur is the best place to bring a woman and young boy, but I reckon you already knew that."

Matthew nodded a second time. Over the years, he'd seen the ugly underbelly of more than one mining town between San Francisco and the Canadian border. He'd known Grand Coeur would be no better. But this was where his employer had sent him, so this was where he and his sister and nephew would live.

"Alice with you?"

"No. I don't expect her and the boy until the end of the week."

"The company told me they wanted a house for the new agent. Couldn't figure out why the spare room upstairs wouldn't do, but I guess it's 'cause of the family."

The comment needed no response from Matthew.

"Might as well show you the place." William turned toward the door leading into a back room. "Ray?"

A few moments later, a young clerk appeared in the doorway. "Yessir?"

"Mind things. I'll be back directly."

"Yessir."

"Come on, Matt. I'll show you where you'll be living."

The two men went outside. The Wells, Fargo coach was no longer in sight. Matthew's replacement driver had already taken it to the station to harness fresh horses for the journey back down to Boise City.

William motioned toward the east. "We'll go thisaway."

Matthew fell into step beside him.

"Your sister and nephew ought to be comfortable. The house is away from the center of the town. Up there on the hillside." He pointed as they turned a corner. "Bit quieter in the evenings, if you know what I mean."

He knew. The saloons did great business at night in a place like Grand Coeur, and the center of town could get rowdy. Better to keep his sister—an attractive widow in ill health—away from the eyes of men starved for female attention.

The street they were on carried them up the steep hillside. Up ahead and to his left, he saw a white church complete with steeple. Off to the right were a half dozen two-story homes. Doubtless the residences of the town's more prosperous citizens. And, surprisingly, it was to one of these houses that William took him.

"Bill, you don't mean this for us."

"I do, indeed." He took a key from his pocket.

"I won't be able to afford the rent."

"Yes, you will. The fellow who built it was killed 'fore he could move in. Company got the house, furnishings and all, for next to nothin'. Not sure how or why. Only know they're rentin' it to you for a song. Now I know who they sent, I reckon I know why they're doin' it. They don't want to lose you when the time comes for you to start drivin' again."

Matthew took pride in the job he did. He was one of the top drivers in the country. Maybe *the* top driver. If a freight company wanted their stage to get where it was going and get there on time with the cargo safe and secure, Matthew Dubois was their man. He could only hope he wouldn't be gone from the job so long that Wells, Fargo forgot they felt that way about him.

William opened the door and the two men entered the house. It wasn't unusually large. Nothing like the palatial homes of many of those who'd made their fortunes in gold and silver around the West. But it was more spacious than any place he'd lived before.

The downstairs had a front parlor, a small dining room, and a kitchen with cupboards, a butler's pantry, and a large stove. Upstairs there were three bedrooms and an honest-to-goodness plunger closet. He'd heard about such things. Just never thought he'd live to see one.

It ought to please Alice.

It would be nice to please his sister. He hadn't done much of that when they were younger. He'd been too stubborn and selfish back then, too determined to have a life of his own that didn't include watching after his baby sister.

If their mother was looking down from heaven, she had to be mighty disappointed by the choices he'd made in the years since her death. Maybe looking after Alice and her son, Todd, would make up for some of those poor choices.

Besides, he supposed a few months living in this house and working in the Wells, Fargo office wouldn't be too bad. He wasn't much for being in one place for long. He preferred wide-open spaces to towns with people packed in like cookies in a tin. But Alice would be strong and healthy before long. Then he'd be back on a coach, holding the reins of a team of horses racing along a narrow road, dust flying up behind him in a cloud.

The parsonage was clean. Shannon could say that for it. Mrs. Rutherford and the other respectable women of Grand Coeur had done their part to welcome the new minister in this way. And the house wasn't quite the shack she'd thought at first, although everything inside was most assuredly rustic and plain. The wooden floors had no rugs. The sofa and beds—donations from members of the congregation, no doubt—were lumpy. And the stove? Oh, mercy! The stove. How was she to prepare a proper meal on it? She was not the most accomplished cook, and until they found a servant who could—

Tears welled in her eyes, and she blinked hard to keep them from falling.

"Shannon, we must thank God for providing for us."

"Yes, Father." She took his hand, bowed her head, and closed her eyes.

"Almighty God, we thank Thee for delivering us safely to our new home . . ."

How would she survive in this horrible place? The people she'd met along the way were mostly uneducated, often dirty and unfamiliar with the basics of good hygiene, all too often gruff and rude. And the way they spoke. My lands! Their voices grated on her ears. She longed for the genteel sounds of her native Virginia. She longed for the gallant young men who had once courted her, riding their fine horses and wearing their fine clothes. But they were all gone now, off to fight in that dreadful war, so many of them dead on the battlefields, never to return. Even her Benjamin.

". . . and may we be a blessing to the people we meet, O God. Help us to be Thy servants and to think of others before we think of ourselves. In the name of Thy Son, Jesus, we pray. Amen."

"Amen," Shannon whispered, hoping her father wouldn't guess how far her attention had strayed during his prayer.

He gave her hand a squeeze before releasing it. "Well." He turned in a slow circle. "We had better make a list of things we'll need to buy at the store. From what Mr. Rutherford said, we can expect prices to be high, so we will need to be careful with our funds."

As if that hadn't been the way of things for the past three years. Once the war began between the North and the South, *if* one could find what one wanted to buy—which all too often one could not—it had come at a premium. But Shannon sensed the deprivation would seem worse in this horrid town in the mountains of Idaho Territory.

Why, oh why had God seen fit to punish her in this way?

Matthew pushed open the restaurant door and was immediately assaulted with the smell of fried foods, tobacco smoke, and the noise of utensils clattering against plates. William had told him Polly's was the best restaurant in all of Grand Coeur, and judging by the crowded dining room early on a weekday morning, he had to be right.

A slender youth approached. The boy was about fourteen, give or take a year, and had a white apron tied around his waist. "You mind sharing a table?" he asked. "We're pretty full up."

"No. Don't mind at all."

"Over here, then."

Matthew followed the boy through the collection of tables to one near the far wall. He recognized the two occupants immediately. The young woman's vibrant red hair—if not her pale beauty—made her unforgettable.

"Want coffee?" the boy asked.

"Yes, thanks."

As he pulled out the lone empty chair, the young woman looked up, her green eyes wide.

"Sorry, Miss Adair. Apparently it's the only place for me."

He could see she was even more surprised that he knew her name; her expression said she had no idea who he was or where they'd met. And why would she remember him? She hadn't given Matthew more than a passing glance when she and her father boarded the coach in Boise City yesterday morning, and it had been just as fleeting when he'd helped her disembark upon their arrival in Grand Coeur.

He looked at her father. "Reverend Adair, hope you don't mind."

"Not at all, sir. Glad to have your company. Mr. . . . ?"

Matthew removed his hat. "Matthew Dubois."

"I'm surprised you're still in town, Mr. Dubois," the reverend said. "I thought the stage returned to Boise yesterday."

"It did. Just not with me driving it."

"Ahh."

"I'm going to be working in the Wells, Fargo office in Grand Coeur for a while. And what about you, Reverend Adair?"

"Saint Stephen's Presbyterian Church was in need of its first minister, and I was called to fill the role."

Matthew nodded. "I figured as much." His gaze shifted to the reverend's daughter and back again. "You've come a long way?"

"From Virginia."

As he'd suspected, given the man's accent. "Things as bad back there as they say?"

"I should think they are much worse than they say."

"And you, sir." Miss Adair's voice was soft and as smooth as honey, but her words held a challenge in them. "Who do you support in this War of Northern Aggression?"

"I don't know that it rightly matters to me who wins, as long as they get things settled soon."

She reacted as if he'd slapped her; her eyes flashed with anger. "How can it not matter to you? Everyone in this country must place their loyalty with one side or the other."

"I've lived most of my life far west of the Mississippi. I figure it's none of my concern what's made folks back there mad enough to kill one another. They'll have to fight it for themselves. I'll take care of me and mine right where I live."

"That is a fool's way to think."

"Shannon!" the reverend said sharply.

She lowered her eyes. "I'm sorry, Father."

"My daughter is tired from our journey, Mr. Dubois. Please accept our apologies."

"No offense taken."

A glance in Shannon Adair's direction convinced Matthew that she wasn't the least bit repentant for her words—and he couldn't help but like her for it. A woman should know her own mind. Leastwise one who lived in a rough-and-tumble gold town.

But even with a mind of her own, he doubted Shannon Adair—or her father—would last long in Grand Coeur. If he were a gambling man, he'd wager the Adairs were from money and had a pedigree as long as his arm. Not the usual kind of folks drawn to this rugged territory.

The waitress arrived with Shannon's and her father's breakfasts and stayed long enough to take Mr. Dubois's order. Not that there were very many choices on the menu. One look at her plate told her that no matter what was ordered, it came with plenty of grease. Her stomach turned at the sight of it.

Oh, what she wouldn't give for some of her favorite breakfast foods, served to her on a tray in bed. She remembered that kind of lazy morning, back before the war, back before her mother died. Back when she'd believed her life in her small corner of the world would go on forever, just the way she liked it, just the way it always had been. Parties and barbecues and horseback rides and dances. Lifelong friends spending warm evenings together on the veranda. Leisurely after—

Loud shouts from the street brought Shannon's wandering thoughts back to the present. As her gaze turned toward the window at the front of the restaurant, several gunshots exploded. They sounded close. She drew back in alarm, her right hand covering her racing heart.

"Perhaps I should see if anyone needs help." Her father pushed his chair back from the table.

Matthew Dubois stopped him. "Better stay put, Reverend. You don't want to get caught in the cross fire if the argument isn't over."

"But someone could be wounded. They might need—"

"Tell you what." Matthew stood. "You eat your breakfast before it gets cold, and I'll see what's happened outside. I figure the sheriff will be out there already. I'll let you know if anybody's asking for a minister." He moved away from the table, wending his way through the busy restaurant with ease.

Shannon lifted her fork, then set it down again.

"Let's bless the food, Shannon."

"I'm not hungry."

Her father cocked an eyebrow.

She leaned back in her chair and crossed her arms over her chest.

"I've lost my appetite. The food is inedible and the company—" She broke off suddenly, knowing she'd gone too far.

Her father rubbed the gray beard on his jaw. His gaze was patient, but it revealed his disappointment. She hated that more than anything. Her father was the most important person in her life. He was all the family she had left now. And he was the kindest and best of men. In a country gone mad with war, his faith kept him strong. He never seemed to mind any hardship that came his way.

In that regard, she was nothing like her father. She missed everything she'd lost. She resented every hardship. And here, far from home, it only seemed that much worse.

"Shannon." He spoke her name softly. A gentle rebuke.

Tears sprang to her eyes. "I'm sorry. I will try, Father. I promise."

"I know you will, my dear." He folded his hands.

The restaurant door opened, allowing a puff of fresh air into the room along with Matthew Dubois. Shannon watched him make his way back to their table. He was a tall man with broad shoulders and strong-looking arms. So unlike too many Confederate soldiers who had become thin and wan for lack of decent food supplies.

Arriving at the table, Matthew removed his hat a second time and hung it on the spindle of his chair. "Nothing to worry about. Just a little disagreement between a couple of prospectors. No one was hurt."

"But the gunfire," her father said.

Matthew sank onto the chair, a slow grin curving his mouth. "They're both lousy shots. Lucky they didn't kill someone else by accident instead of each other. The deputy took them to his office to cool off."

Was everyone so blasé about gunfights on the streets of Grand Coeur, or was it only this man who found humor in it? But what else could she expect from someone like him? He was obviously no gentleman.

The waitress arrived and set a breakfast plate before Matthew.

"I was just about to bless the food," her father said the moment the young woman moved away.

Matthew nodded and bowed his head. A second later, Shannon did the same, even though she knew no amount of praying would make the hotcakes, sausage, and fried potatoes on her plate palatable. But, for her father, she would try to pretend otherwise.

Matthew felt a little sorry for the young woman to his right. If ever he'd seen a fish out of water, Shannon Adair was one.

He couldn't claim to know any genteel ladies of the South. Most of his acquaintances were good, plain, hardworking souls who'd come west to better their lot in life. He'd wager Miss Adair had never worked hard at anything besides deciding what color frock to wear to a party. No wonder she looked so unhappy.

As he ate his breakfast, he answered the reverend's questions as best he could, finally adding, "If you want more than general information about Grand Coeur and the area, I suggest you pay a visit to Bill Washburn over at the Wells, Fargo office. He's been here since not long after they found gold in these parts. He'll know the most trustworthy merchants in town and can steer you clear of the ones who'll rob you blind if you give them a chance."

"Are there many such people?" Shannon asked.

"No more than any other town that springs up during a gold rush." He set down his fork, his plate empty. "Time'll come when the gold plays out and the prospectors move on. Most of the saloons'll close, and then the folks who're left will decide if there's enough round here to keep a town going." His gaze shifted to her father. "They built you a fine church, Reverend Adair. Must mean there's a good number of God-fearing folks who mean to put down roots and stay after the boom is over."

"Will you be staying, Mr. Dubois?" the reverend asked.

"Me? No." He shook his head. "I'm not the kind of man to stay too long in one place. Once my sister, Alice, has regained her health, I'll be back to driving the coach. I don't reckon that'll be too long."

"I'm sorry to hear your sister is ill. Would she like me to come and pray for her?"

"I'm sure she would, but she isn't here yet. I expect her and her boy to arrive in a few days." He pushed back his chair from the table. "Thanks for your company. Time for me to get over to the office."

"It was our pleasure, Mr. Dubois. We look forward to seeing you again. Perhaps in church?"

Matthew grinned. "More'n likely, Reverend." He set his hat on his head, then bent the brim in Shannon's direction. "Good day to you, Miss Adair."

"Mr. Dubois."

The day seemed incredibly long to Shannon. No matter how much work she accomplished, it wasn't enough for her to feel settled into her new home. She feared it would never be enough for that.

Supper was over, the dishes washed and put away, and daylight still spilled through the parlor window. But her father didn't seem to notice the earliness of the hour. He rose from his chair, yawned, stretched, and then bid her good night. "Don't stay up too late, my dear."

"I won't, Father." She went to him, rose on tiptoe, and kissed his cheek.

At the click of his bedroom door closing, she went into her own room. It was no more than a quarter the size of her room at Covington House, the family home of her mother, Adelyn Adair. The only home Shannon had ever known. This room barely had enough space for the narrow bed, a wardrobe and dresser, and the writing desk that had somehow made it all the way across the country without serious injury.

She sat at the desk and ran the palm of her hand over the surface, treasuring the memories that sprang to mind. How many times over the years had she seen her mother seated at this desk, writing in her journal or penning letters to friends? The memory was enough to make her want to do the same. She had much to share with her dearest friend in all the world, and perhaps writing to Katie would help to ease the homesick feeling roiling in her chest.

My dear Katie,

I pray that this letter will reach you and that it will find you well. Father and I arrived in Grand Coeur yesterday afternoon. The journey here was perilous at times, just as we knew it would be. We were able to travel only a small distance by railroad as the Confederacy has greater need of its trains for transporting our soldiers and the wounded than to carry a minister and his daughter out of the South. The greatest portion of our trip was spent in a stagecoach.

My dearest friend, you cannot comprehend what that was like. Hundreds of miles in the confines of a carriage that is suspended on leather straps, rocking and swaying as three pairs of horses pull it as fast as they can. Every ten to fifteen miles, there was a station where we stopped and the horses were changed for fresh ones. Sometimes we were able to have a meal, but the food was barely passable anywhere. A few times there was word of Indians attacking stages along the way. I tell you, I was more in fear for my life once we were west of the Mississippi River than I ever was with Yankees threatening us in Virginia. And the dust. I felt it coating my tongue and teeth, day after day.

I was never so glad as I was to reach the end of our journey, although Grand Coeur is not a place I should like to live for long. It is rough and dirty and the inhabitants are equally so. Father has not changed his opinion, however. He believes God has called him here to serve these men and women.

Of the latter, there are not many. Perhaps two or three hundred women out of more than five thousand men. And as you might expect, too few of those can be called ladies. I shall not write more in that regard. I'm sure you understand. Still, there are some respectable, married people who call Grand Coeur their home. Very few, but some.

Shannon paused and read what she had written thus far. How gloomy she sounded. Shouldn't she try to offer some cheer to her friend? Katie Davis and her widowed mother hadn't had an easy time of it, and until the Confederacy ran the Union Army out of Virginia once and for all, things would not improve for the Davises or their neighbors.

She drew in a deep breath and continued writing.

All is not terrible here, Katie dear. I would not have you think so. There is beauty in these mountains, and Father has a fine church in which to serve. The people of the congregation used skilled craftsmen to build it. Our home is small but comfortable enough for two people.

I am not at all sure what I will do with my time now that we are here. There is no proper society. How I wish you and your mother could have come with us. It would be good to know that you are safe and well fed. Of course, you would like Grand Coeur no more than I do. Still, I wish my dearest friend was with me. Never in our lives have we been so far apart.

I already miss helping Dr. Crenshaw at the hospital. You know how much I admire Miss Nightingale and all she has done in the cause of nursing. I wonder if the day will come when nurses are no longer expected to be male or, if female, married women with gray hair. I should never have been allowed to do the things I did if not for the desperate situation brought about by war.

How will I be of use to anyone in this place? Father does not wish me to wander too far from the most acceptable areas of Grand Coeur, and I know I shall find that terribly confining. I shall have to change his mind slowly, but change it I shall. You know how stubborn I can be. Not the best of character attributes for a minister's daughter.

I was informed by a Wells, Fargo agent that their mail service between the West and the East has not met with much interruption over the past year or two. But he could not make any promise regarding letters going into the South. So I will pray that God will find a miraculous way for this letter to reach you. I send it with my love.

Your devoted friend,

Shannon Adair

The first few days of living in the small parsonage and trying to buy the things she and her father needed did nothing to improve Shannon's poor opinion of Grand Coeur. It was dirty and noisy. In the cool spring mornings a haze of smoke from woodstoves blanketed the mountain valley, and when it rained—as it had three days ago—the streets turned to a sea of mud. Worst of all, there were few people of quality with whom she might associate in this dreadful place. She felt trapped, like a wild animal in a cage.

Her father, on the other hand, seemed happier and more alive than he had in a long while. Last evening, seeing her disgruntled mood, he'd said, "'The harvest truly is plenteous, but the labourers are few; pray ye therefore the Lord of the harvest, that He will send forth labourers into His harvest.' We are those laborers, my child."

Shannon thought it patently unfair that he should use Scripture to chastise her. There was no way for her to respond except in agreement.

Late on Saturday morning, Shannon put her father's lunch into a basket and carried it over to the church. Before she reached the rear door of the building, she heard his voice, raised to be heard in the farthest corner of the sanctuary. Practicing his sermon, as he had every Saturday since before Shannon could remember.

She paused, allowing a memory to wash over her, picturing herself as a little girl, holding her mother's hand as they took her father's lunch to him, just as she did now. The warm air had been sweet with the scent of flowering trees, and the sky had been a sharp cloudless blue that almost hurt the eyes. Together, they'd sat down and laid out the food and waited as he ate it. The love her parents felt for each other had been a palpable thing, understood even by a child, and Shannon had felt warm and happy because of it.

How much she missed her mother. How she wished she was more like her. Despite Adelyn Adair's privileged past, she would have known how to make a proper home in this godforsaken place. And without a single complaint too.

Tears welled in Shannon's eyes, but she blinked them back. They did no good. Crying changed nothing. They hadn't kept her mother alive nine years ago, they couldn't bring her back now, and they certainly wouldn't change Shannon's basic nature.

With a deep sigh, Shannon continued on. When she reached the door, she opened it slowly, not wanting to make a sound. Not that it mattered.

"Come in, Shannon," he called to her as she stood in the small antechamber.

A soft laugh escaped her, chasing away the last remnants of sorrow. As she stepped through the doorway into the sanctuary, she said, "How did you know I was there?"

"A hungry man can smell warm cornbread a mile away." He came down from the raised pulpit and took the basket from her. "And what else is beneath that towel?"

"Cold ham and peas."

Although her father said nothing aloud, the look in his eyes spoke for him. Pleased over such a little thing. But he loved ham, and pork wasn't easily found in the South these days. Even when one could find a favorite food, it cost a small fortune. Why, white potatoes had been selling for twenty-five dollars a bushel when they left Virginia.

Shannon supposed that was one reason to be thankful for her father's call to this church. A wider variety of foods was available in the mercantile, and the butcher shop seemed well supplied. Prices were still high, but not as bad as back home.

Back home.

The very words caused her chest to tighten. Would they ever go back home again? Would they be able to return to Covington House and the life they'd known? Could she hope her father would change his mind after a few months in this town? Or at least when the war was over?

Her father led the way to the back of the sanctuary. There they sat in the last pew and he set the basket between them. After thanking God, he removed the napkin that covered his plate of food.

"Mmm. Just what I needed."

Shannon gave him a smile, knowing that was another thing he needed. He wanted to believe she was just as happy to serve the good people of Grand Coeur as he was. Her mother would have been. Oh, if only she were more like her mother.

"Shannon." Her father spoke her name softly.

"Yes?"

"'For I know the thoughts that I think toward you, saith the LORD, thoughts of peace, and not of evil, to give you an expected end.' God has a plan, a good plan, for your life."

"Yes, Father. I know."

"But we must act on our beliefs, dear girl. If you truly believe it, how can you resent that He has brought you here? It could be the very place that takes you to that expected end."

"I don't resent it, Father." She managed to make the words sound as if they weren't a lie. "I just . . . I just miss home. I miss the people I know and love." At least all of that was the truth. "Everything here is so strange, so . . . so . . . unrefined."

He reached out and gently touched her cheek, saying nothing. And yet in his silence saying so much.

I must try to do better. To be better. I will try.

Matthew stood on the boardwalk outside the Wells, Fargo office, looking east, waiting for the stagecoach to roll into sight. It was late by half an hour. He wasn't happy about that, no matter the reason. But since Alice and Todd were supposed to be on this stage, it made him anxious, a foreign feeling. Another quarter of an hour and he would get a horse from the livery and go looking for them.

As if in answer to that thought, he heard the jangle of harness and the thunder of twenty-four hooves striking the earth. A few moments later the horses came into view, the driver already drawing back on the reins, slowing them from gallop to canter to trot to walk. The coach bounced and swayed as it rolled to a stop right in front of him.

Before the driver could climb down from his perch, Matthew stepped off the boardwalk and opened the coach door.

Relief and alarm simultaneously shot through him when he saw Alice and her boy. Relief because they were in the coach and had arrived unharmed. Alarm because Alice looked far worse than he'd anticipated. But then, it was years since the two had seen each other. More than a decade. Maybe she was thin and pale by nature.

"Matt," she said, scarcely above a whisper.

"It's good to see you, sis. Been a long time." He held out his hand for her.

She ignored it, instead putting her hands on the boy's shoulders. "Matt, this is my son, Todd. Todd, this is your Uncle Matt."

The youngster looked a lot like his mother. He had the same dark brown hair, the same big brown eyes, the same small dimple in his chin.

"Howdy, Todd."

The boy shrank back against his mother.

Alice offered an apologetic smile. "He's tired. It's been a long journey."

"Well, let's get you out of this coach and up to the house. Then you both can rest."

This time when he offered a hand to his sister, she took it. He helped her disembark. Todd hopped down without aid, quickly taking his mother's free hand.

Matthew was about to ask the driver to take Alice's things inside the office for him to retrieve later, but William—who'd come outside—was one step ahead of him.

"You go on, Matt," his friend said from the boardwalk. "I'll make sure everything gets up to the house for you."

"Thanks, Bill."

As he guided Alice away from the coach, she asked, "Aren't you going to introduce me?"

"You can meet Bill later. Right now you need to lie down and rest. And you probably need something to eat as well."

"I'm not hungry. I won't be until the world stops rolling."

Come to think of it, she did look a bit green about the gills. Maybe that was the reason for her sickly appearance. He'd been driving coaches for so long he paid no attention to the rocking and swaying. Obviously his sister was not like him in that regard.

He shortened his stride, letting her set the pace as they left the main street of Grand Coeur and climbed the hillside toward the home they were to share. For a matter of weeks or for a number of months? He wasn't so sure which.

A knot formed in his stomach. He'd been nineteen years old the last time he'd stayed in one place longer than two or three weeks. He'd had a streak of wanderlust from the time he was a boy, and driving a coach for Wells, Fargo had been the perfect job for him. The company opened up new offices all the time. Wherever there was a new gold or silver strike. Wherever a town sprang up in the Rockies or in the deserts of the Southwest or along the Pacific Coast. And every time a new office opened, a new route was created. Over the past thirteen years, he'd seen just about every corner of the country west of the Mississippi River.

"How much farther?" Alice asked, bringing his roaming thoughts back to her.

He motioned with his head. "Not much. That's the house up there. Do you need to stop and rest a bit?"

"No." She shook her head. "I can make it that far."

Despite her refusal, Matthew stopped anyway. He put his right arm around her back at the waist and gripped her left forearm with his left hand. Then they continued the climb up the hillside.

What exactly is wrong with her?

He should have asked when she first wrote to him, but her letter hadn't made it sound like anything serious. Just that she'd been ill and needed time to recuperate. She'd been alone since the death of her husband, just her and Todd, no other family. She hadn't wanted to impose any longer on friends and neighbors in the small Wisconsin town where she'd lived with her husband until he went off to war.

Matthew feared his lack of curiosity—not to mention his lack of true concern—showed a serious flaw in his character. He hadn't been much of a brother to Alice up to now. Maybe he'd be able to atone for some of that while Alice and Todd were in Grand Coeur. He'd help her build up her strength, then he'd make sure she and the boy got settled wherever she wanted before he went back to driving a stage.

It seemed a good and reasonable plan for now.

Delaney walked along the forest path, hands behind his back.

"Adelyn, I am more certain than ever this is where God called us to be. But how do I help Shannon find her way in this new place? I fear she is as determined as ever to change my mind, to have me return with her to Virginia. She seems unwilling to care about others who were not raised the way she was raised." He shook his head. "If you'd seen her with that stagecoach driver earlier this week. Is it arrogance I see in her eyes? Does she believe herself so much better than others simply because she was born in Virginia, born into privilege? I hope not, for if so, I have failed her completely. Perhaps it's a good thing that the war has taken so much of the money we had before."

It was true. The Lord worked in mysterious ways. No wonder the

Bible told Christians to thank God in all things. Mere mortals couldn't see the end from the beginning as the Almighty could.

If she had something to do, Adelyn. Like the nursing she did back in Virginia. I wasn't sure I approved completely when she first began working in the hospital, but it seemed so much what God called His children to do in Isaiah 61. Binding up the brokenhearted, giving comfort to the afflicted. She was a good nurse. Perhaps God will open another door I cannot imagine, for I certainly never imagined that one.

"Thy will, not ours, be done, Lord. Thy will and not ours."

When Alice awoke, the light coming through the bedroom window had begun to weaken. *It must be near suppertime.*

She pushed herself up against the pillows at her back and let her gaze roam over the room. It was nothing like she'd expected. Larger than the home Edward had built before they were married.

Edward.

Would it ever cease to hurt to think about him?

Yes. Yes, it would cease. It would cease because it wouldn't be long before she joined him in heaven. She had come to Idaho Territory to die. But before she could let go of her ties to this earthly life, she had to make certain her son would be all right. She had to make certain he had a home with someone who would love him.

She prayed to God she would find that someone in her brother. Matthew was the only family Todd would have left when she passed over.

Alice closed her eyes and pictured her brother again. She had been as amazed at the changes she'd found in him as he was in her. The tall, stick-thin boy had become a tall, broad-shouldered man. While he'd held her with tender care as they climbed the hill to this house, there had been strength in his arms.

Sadly, her brother was a stranger to her in many ways. The letters they'd exchanged over the past eleven years had been few and far between. He was a poor correspondent, and she little better. Now she needed to know him, needed to know that he was the kind of man who could love her son.

Pain sliced through her abdomen. A pain that was familiar to her by this time. A cancer, the doctor had told her. A growing tumor. One that couldn't be stopped.

Let me have long enough, Lord. Let me make certain Todd will be all right. Please.

Back home in Virginia, Shannon had known all of the fine families who were members of her father's congregation. She had gone to school with many of the daughters. She had been courted by some of the sons. And of course she had become engaged to Benjamin Bluecher Hood, the handsomest young man in the county. But here in Grand Coeur, she knew no one, save for the Wells, Fargo stagecoach driver and the gentleman who'd met them upon their arrival.

As she sat in the chair near the small pump organ, she watched people coming into the sanctuary, wondering who they were and what had brought them to this town. The vast majority were men—and not the sort one would deem gentlemen. They were a rough-hewn lot, many with scraggly beards that begged for a trim. The few women who passed through the church doors wore plain, everyday dresses.

But who was she to judge? Her own dress could hardly pass for the latest fashion. Not after three years of war and the blockades that had closed the Southern harbors.

Shannon closed her eyes and drew in a deep breath, a wave of homesickness washing over her. She hadn't known it would be this hard to be away from Virginia, that it would hurt this much, that she would feel so alone.

"Shannon," her father said softly.

She opened her eyes and saw him tip his head toward the organ. She quickly moved to the bench and waited for his signal, as she'd done hundreds of times before.

"Welcome." Her father spread his arms wide, as if to embrace every member of his new congregation. "Please stand with me and sing 'Rock of Ages.'"

At her father's slight nod, Shannon began to play. The organ was new, just as everything else in the church was, and it played beautifully. She was thankful for that, for it drowned out the off-key voices that peppered the sanctuary. Father liked to remind her that the Lord loved a joyful noise raised in praise equally as much as He loved a song that was pitch-perfect.

At the close of the hymn, she returned to the nearby chair, took up her Bible, and placed it on her lap.

Her father's sermon that morning was on the importance of trusting in the Lord no matter the storms that buffeted His children. Shannon tried to listen, tried to take his teaching to heart, but her thoughts insisted upon wandering as her gaze scanned the motley congregation before her.

She stopped when she recognized Matthew Dubois in the last pew. It surprised her, seeing him there, a woman and boy by his side. Then she remembered his sister and her son had been expected. *That must be them.* Yes, there was some resemblance between Matthew and the younger woman, although the sister exhibited none of Matthew's robust health. Even from where she sat Shannon could see that. What was wrong with her? What treatments had the doctors prescribed? Perhaps if she consulted one of her books on nursing—

Her father's voice raised to emphasize a point, and it pulled Shannon's attention back where it belonged. Thank goodness she hadn't missed his cue for the closing hymn.

Matthew hadn't been keen on coming to church that morning. Not because he didn't want to be there, but because he'd thought Alice should stay in bed and recover from her journey. But his sister had been adamant. She'd wanted the family to attend service together, the three of them.

Family. It was almost a foreign term to him. Had been since his parents died the year he was twenty-one and Alice fifteen. That was the same year he'd started working for the express company in San Francisco. His sister had been in the care of neighbors in Oregon, so he hadn't worried about her. He'd sent money to see that she had what she needed. And he'd meant to go back to see her. Soon. Someday. But someday had never come. Just over a year later, sixteen-year-old Alice had married Edward Jackson and moved with her new husband to Wisconsin. After that, there'd been no point in Matthew going back to Oregon, no point in settling down in any one place. That's how he'd lived for more than a decade.

But his first week in Grand Coeur hadn't been all that bad. He'd kept busy, learning again the duties of an express agent from William Washburn. In the evenings, he'd readied the house for his sister and nephew's arrival. He'd even convinced himself that he might not mind staying in one place as much as he'd thought. Not for a couple of months. Surely that was all it would take to restore Alice to good health.

The congregation rose to sing a final hymn, Shannon Adair once more playing the organ.

A smile crept onto his lips. Miss Adair was an accomplished young woman and very easy on the eyes. No argument there. But if her nose was stuck any higher in the air when she looked at him and others, she'd be in danger of tipping over backward.

With the closing prayer said, Reverend Adair walked down the center aisle of the church and waited by the exit to shake hands. His daughter remained at the organ, playing some familiar hymns.

Matthew stepped into the aisle and offered his arm to Alice. She slipped her hand into the crook and allowed him to guide her toward the door, Todd on her other side.

"Pleasure to see you again, Mr. Dubois," the reverend said, shaking his free right hand. "And this must be your sister."

"Yes. Reverend, may I introduce Alice Jackson and her son, Todd."

"How do you do, Mrs. Jackson?"

"Good day, Reverend. I enjoyed your sermon a great deal. I shall endeavor to put it into practice."

"God bless you. Would that many in the congregation do so."

"Was that your daughter playing the organ?"

"Yes, indeed."

"I hope to get to meet her and tell her how well she plays. I've always envied those with musical abilities."

"I'll make certain the two of you are introduced soon. Like you, she is new to Grand Coeur. I know she will welcome the opportunity to make a friend close to her own age."

"Then I shall look forward to it."

Matthew felt Alice's grip tightening on his arm and sensed she was tiring even as they stood there. He bid the reverend a pleasant afternoon and escorted her down the steps. As he'd done the day before, he allowed her to set the pace as they walked toward home, and once again he was reminded that he hadn't yet asked her for more details about her ailment. He needed to change that and would do so as soon as she was rested.

After a Sunday dinner of chicken potpie, Delaney Adair lay down to rest and was soon asleep. Not wishing to wake him, Shannon went outside onto the small porch and sat on one of two chairs placed there.

The day was pleasant, warm but not hot, and without the humidity that made one's clothing stick to the skin. Shannon could appreciate that. And she supposed the surrounding hillsides would be pretty if they were still covered in trees. At least the tall pine growing by the corner of the house had been spared.

The church and parsonage were built on a hillside, giving Shannon a view of Grand Coeur. Not that it was a pleasant view. But the early morning haze of wood smoke had drifted away on a gentle breeze, and that was a blessing.

We aren't leaving.

The thought caused her chest to tighten. Ever since their arrival the previous Monday, Shannon had clung to a fragile hope that her father would come to his senses and choose to return to Virginia. But it was futile to go on thinking that way. Father wouldn't change his mind unless God changed it for him.

I could have stayed behind.

Yes, she was a grown woman. If she'd insisted on remaining in Virginia, Father would have allowed it. He could have left her in the care of close, trusted friends. But to be separated from him by so great a distance? Especially in wartime? No, she had to be with him. He needed her.

It's time I accept it. We're here to stay. But perhaps when the war is over he'll change his mind.

A movement out of the corner of her eye drew her gaze. About halfway between Shannon and the church she saw a boy on his hands and knees, looking underneath an uneven stack of lumber.

"Come here," he said. "Come on."

What on earth? She rose from the chair and moved to the corner of the porch.

"Come on." He reached with one hand into an open space in the lumber. "I won't hurt you. Come here."

"Boy, what are you doing?"

He sat back on his heels and looked around. When he saw her, he got to his feet. "There's a puppy under there."

"A puppy? Are you sure?" She thought it far more likely it was a skunk or some other wild animal.

"I'm sure. I followed him here."

She remembered where she'd seen the boy before. In church. He was Matthew Dubois's nephew. "You had best go on home and leave it alone."

The boy didn't answer—nor did he move away from the lumber.

Shannon went down the three steps and walked toward him. "What's your name?"

"Todd. Todd Jackson."

"Does your mother know you're wandering about?"

His eyes narrowed as he shook his head, and Shannon saw a mixture of stubbornness and uncertainty in his gaze.

"If it's a skunk, we will regret being this close," she said. Merciful heavens! How she hoped it wasn't a skunk.

"It ain't a skunk." He knelt on the ground again, sticking his rump into the air as he peered beneath the wood. "If my arm was longer, I could get him."

It was against her better judgment, but she decided to join him on the ground. "Where is it?"

"See there. You can see his yellow coat."

She lowered her cheek until it almost touched the ground. Yes. There it was. And there was just enough light for her to see the baby animal couldn't be a skunk. It appeared to be yellow or maybe cream colored. Definitely not black-and-white. What else could it be besides a puppy? What sort of wild animals did they have in Idaho?

"Can you reach him?" Todd asked.

Stick her hand into that shadowy space? There could be spiders or a snake or—

The sound of a throat clearing broke into her thoughts. "Maybe I should do that for you."

She straightened at once.

Matthew stood off to the side of the lumber, wearing a crooked grin. He was laughing at her. And no wonder. Her rump had been stuck up in the air just as the boy's had been. Heat rushed to her cheeks.

"Allow me," he said, offering his hand.

She didn't want to take it, but she did.

With a gentle pull, he lifted her to her feet. A moment later, he'd taken her place on his hands and knees. "What're we looking for, Todd?"

"A puppy. See him? Right there."

"Yes. I see him. Move over a bit." He stuck his arm under the lumber, and a few moments later he withdrew it, a golden ball of fluff in hand. He gave it to the boy.

Todd's face lit up. "Thanks, Uncle Matt."

"You're welcome, kid." Matthew ruffled the boy's hair, then stood, brushing off his trousers before straightening. "Thanks for helping him, Miss Adair."

The warmth in her cheeks grew hotter still. "I didn't do anything."

"You tried. I appreciate that." He glanced at the puppy, clutched close to Todd's chest. "Do you know who it belongs to?"

"No. I've never seen it before."

"Seems young to be running around by itself." He looked up the hillside. "Its mother must be somewhere nearby. Todd, where'd you first see it?"

"By the house."

"*Our* house?"

"Uh-huh."

"Well, come on. We'd best see if we can find its owner. Must belong to one of our neighbors."

That stubborn look returned to the boy's face. "I wanna keep it."

Shannon didn't have a great deal of experience with children, but she was quite sure she had more experience than Matthew Dubois. She wondered how he would handle the matter, hoping—in that small, dark, rebellious, sinful corner of her heart—that he would fail miserably, if only because he'd laughed at her.

He dropped to one knee and looked the boy in the eyes. "What if this was your puppy and you'd lost it? Would you want someone else to keep it rather than try to find its rightful owner?"

Todd's mouth pursed. That he wanted to say anything that would allow him to keep the puppy was crystal clear. But honesty won out. He shook his head.

Matthew stood. "Then let's go find who lost him." He looked at Shannon again, that crooked smile slipping back into place. "Thanks again for helping the boy."

Odd. This time his silly grin didn't make her angry . . . and she was almost sorry to watch him walk away.

Ruth Ann Rutherford's appearance was remarkably like that of her husband—rotund build, ruddy complexion, bulbous nose. She also seemed to enjoy the sound of her own voice, for she chuckled at what she'd said even if others didn't. It was Ruth Ann who brought the Adairs a housekeeper and cook.

"This is Sun Jie," she said, motioning toward the petite Chinese woman who stood slightly behind her and to one side.

She was a tiny thing, perhaps five feet tall, though barely that. Her black hair was pulled back, tight to the skull, braided and captured at her nape. She was dressed in a kind of robe made of bright purple cloth, and beneath it her legs were encased in matching silk trousers. Somewhat like pantaloons, Shannon supposed, only meant to be seen rather than hidden beneath skirts and hoops and petticoats.

Shannon wondered how old she was. She looked to be no more than twelve or thirteen. Perhaps she would make a decent lady's maid, but a cook?

Mrs. Rutherford continued on, "Sun Jie's husband, Wu Lok, owns the mercantile at the corner of Lewis and Clark Streets. I think Henry sent you to do your shopping there last week. Don't worry. She speaks pretty good English. Better than most of her kind, I'd say."

Her husband? Shannon felt her eyes widen. Was it usual for the Oriental girls to be married at such a young age? What would her father have to say about that?

Sun Jie bowed at the waist. When she straightened, her dark eyes met Shannon's briefly before training once again on the floor.

"Sun Jie," Ruth Ann said, "this is Miss Shannon Adair and her father, Reverend Adair."

Again the girl bowed. "How do you do?" She spoke slowly but with precision.

"Sun Jie and her husband are converts to the Christian faith," Ruth Ann added with a smile. "Otherwise I would never suggest that you hire her to care for your home. But she's one you can trust."

Shannon glanced at her father in time to see a flash of irritation in his eyes, but he subdued it so quickly she doubted Mrs. Rutherford could have recognized it. Shannon, on the other hand, was well attuned to his moods and his looks.

Her father motioned toward the chairs in the parlor. "Please, Mrs. Jie. Won't you sit down so we can become acquainted?"

"They put their last names first, Reverend," Ruth Ann said in a stage whisper, as if the young woman couldn't hear her that way. "Easier to just call her Sun Jie."

"Ah." He smiled. "Well, I do thank you for bringing Sun Jie to meet with us, Mrs. Rutherford. I wouldn't want to impose on any more of your time while we conduct the rest of the interview. Please give my regards to your husband. Both of you have been so kind and thoughtful to us. Shannon and I can't thank you enough."

As he spoke, he eased the woman toward the door until she found herself standing on the front porch and could do nothing except acknowledge his thanks and depart.

Shannon smiled as she turned toward Sun Jie. "Please. Do sit down so we can talk."

The girl complied.

Until her arrival in Grand Coeur, Shannon had never seen anyone from China before, but she'd learned there were many Orientals in the gold camps. Her first thought had been that the color of their skin and the shape of their eyes were so different from those who'd peopled her world. But now, as she looked at Sun Jie, she forgot the differences and noticed only a delicate beauty.

"How old are you, Sun Jie?"

Without looking up she answered, "Twenty-three."

"Twenty-three?" Shannon could scarcely believe it. Only two years younger than herself.

Her father returned and took the seat beside her. "Sun Jie, my daughter and I could ask you many questions, but why don't you just tell us about yourself. Would that be all right?"

Sun Jie nodded.

"Why not begin with how you came to faith in Christ."

Breaking for lunch, Matthew left the Wells, Fargo office and strode up the hillside toward the company house. Neither Alice nor Todd had been awake when he left for work that morning, and he was curious to see how the two of them fared.

Despite her lengthy nap Sunday afternoon, his sister hadn't seemed any more rested by the time they sat down to supper. She'd tried to convince him that she should do the cooking, but he hadn't let her. The point of her coming to Idaho, after all, was so she could regain her health. And the sooner that happened, the sooner he could be back to driving a coach.

When he rounded the corner onto Randolph Street, he saw his nephew playing with the pale-gold puppy in the small yard in front of the company house. This morning he'd asked a number of people in town if they knew where the pup belonged.

"Plenty of stray dogs hereabouts," one man had answered. "Not like men've got time or place for pets."

Looked like the pup had a new home.

Matthew'd had a dog as a boy. A black-and-white spaniel called Trip. Just like here, most farmers had little use for pets. A dog on a farm was expected to work almost as hard as its master. Run off critters that tried to break into the henhouse or kill a sheep. Help a man when he was hunting. That sort of thing. Trip had been the best.

When Todd saw his uncle striding up to the gate, he pulled the puppy into his arms, pressing him tight to his chest, clearly afraid Matthew was about to announce the pup's true owner had been found.

"It's okay," he said, feeling sorry for the kid. "Looks like you can keep him."

"I can?" His sudden grin looked a mile wide.

Funny how good that made Matthew feel. "How's your ma?"

"She's okay. She's restin'." Todd stood. "She helped me name the puppy."

He cocked an eyebrow.

"I'm callin' him Nugget."

"Good name."

"It's 'cause of his color. You know. Like gold."

"Yeah, I got it." He motioned toward the front door. "Let's go fix something to eat. Your ma's probably hungry."

"I'm hungry too."

"Makes three of us."

Matthew found his sister reclining on the sofa in the parlor, a blanket covering her legs. Sunlight streamed through the large window, illuminating dust motes in the air.

Alice smiled when she saw him. "Is it that time already?"

"It is. Are you hungry? Todd is."

"I could eat something."

"Cold beef with cheese and some bread and butter sound okay?"

"Whatever's easy." She closed her eyes, as if exhausted by the brief conversation.

He left the parlor and went into the kitchen.

A doctor consultation was in order, he thought, as he prepared the meal for the three of them. He needed to know what to do for Alice. She hadn't been forthcoming when he'd asked questions about her illness. His gut told him she needed more than simple rest, but he didn't know what that might be. He'd hardly been sick a day in his life. A cold every now and again, but nothing that put him to bed. And he'd broken his left arm when he was a boy.

He wondered if Alice remembered that. She'd been pretty small when it happened.

Taking up the lunch tray, he carried it into the parlor and set it on the low table before the sofa. His sister looked at him, and there was something in her eyes that caused a twinge of alarm. She seemed . . . disconnected . . . departed. Then she gave him a small smile and he thought he must have imagined it.

"Eat up." He took up some pillows to put behind her back. "You need your strength."

He was going to contact the doctor before this day was out.

Shannon stood on the porch, watching Sun Jie make her way down the street toward the south side of Grand Coeur. That was where—Mrs. Rutherford had informed them in front of their new housekeeper—the area known as Chinatown was located.

She could almost hear her father preparing his sermon now. She'd recognized his annoyance with the woman's condescending attitude.

Delaney Adair was a Southerner through and through. No man could say that he wasn't. But he'd disagreed with many of his friends and neighbors back in Virginia on the issue of slavery and the supposed inferiority of the colored races. He believed, deep in his soul, that all men were the same—white, black, yellow, red. He believed they should all be free to live and serve God as He called them. While her father was in favor of a state's right to govern, while she was certain he would support the Confederacy once the new nation was free of Yankee invaders, Delaney Adair would also press for the emancipation of the slaves. He even admired Abraham Lincoln for that very act.

Imagine. A Southern gentleman admitting that he admired President Lincoln. It had cost him a number of friends, but he'd stood firm in his belief. Shannon reluctantly admired him for his unwavering stance before popular opinion.

"God would not have us discriminate between the races," her father had told her on more than one occasion. "He would not have us be another's master. He would have us respect one another. Respect even our differences. Serve one another out of love."

Yes, she admired her father above all men. But she often wished he would keep such thoughts to himself.

Shannon turned and reentered the house. Her father was seated in one of the mismatched chairs, his Bible open on his lap, a pair of glasses perched on the end of his nose.

"It appears you won't have many meals to prepare for your father after today," he said.

"I like cooking for you." She leaned over and kissed his forehead.

He chuckled. "When it suits your mood."

She playfully slapped his shoulder.

But he turned serious again. "God has great work for us to do in Grand Coeur. There are men here from around the country, from around the world. 'The harvest truly is plenteous, but the labourers are few; pray ye therefore the Lord of the harvest, that he will send forth labourers into his harvest.' That's why the Lord has called us to this territory, Shannon. We are the laborers He needs to bring in the harvest."

She nodded, although she wasn't convinced. At least when it came to her part in this master plan.

"Think of it, daughter. It isn't just these miners who so desperately need Christ. Sun Jie and her husband are believers. Perhaps we can be of help in the conversion of more Chinese. The gospel is the good news to all. Not simply to those of European roots. How exciting this could be."

It seemed to Shannon that she was there by default. God had called her father, and the Lord got her in the bargain.

"Yes, Father," she answered softly. "It is exciting."

She turned away, and her gaze fell upon the table near a window where she'd set out the cherished portraits and photographs brought from home. There were portraits of her grandparents and another of her mother that had been made the year before she died. There was a photograph of a number of young women of the county—good friends, all—taken in 1860, the year before the war began. What innocents they'd been. And there was a photograph of Benjamin, the man she was to have married. But the Yankees had killed him at the Battle of Malvern Hill, just one of more than twenty thousand gallant men of the Confederacy killed in that weeklong campaign in Virginia.

She crossed the room and took up the framed photograph. How handsome Benjamin had looked in his uniform, his black hair combed back, his mustache and goatee neatly trimmed.

I should have married him before the war started. Maybe he wouldn't have joined the army so soon. Maybe he wouldn't have died. Why wasn't I in more of a hurry to wed him? Now who will I marry?

Shame washed over her. What a horrid person she was. Benjamin had been killed on the battlefield, and here she was thinking of herself and how her life had been inconvenienced. So different from what she'd thought it would be. If her father could read her mind . . .

Perish the thought.

Delaney returned to the church that afternoon. He'd planned to begin work on his sermon for the following Sunday, but instead he found himself on his knees at the altar.

"Rejoice evermore. Pray without ceasing. In every thing give thanks: for this is the will of God in Christ Jesus concerning you . . . Rejoice evermore. Pray without ceasing . . . Pray without ceasing . . . Pray without ceasing."

Earlier this afternoon he'd felt great excitement at the prospect of being able to help Sun Jie and Wu Lok bring the good news to other Orientals in Chinatown. But as he'd walked from the house to the church, truth had pierced his heart. The Orientals needed the Lord no more and no less than the godless men who nightly frequented the saloons of Grand Coeur. And neither people group would be easy to reach. He couldn't depend upon them to suddenly appear at one of his services. Prejudice would keep the Chinese from the white man's church, and strong drink and riotous living would keep most of the miners away. If he meant to win souls, he would have to go out to meet them where they were.

He'd seen his daughter's reluctance when he'd shared his excitement, but now he felt reluctance himself. Throughout his ministry, he'd enjoyed the society of people quite like himself. That was no longer the case. What if he wasn't up to the task? What if he hadn't the knowledge he would need? Or even the compassion. If his daughter had been spoiled by the life they'd enjoyed in Virginia, then it was no less true of himself. Until the war began, he'd lived in comfort and plenty. Even now he wasn't without financial resources.

"In every thing give thanks: for this is the will of God in Christ Jesus concerning you."

"Lord, I thank Thee for bringing us to Grand Coeur. I thank Thee that my daughter is out of harm's way, that the war can't endanger her here. Be with our loved ones who are still in Virginia. Be with our soldiers and their families. I thank Thee for this church and for the congregation I have come to this territory to serve. Lord, empower me by Thy Holy Spirit to reach out and evangelize. Show me common ground with those who are different from me. Fill me with Thy compassion."

"Pray without ceasing."

"Lord, please help my daughter find contentment here. Please send her a friend so she won't feel alone." He remembered the way she'd looked at the photographs earlier and the loss that had flickered in her eyes as she'd remembered Benjamin. "Please heal her heart and perhaps allow her to find love again."

"I'm sorry, Mr. Dubois. There is no easy way to say this: your sister is dying."

Matthew stared at the doctor as if he were speaking another language. "Dying?" He looked toward the bedroom door. "But I thought all she needed was to rest and regain her strength." He raked the fingers of his right hand through his hair. "Are you sure?"

"I'm sure." Hiram Featherhill, a man not much older than Matthew, removed his spectacles and cleaned them with a handkerchief from his breast pocket. "Her heart is weak. Most likely the result of a prior infection such as scarlet fever. But I daresay it's a cancer in her abdomen that will rob her of life first."

"Did she know she was dying when she came here?"

"I should think so. Her physician in Wisconsin must have told her the seriousness of her condition."

Matthew nodded. "How long does she have?"

"A few months at most."

Alice was going to die and leave her son an orphan. Matthew would be Todd's only living relative.

God help him.

Matthew walked to the end of the upstairs hallway and looked out the window. A haze lay over Grand Coeur that morning, as it did most mornings when there wasn't a breeze. From the vantage point of this house on the hillside, he could see the three long streets that ran east-west and several shorter streets that ran north-south. Someone had carefully platted what would be the main thoroughfares of the town, making the streets wide and straight. But as he looked farther out from the center of town, the streets became less defined, narrower and more crooked. The buildings were of all shapes and sizes, a large boardinghouse next to a small shoe shop, a restaurant a stone's throw from a livery stable. And plenty of saloons. All those lonely men with gold dust in their pockets needed a place to go at night because their wives and sweethearts—if they had them—lived far away.

He faced the doctor again. "What is it I need to do for her?"

"I think it best that she not be left alone. She shouldn't exert herself. Perhaps you could send to Boise City or Idaho City for a nurse." His brows lifted. "I know. Check with the new reverend. He might be able to direct you to a woman in his congregation who could stay with your sister while you're working."

"I'll do that." He glanced toward the door. "May I go in to her now?"

"Of course. Just don't stay too long. You don't want to overtire her."

"No, I won't."

"Send for me if you need me." Dr. Featherhill put on his hat.

"I will."

Matthew waited until the doctor started down the staircase before he walked to Alice's room and opened the door. She lay with her back toward him, and he wondered if she was asleep.

She wasn't. "I'm sorry, Matt." She rolled onto her back and looked toward him.

"What for? You can't help that you're sick." He walked to the bedside and took her hand in his.

"I . . . I should have told you what was wrong with me before I came. I guess I hoped for a miracle, that I wouldn't ever have to tell you, that I would be able to live and watch my son grow to manhood. That's what I've prayed for."

"Maybe the doctor's wrong."

Her smile was a pale shadow of the kind he remembered when they were kids. "He's not wrong."

"Alice, I should have been there for you. All these years without seeing you . . . I should have sent for you after Edward died. You shouldn't have been alone all this time."

"It isn't your fault we haven't been closer. I married and moved away. That was my choice, Matt. Your place was in the West. I always understood that."

Their brief conversation had taxed Alice's limited energy. Her breathing seemed more labored, the circles beneath her eyes darker. Better to leave so she could rest, he decided. They could talk more later.

But for how much longer? How many opportunities would he have to get to know his sister better? Not many. A few months, the doctor had said.

He leaned down to kiss her forehead. "Rest, Alice. I'll check back on you in a short while."

"We need to talk . . . about Todd."

"I know, but it can wait for now. You need to sleep."

"We can't wait long."

Strange, the pain those words caused him. He'd given his younger sister so little thought through the years. He'd known she was married and cared for by her husband, and there had always been "someday." Someday he would go visit her in Wisconsin. Someday he would write more often. Someday . . .

God, why? I don't understand why she has to die. Better if it were me. I don't have a child to raise.

Only it looked like he would have one to raise soon.

Sun Jie cleared the table after lunch and put the dishes into the wash pan.

"Thank you, Sun Jie," Shannon's father said. "It was delicious."

Before the housekeeper could respond, there was a knock upon the door.

"I'll get it, Father." Shannon crossed the room and opened it. Her gaze lowered to the boy on the porch. "Well, hello, Todd. Have you followed another puppy to our woodpile?" She smiled as she asked the question.

"No, ma'am." He shook his head. "Uncle Matt told me to come for the reverend. Asked if he could come to our house." His expression was, she realized now, forlorn. "I think it's about my ma."

"What about your mother?"

"She's sick."

Shannon turned. "Father."

"Yes?"

"You're needed at the Dubois home."

The reverend came to stand beside her.

"This is Todd Jackson. You met him and his mother at church last Sunday. He says his mother is sick, and his uncle, Mr. Dubois, has requested that you come to their house."

"Then I shall go straightaway."

Something about the small boy's expression tugged at Shannon's heart. "If it's all right, I'll join you, Father."

"Of course it's all right. Let me get my Bible, and we'll go at once."

A short while later, Shannon and her father followed Todd along a narrow street that climbed the hillside. Ahead of them and to the right, she could see several two-story homes that were a cut above anything else she'd seen in the town. Although not overly large, they had been designed and built with care, unlike the many shacks elsewhere in Grand Coeur that seemed to have been thrown together with whatever materials were available at the time.

"That's our house," Todd said, pointing to one of the homes she'd been looking at.

The news surprised her. Matthew Dubois hadn't seemed to be a man of either influence or money. He was a stagecoach driver, after all. That wasn't the sort of work that made a man wealthy, was it?

"Judge not, that ye be not judged."

How many times had her father quoted those words to her? Too many. Would she ever learn to heed his instructions the first time? Oh, she hoped so. She would love to become as good at heart as her father. She feared God would never work that particular miracle. And it would, indeed, take a miracle to make her as good as her father.

When they arrived at the house, Todd opened the door and ran in ahead of them, calling for his uncle. Shannon and her father waited on the veranda.

"Reverend Adair." Matthew Dubois stepped into view. "Miss Adair. Thanks for coming. Please. Come in."

After his visitors stepped into the entry hall, Matthew took them into the parlor, where he invited them to sit. As soon as they'd done so, Shannon's father said, "I take it your sister's condition has worsened."

"Yes." Matthew glanced toward the stairs. "The doctor tells me she's dying."

Shannon's breath caught in her throat. Dying? But she was so young. Only a year or two older than Shannon.

"He doesn't think she'll last more than a few months."

"I'm so sorry, Mr. Dubois. Would you like me to pray for her?"

"Yes. Of course. But that wasn't the main reason I sent for you. I'm hoping you might be able to recommend someone—a woman in your congregation, perhaps—who could help care for Alice when I'm at work. I know you haven't been here any longer than I have, but I was hoping... I thought..." His sentence faded into silence, unfinished.

Shannon thought back to the Sunday service. She and Mrs. Jackson had been two of a handful of women in the church. The only one she'd met thus far was Mrs. Rutherford, but she hardly seemed the right nurse for a dying woman.

"I could do it, Father."

She saw Matthew's eyes widen at her suggestion. The look said she was the last woman he would want caring for his sister. She stiffened her spine and tilted her chin.

"I assure you, sir, I'm a good nurse. I've spent a great deal of time in the past year helping to care for Confederate soldiers wounded in battle. I'm not squeamish nor given to fainting spells."

She looked at her father and was rewarded with a small smile. Then he turned to Matthew. "It seems my daughter would like to help care for your sister, if you'll allow it. And she is telling the truth. She's come to be a fine nurse. The physician at the army hospital near our home in Virginia told me so himself."

"If you're sure, Miss Adair," Matthew said after a period of silence.

"I'm sure," she answered.

"Good." Her father gave a firm nod. "It's settled, then. Now, why don't you show us to Mrs. Jackson's room."

The small group climbed the narrow staircase, Shannon bringing up the rear. The door to Matthew's sister's bedroom stood open. Inside, the curtains had been drawn, letting in only a small amount of light. Alice Jackson lay on her side. The blanket covering her barely moved as she breathed in and out.

"Alice?" Matthew said softly.

She opened her eyes and sent him a brief smile.

"The reverend and his daughter are here to see you." He helped her to turn onto her back and sit up slightly with the help of pillows against her back. "Miss Adair has offered to stay with you while I'm at work."

"Miss Adair." Alice smiled again, though it didn't linger on her lips. "I've looked forward to meeting you. You played so beautifully at church on Sunday."

"Thank you."

Shannon's father pulled a straight-backed chair close to the bed and sat on it. "I would like to pray for you, Mrs. Jackson. Is that all right?"

Alice nodded, and her eyes closed again. Shannon suspected it wasn't so much because the reverend was about to pray as because the brief exchange had sapped her strength.

Matthew wasn't ungrateful for the assistance, but he hadn't expected Shannon Adair to volunteer to care for Alice. She didn't seem the type to take care of a woman she'd never met. It surprised him even more to learn that she'd nursed wounded soldiers. He would have expected her to consider herself too good for such pursuits.

He'd obviously misjudged her. Shannon had looked upon Alice with true compassion when they were all upstairs in the bedroom.

Before returning to the Wells, Fargo office, Matthew gave Shannon a quick tour of the house so she would know where to find things, and he passed along the instructions Dr. Featherhill had given him for Alice's care. In truth, there wasn't much that could be done for her. The physician had left a tincture of Hawthorn to be taken daily for her heart and, when the time arrived that the pain became too much, laudanum for the cancer.

When Matthew entered the office, William rose from his desk behind the counter. "I was gettin' worried. What'd the doctor say?"

"It's not good." He removed his hat and hung it on a peg near the door. "She's dying."

"Oh, Matt. I'm right sorry to hear that news."

He nodded.

"What's to become of the boy?"

"I'm not sure."

"We need to talk . . . about Todd . . ."

Matthew pictured his sister as her words repeated in his head.

"We can't wait long."

No, they couldn't wait long. Time was running out. It was written in the pain on her face and could be heard in her labored breathing.

God help me. What will I do about Todd when she's gone?

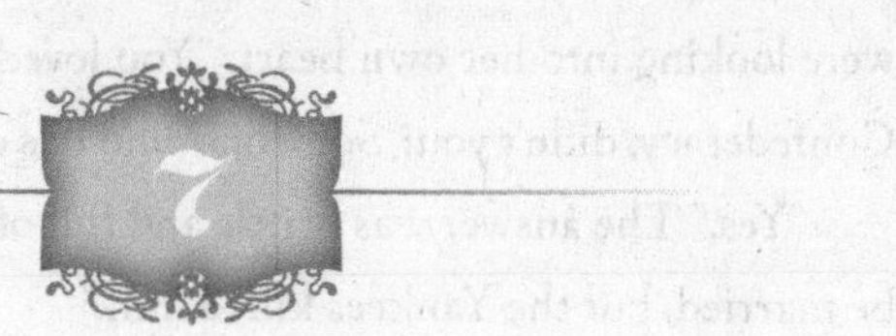

Alice slept away the first morning Shannon Adair came to care for her. Her body wouldn't allow her to do anything else. But after a bowl of hot soup for lunch, she was ready to become better acquainted with the pretty young woman from Virginia.

"Tell me about yourself, Miss Adair," she requested when Shannon returned to the bedroom after taking away the luncheon tray.

Shannon sat on the chair beside the bed. "What would you like to know?"

"Tell me about your family."

"Father is my only family now. My mother passed away nearly ten years ago. I have no brothers or sisters."

"I was fifteen when my parents died."

"And it was just you and your brother after that?"

Alice nodded. "But he left Oregon to find work with the express company. That's where our farm was. In Oregon Territory. That's where I met Edward, my husband. After we married, we returned to his hometown in Wisconsin." Her voice faltered, and she turned her gaze toward the window. "He was killed the first year of the war."

"Serving the Union?" Something altered in Shannon's voice.

Alice didn't have to wonder at the cause of it. It was as if she were looking into her own heart. "You loved someone fighting for the Confederacy, didn't you? Someone who has died in the war."

"Yes." The answer was brittle and full of resentment. "We were to be married, but the Yankees killed him."

"I'm sorry, Miss Adair. I'm sorry you've had to experience the same kind of pain that so many other women are feeling because of the war." Alice reached over and touched the back of Shannon's left hand. "We shall be friends, you and I."

Shannon was not accomplished at hiding her emotions. Alice could see the struggle going on within the young woman. The goodness in her wanted to be kind and caring toward Alice. The hurt and anger wanted to refuse her offer of friendship. Alice even understood the feelings. She'd hated the Rebels for many months after she received word of Edward's death. But hate changed nothing. At least nothing for the better. And so she'd given it up and surrendered her heartache to God.

Shannon's father refused to hate Northerners. Even as the war raged around them, the fighting sometimes coming almost to their back door, still the good reverend had refused to hate. Even when they'd learned Benjamin had been buried with thousands of other Confederate soldiers, her father had maintained that God loved the Yankees and the Adairs must too.

Love them? Not hardly. They'd stolen her chance at happiness. She would always hate them and pray for their defeat. How could any self-respecting Southerner do otherwise? And yet she was tempted to like Alice. If not for the war, would they have become friends?

"I've upset you," Alice said softly. "I'm sorry."

"No. It's all right."

"The war shouldn't matter between you and me. Two women who both know what it means to lose the men they love in battles far away from us."

Alice was wrong. The war did matter between them. Shannon had wanted to marry Benjamin, had planned to marry him. She'd loved him. At least she'd thought so. Only sometimes her feelings for him seemed to have belonged to someone else. Without his photograph, would she remember what he'd looked like? She wasn't sure she would, and she felt guilty for it.

She didn't like feeling guilty.

Shannon rose from the chair. "I'm going to fix myself a cup of tea. Would you like one too?"

Alice looked up at her, her expression a combination of sorrow and weariness. "Thank you. No. I think I shall sleep again. Perhaps a little later."

Shannon went to the window and closed the curtains, once again casting the bedroom into shadows. Then she left without another word. When she reached the kitchen, she stopped and made a slow turn. It was a wonderful room with an icebox and a stove that hardly looked used. Several windows let in plenty of light. Oh, how she could envy Alice Jackson such a kitchen.

Only Alice most likely would never prepare a meal in this room. Alice was dying.

Unexpected tears sprang to her eyes. She didn't want to feel sorry for Alice or for Alice's son or her brother. And yet she did. Shannon knew something about losing one's mother, knew what a hole it had left in her life—an empty space that nothing else seemed to fill. At least she had been sixteen. Todd was only nine, and he'd already lost his father. Now he was losing his mother too. The only family he would have left was the uncle he'd met for the first time last week.

"What're you doin'?"

At the sound of Todd's voice, Shannon quickly wiped away any trace of her tears. Then she turned. The boy stood in the doorway that led from the kitchen onto the veranda—a veranda that wrapped around three sides of this house on the hillside. Cheerily, she answered, "I was thinking what a lovely room this is." It wasn't truly a lie. She had thought that a short while ago.

"Just a room." Todd held the pup named Nugget in his arms, and as he spoke he rubbed his chin against the puppy's golden head. "How's Ma feelin'? Can I go up to see her?"

Shannon forced a confident smile. "She seems stronger to me, but she's sleeping now. I left her to rest while I came down to fix some tea. Do you need something?"

The boy shook his head but came into the kitchen and sat on one of the chairs at the table in the center of the room. Shannon's mother never would have allowed a dog in her kitchen, but Shannon suspected Alice Jackson wouldn't mind.

"Why don't I fix you some hot chocolate? You would like that, wouldn't you?"

From the moment Matthew had been hired as a clerk for Wells, Fargo in San Francisco, his goal had been to become a driver. He'd worked his way from clerk to agent in a matter of weeks, and in a matter of months, he'd become an express messenger. In that capacity, he'd sat beside the stagecoach driver, armed with a sawed-off double-barreled shotgun, a breech-loading rifle, and a Colt revolver. It had been his responsibility to protect the important documents and express mail entrusted to him, not to mention the valuable minerals—called "treasure"—that were placed in the safe beneath the driver's feet. He'd made numerous trips between the Missouri River and the Rocky Mountains in those early years, catching what sleep he could while the stage crossed sagebrush-covered plains or climbed rugged mountain passes.

But drivers were at the top of the staging hierarchy, and that's where Matthew had wanted to be. At the top. He'd wanted to slip on those silk-lined buckskin gloves and lace three pairs of reins between his fingers. He'd wanted to snap the whip above the heads of the horses or mules and feel them give another measure of speed. Sure, drivers were exposed to all extremes of weather—rain, wind, snow, sleet, the dry heat of a summer's sun and the icy cold of a winter's night—but no more so than a poor fool messenger.

He'd finally gotten his chance to drive at the age of twenty-five, and that's what he'd done for the last seven years.

One thing he'd learned from his many years driving stagecoach for the company—speed was addictive. At first he'd driven hard to keep on schedule. Sometimes he'd done it to avoid getting scalped. But after a while, he'd just craved the rush that came with the race from one location to another.

After ten days in Grand Coeur, Matthew missed that speed more than he'd thought possible. He found the work of an agent even more confining than he had eleven years before. He spent almost the entire day indoors, buying gold dust, drawing checks, receiving packages and preparing others to be sent out, serving as the telegraph operator, transferring bank funds. There were three of them in the office—Matthew, William, and Ray—and even so they could barely keep up with the demand for the company's services. But he refused to complain. At least he could provide a home for his sister and her boy. He was thankful for that, despite wishing he was back on the driver's seat of a stage.

Such were his thoughts when he arrived home that evening. Opening the front door, he was met with delicious odors drifting toward him from the back of the house. Fried chicken, if he wasn't mistaken. His stomach growled in anticipation.

He moved toward the kitchen.

Shannon stood at the stove with her back to him, an apron tied around her waist, taking pieces of chicken from the skillet and placing them on a platter. Todd sat at the table in the center of the room, the puppy on his lap.

"Uncle Matt!" the boy cried when he saw him. He slid from the chair and set Nugget on the floor. "I helped Miss Shannon make biscuits."

"You did, huh?"

"Yup."

Shannon turned to face him. There was a sheen of perspiration on her forehead and her face was flushed from the heat of the stove. Oddly enough, it seemed to make her even prettier than he'd thought her before. Not that he wanted to notice that about her.

"Miss Adair, I never expected you to cook for us." Although he was glad of it. His experience didn't extend much further than warming a can of beans. His stomach growled again.

"I enjoy cooking on occasion," Shannon said. "My father says my fried chicken is superb."

"I'm sure it is."

She carried the platter of chicken to the table and set it next to a plate stacked with biscuits. "I hope your sister will be enticed to eat a bit more than she did for lunch. She told me fried chicken is one of her favorites."

Matthew wouldn't have known that about Alice, of course. It hadn't occurred to him to ask.

Shannon untied the apron and draped it over the back of a chair. "Mrs. Jackson slept a great deal of the day, but I think she might be a little stronger than she was yesterday. Her pain seems to have lessened and her breathing seems less labored."

"That's good to know."

"Please see that she eats as much as she can. She needs to rebuild her strength, and she can't do that if she only picks at her food."

"I'll do my best."

Shannon nodded. "Then I shall go home. I'll be here first thing in the morning." She moved toward the front door.

Matthew turned and followed her. "Thank you, Miss Adair, for your help. Don't know how I'd manage otherwise. I know a little about dressing wounds from gunshot and arrows and a thing or two about trying to save a man's frostbitten fingers. But what's wrong with Alice . . ." He shook his head, embarrassed by the helpless feeling that washed over him.

A look of sympathy flickered in her eyes, then was gone.

Just as well. He didn't need her feeling sorry for him any more than he needed to be thinking she was attractive. All he needed was for her to use her nursing skills to care for his sister.

Night blanketed the town of Grand Coeur. Even the saloons had grown silent in this wee hour.

Alice leaned her shoulder against the wall and stared out the window into the inky darkness, her thoughts troubled. Her brother still wasn't ready to talk about what he would do with his nephew once cancer sent Alice to heaven. She supposed she couldn't blame him for that. It had taken many weeks for her to come to grips with the truth. She was dying. Someone else would have to raise her son to manhood.

Despite the years they'd spent apart, she loved her brother and she understood him. She knew he yearned to be back driving a stagecoach, although he was careful not to say so. She knew he was already restless from a more sedentary way of life. How long could he stand working as an agent before boredom sent him back to what he loved best?

He needs a wife. He needs to marry a woman who will love Todd and take care of him when Matt is away.

Pain pinched her heart. She hated the idea that Todd might learn to love someone else as his mother, that she might be replaced in her son's heart. Would he forget her completely?

She shook her head, trying to drive away the thoughts. She couldn't think of herself now. She had to think of what was best for her boy. And what was best was for him was to be with family, to be with his uncle.

"And his uncle needs a wife," she whispered. "But where is he to find one with so little time left? Especially here in Grand Coeur."

She went to her bed and slipped between the cool sheets as her thoughts returned to earlier that evening when Matthew and Todd had joined her in this bedroom for supper. All three of them had enjoyed the meal prepared by Shannon Adair.

Shannon Adair.

She was young and attractive, a Christian, the daughter of a minister, and she seemed fond of Todd. Why not her? But something told Alice she would have to approach the matter carefully.

Very carefully.

Shannon sat near the window of Alice's bedroom, thumbing through the pages of one of her most prized books, *Notes on Nursing* by Florence Nightingale. She paused in the section on taking food.

> Every careful observer of the sick will agree in this that thousands of patients are annually starved in the midst of plenty, from want of attention to the ways which alone make it possible for them to take food. This want of attention is as remarkable in those who urge upon the sick to do what is quite impossible to them, as in the sick themselves who will not make the effort to do what is perfectly possible to them.

Shannon lifted her eyes from the page to look toward her patient. What more could she do to help Alice take the nourishment she needed to improve her health? She barely ate enough to keep a bird alive. Even the fried chicken Shannon had prepared yesterday hadn't tempted her to eat more than a few bites. Perhaps it was too rich for her stomach. But she could not grow strong on chicken broth or beef tea alone.

Perhaps Shannon was expecting too much. According to Dr. Featherhill, Alice had only a few months at most to live. Still, Shannon had nursed dying men back from the edge of the grave. With good care and prayer, many patients had defied the predictions of doctors.

She looked down at the book and continued to read.

> I am bound to say, that I think more patients are lost by want of care and ingenuity in these momentous minutiae in private nursing than in public hospitals. And I think there is more of the *entente cordiale* to assist one another's hands between the doctor and his head nurse in the latter institutions, than between the doctor and the patient's friends in the private house.

"What are you reading?"

At Alice's question, Shannon looked up again. "Nothing important." She set the book aside and rose from the chair. "Can I get you something? How about some beef tea and bread?"

"Perhaps later. I would rather talk with you awhile. Please."

Shannon was not surprised by Alice's request. The woman had asked the same thing numerous times over the past two days. Shannon found it impossible not to comply. After all, wasn't that part of her job as a nurse? To do everything possible to make the invalid comfortable? But these too frequent tête-à-têtes felt much too . . . intimate to her. She would prefer their relationship remain a professional one, as nurse and patient. That was difficult to do as she learned more about Alice.

"I was thinking about your home in Virginia," Alice said softly. "The way you described it. I can see it clearly in my mind."

Shannon settled onto the chair beside the bed.

"It's hard to say good-bye to the places we've come to love, isn't it? I was just sixteen when Edward and I left Oregon Territory and returned to his family home in Wisconsin. Of course, I wasn't leaving anything so pretty as Covington House must be, but it was difficult all the same."

"I'm sure it was."

Alice smiled. "We women do seem to always be following a man somewhere, don't we? Me, going with Edward back to his boyhood home. And now coming here to be with Matthew because this is where his job is. You, joining your father where he pastors a new church."

Shannon couldn't argue. It did seem to be a woman's role to do the following. "I suppose, if not for the men in our lives, we women would never stray far from the places of our births. The entire population of the world might still be living within a short distance of the Garden of Eden if left to the gentler sex."

Alice laughed aloud. The response brought color to her cheeks and a sparkle to her dark eyes.

She must have been quite pretty before she took sick.

"I must remember to tell Matt what you said. He'll find it funny too."

Shannon remembered that moment by the woodpile, when she'd been on her hands and knees, rump in the air, looking for the puppy. She hadn't cared at all for his laughter then, and she wasn't sure she wanted to give him another reason to laugh at her now.

"When we were young, my brother loved to tease me." Still smiling, Alice closed her eyes. "But he was good to me and looked out for me too. As a girl, I thought the sun and moon rose at his request. Of all the things I remember about my girlhood, I think it's the sound of his laughter I like the best."

Begrudgingly, Shannon admitted to herself that Matthew Dubois did have a pleasant laugh.

Alice released a sigh. "If not for Edward's death and my illness, I wonder if I would ever have seen my brother again. But here we are. Together." She looked at Shannon. "The Lord does indeed work in mysterious ways. We see only the threads on the back of the tapestry. God sees the whole design."

Quiet faith. That's what Shannon saw in the eyes of the woman on the bed. No self-pity. No anger over what lay before her. Peace. A peace that passed understanding.

Have I ever known peace like that?

She feared not—and she found herself strangely envious of the dying woman.

Delaney Adair followed the boardwalk through town. When he made eye contact with others, he smiled and dipped his head in acknowledgment, but he didn't stop or try to make conversation. His thoughts were busy elsewhere. He was busy praying, beseeching the God of heaven on behalf of lost souls—and it was quite clear to him that there were plenty of them in Grand Coeur. On Main Street alone he'd counted seventeen saloons and six brothels.

A block back, he'd seen some women from one of those latter establishments sitting on a second-story veranda. Although morning had given way to midday already, they'd been clad in night attire. Revealing attire, at that. One of them had even called out to him, inviting him to come inside and partake of her pleasures. He recoiled at the thought.

Poor lost souls, indeed.

Then he recalled the story of Hosea and the example of unrelenting, all-pursuing, unconditional love that book of the Bible provided to God's children. Perhaps the Lord would have him go back to that brothel and speak to that woman. Perhaps Delaney had missed a door God had opened. Perhaps the scantily clad female was among the fruit he was here to harvest.

Lord?

He waited but felt no urging.

Richmond had its brothels, of course, as did other towns in Virginia and elsewhere in the South, but Delaney had never felt called to visit those establishments or reach out to those women. Why was that? Because they were tucked away in corners of the city where he never went? Corners where they couldn't be seen?

Make the way clear, Lord. Help me to heed Thy voice.

His thoughts turned to his daughter. He didn't like the idea of her being exposed to such blatant sin. If a prostitute would call out to a man wearing the collar of a clergyman, might she not be just as bold with a decent young woman? He might want to limit Shannon's exposure to those in town. Only how was he to do that? His daughter was not the sort to want to be closed away day after day. He supposed it was good she had her nursing duties to keep her occupied.

Grant me continued wisdom as a father, Lord. Help Shannon become all that You want her to be.

He stopped and looked behind him at the length of the street. God had called him to this town. He had called him here as His servant, to bring His word and His love to a fallen humanity. At first his flock would be believers, most of them merchants and their wives. A few would be miners and some with less respectable jobs. But wouldn't it be something if the pews of the church began to fill with the broken and forgotten? With men and women to whom Jesus would say, "Neither do I condemn thee: go, and sin no more."

He clasped his hands behind his back as he turned again and began to pray afresh.

On Saturday afternoon, as soon as Matthew returned from work, Shannon went into town to do some shopping for the Adair household. However, before she reached the mercantile, a window display caught her eye. A dress shop, and in the window was a beautiful carriage dress of tartan glacé. The bodice was cut low and square. The full skirt was gored and slightly trained, belled by the crinolines underneath.

It seemed ages since she'd seen anything so pretty as that dress, and the deep green and blue colors would be perfect with her complexion. Her practiced eye caught the subtle changes to the pattern from the dresses she'd worn for several years. Fashion hadn't stood still just because the Union and Confederacy were at war. Dress designers had been busy in France and England and other places in the world.

She entered the shop, her heart beating faster than usual. A small bell above the door announced her arrival.

A tall, thin woman pushed aside the curtain that divided the shop from what Shannon assumed to be a workroom in the back. Her appearance was austere, her attire an unrelieved black from head to toe. "Good afternoon," she said. "How may I help you?"

"The dress in the window. It's lovely."

"Yes. The very latest from England." She showed a quick smile, then asked, "Would you like to try it on?"

What would her father say if she came home with a new dress? Before the war he wouldn't have given it a great deal of thought. Now? He might think it an unnecessary expense. Rightly so, she supposed. But could it hurt to try it on? Just a peek. She needn't buy it simply because she looked at it in the mirror.

"You must be the new minister's daughter," the woman said. "I'm Mrs. Treehorn. This is my shop."

"I'm Miss Adair."

"A pleasure to meet you, Miss Adair." She motioned toward the back of the shop. "I don't believe the dress will require much in the way of alterations. You look to be the right size. Let's see if I'm right."

Less than an hour later, Shannon stepped onto the boardwalk outside the shop, the owner of a glossy tartan dress in the latest style. Mrs. Treehorn had promised it would be delivered to the parsonage on Monday afternoon. That would give her just enough time to prepare her father for the bill.

Shannon would begin by telling him she'd met a woman who was recently widowed, her husband killed in an accident while panning for gold in the mountains to the north of Grand Coeur. So tragic. Mrs. Gladys Treehorn's only way to support herself and her adolescent children was with her sewing, and while most of her customers were men buying woolen shirts and pants, it pleased her to be able to make dresses for the women of the town, few in number though they might be. Surely Shannon's father would approve of her helping the widow by purchasing one of those dresses.

She must hope the good reverend wouldn't see through her flimsy reasoning and know that she'd thought only of herself, not the dressmaker, when she'd agreed to buy the gown. But now she must hurry. She must get to the mercantile and return home before her father finished practicing his sermon.

She turned and stepped right into the chest of a tall man.

His fingers closed around her upper arms. "Careful there, miss." His voice was genteel, his accent blessedly familiar.

Shannon took a step back and looked up.

His eyes were blue, his skin bronzed by the sun, his hair the color of straw. He had a mustache that she thought might make him look a few years older than he was. A smile spread slowly across his lips as he tipped his hat. "I trust you are not harmed."

"No. Of course not." She placed her right hand over her collarbone, willing her pulse to slow down.

The man bowed slightly at the waist. "Joe Burkette at your service."

It wasn't proper etiquette to introduce herself to a man on the street. She should do nothing more than nod, if that, before continuing on her way.

But he saved her from cutting him, which she truly did not want to do. "Miss Adair, I presume?"

Truly it must have been a rare thing for a young woman to arrive in Grand Coeur if everyone guessed she was the reverend's daughter immediately upon meeting her.

Joe Burkette's smile broadened. "It's the red hair, miss."

"I beg your pardon."

"Just about everybody's heard about the color of your hair."

"Oh." She felt a blush warming her cheeks.

"You're from Virginia, I hear."

She nodded.

"I'm from Greensboro, North Carolina."

A wave of homesickness washed over her. She'd formed friendships with several girls from North Carolina when she was in school.

"Perhaps you would allow me to escort you home, Miss Adair. You really shouldn't be out alone. Grand Coeur can be a rough place."

"No. Thank you. I . . . I'm not going home yet." She pressed her lips together, horrified that she had said so much. Where were her manners?

"Then please allow me to walk you to your destination."

Surely it was better to agree than to stand there declining his chivalrous offer. She nodded as she pointed in the direction they needed to go. He turned and fell into step beside her.

"Where in Virginia are you from, Miss Adair?"

"My father's family was from Richmond, but after he married my mother, they settled near her parents' home. Perhaps you know of Brandon and Elizabeth Covington."

"I do indeed. My grandfather went to school with Brandon Covington."

This news brought a smile to her lips. How could it help but do so? It felt as if she'd met an old family friend, someone she'd known since childhood.

He continued, "I suppose there is some comfort in knowing my grandfather didn't live to see so many suffering in this war. With all the bad news that's coming out of the Confederacy, it's—"

She stopped walking. "I've heard little news of the war since arriving in this territory, Mr. Burkette. Kindly tell me what you have heard."

"It isn't good, Miss Adair. Grant has pushed Lee's Army of

Northern Virginia down past Spotsylvania. The most recent news we've had says there's a big battle taking place in Cold Harbor."

"Cold Harbor?" But that was less than twenty miles from Richmond.

"I've upset you, Miss Adair. I'm sorry."

"No, Mr. Burkette. I'm glad you told me. I don't want to forget what's happening just because we live so far from home."

He nodded. "Spoken like a true Southerner, Miss Adair."

Matthew sat in the chair beside his sister's bed, watching as she sipped the last of the soup.

As if she felt his gaze upon her, Alice looked up. "We must speak about Todd."

"What about him?"

"You're all the family he has left in the world."

"Alice—"

"Promise me you'll be there for him, Matt. When my time comes, I'll be able to die in peace if I know you'll see that he's loved and cared for."

Because I wasn't much of a brother to you when we lost our parents.

There was sadness in her eyes, but forgiveness too. "He adores you already. I can tell he does. He's a good boy, Matt. He won't be any trouble."

Won't be any trouble? What about when Matthew returned to driving stage? Was he supposed to throw the boy into the boot of the coach or strap him onto the roof? But he couldn't say those words aloud. He couldn't tell Alice he wouldn't take care of her son.

"Promise me," she repeated, softer this time.

If he made her that promise, he might be stuck in Grand Coeur or some other gold camp just like it for years to come. Or worse, he might end up back in San Francisco; he wasn't cut out for that. A little under two weeks of working as an agent, and Matthew already felt like he was trapped in a cage. Todd was nine. How many years before Matthew could return to the road without guilt? Six? Seven? More? Would Wells, Fargo even want him as a driver by then?

"You don't want to give up driving coach. I know that."

"Alice . . ."

"It's all right. I understand. But I have a suggestion. Would you listen to it?"

He nodded.

"If you were to take a wife—"

"Take a wife?" He straightened on the chair.

"Please, Matt, listen."

Reluctantly, he nodded again.

"If you were to marry a woman who would care for Todd, who would treat him with love and kindness, you could return to driving stage and know that he was well cared for while you were gone. Surely you could return to the place you made your home frequently enough that you could father him to some degree."

Marry. He'd given little thought to taking a wife. Just as well since driving stage allowed little opportunity to meet the kind of woman he'd want to marry. He wasn't about to tie himself to just any petticoat. If he were to wed, he would want . . .

Shannon Adair's pretty image—pale, delicate complexion; fiery red hair; flashing green eyes; stubborn, uptilted chin; the unmistakable air of superiority—drifted into his mind, pulling him up short. In fact, it made him want to laugh aloud. Because even if he wanted that Southern belle, he knew good and well she would never want him.

"Just think about it, Matt," Alice said, drawing his attention back to her. "Please."

"All right. I'll think about it." He stood and picked up her tray. "Now stop worrying and get some rest."

Downstairs, he left the tray in the kitchen and stepped outside onto the veranda.

"Verily I say unto you, Inasmuch as ye did it not to one of the least of these, ye did it not to me."

He recognized the voice in his heart. He knew the Almighty expected more of him than what he'd given. Todd was his nephew. He had an obligation to the boy. He had an obligation to his sister. But marriage? Did his obligation go that far?

In the town below, long shadows stretched toward the east. Soon the sun would sink below the mountain peaks. With sunset would come cooler temperatures—and more activity in the saloons that lined the main streets of Grand Coeur.

Miners were a lonely lot. Most who were married left their wives back in civilization somewhere. When they found gold dust, it was seldom more than what was needed to buy some groceries to fill their bellies and a little whiskey to warm them. But it was also almost always enough to keep them hoping that in another week or two or four or ten they would find the mother lode. They came to towns like Grand Coeur and Idaho City and Placerville with dreams of getting rich. Those dreams rarely came true.

At least Matthew had never caught gold fever. Maybe it was because he'd driven coaches in and out of towns like Grand Coeur for too many years. He'd seen what that particular disease could do to a man. It could make him do crazy things he would never otherwise consider doing, up to and including murder.

Given enough time, Grand Coeur could become a pleasant place to live. The gold would play out. Miners would move away. Brothels and saloons would close down. Families would move in. A school would be built. More businesses would open.

"Promise me you'll be there for him, Matt."

Could he make that promise to his sister and mean it? Could he give his word to be there for his nephew, even if it meant marrying in order to give him a mother and a stable home life?

God, help me know what to do.

As his brief prayer lifted toward heaven, he thought of his parents. God-fearing, the both of them, and they'd raised their children to be the same. But would his faith be enough now? Did he have what he would need to take a half-grown boy and guide him into manhood?

Heaven help him if he didn't.

On the first Sunday in June, there were at least another twenty men in the congregation than had been there the previous Lord's Day. It appeared news of Reverend Adair's fine preaching was spreading.

From her chair near the organ, Shannon was pleased to see that Joe Burkette, whom she'd met the previous day, was among the newcomers that morning. And the way his eyes kept turning in her direction, she couldn't help thinking she might be the reason he'd attended, that he'd come to see her rather than to hear her father preach the Word of God.

She shouldn't be pleased by that thought, but she was. It flattered her to have a handsome Southern gentleman notice her. Back before the war, she'd enjoyed the attentions of many such gallant men of Virginia.

Shannon pictured herself in one of her beautiful ball gowns, dancing in the arms of her dear Benjamin, resplendent in his uniform of gray with gold trimming. Oh, she'd been the envy of all the young ladies of the county when he'd asked for her hand in marriage. Benjamin Bluecher Hood had been quite the catch, heir to a great tobacco plantation.

But Benjamin was dead, and his family's plantation had been

destroyed by the invading Union Army. Oh, how she hated the Yankees.

Father would be ashamed of me.

She lowered her eyes again.

"My dear girl, there is enough blame to go around. The Confederacy is not without fault in this civil war," her father would say to her, as he'd said before. "And besides, we must love our enemies. We must do good to those who spitefully use us."

She knew that was true, of course, but it was hard after all she'd seen and endured. At the very least she knew her father would never have accepted assignment to this territory if not for the war. They could have gone on living in Virginia, living the genteel lives they'd always known, spending their time with beloved friends.

"'We know that all things work together for good to them that love God, to them who are the called according to His purpose,'" her father would add. "Even from war, Shannon. He can work good even from war, for He is sovereign."

She wanted to believe him. She wanted to believe that one day she would look back and see that God had brought good out of so much misery and loss. But it was hard to do. Hard to believe when tens of thousands had died on the battlefields or from sickness. When tens of thousands more had been severely wounded, many of them losing limbs or eyes. When civilians were left in hunger and want or forced to move far from the homes they loved. What good could come out of that?

She felt an awkward hush in the sanctuary and looked toward her father—who was likewise looking at her, waiting. Realizing she'd missed her cue, she moved to the organ bench and began to play the closing hymn, hoping her face didn't look as flushed as it felt.

Miss Adair's embarrassment, Matthew noted as he joined the rest of the congregation in song, had brought a pink hue to her cheeks that he could see even from the last pew of the sanctuary. Rather than detracting from her beauty, the heightened color only made her more so. She was without a doubt the prettiest female in the church that morning. And she was likely the only unmarried one, other than his widowed sister.

Unmarried.

Married.

It was a ludicrous idea, what Alice had suggested: that he should take a wife.

Matthew married to Shannon Adair.

That was an even more ludicrous idea. Even if he wanted to marry her, she would never want to marry him. She thought him a fool—or something worse—because he refused to choose a side in the war. And maybe she was right. Maybe he was a fool for not giving the war much thought. It seemed far away, but he supposed it wasn't. If the Confederacy won the conflict, it would change this nation forever. If the Union won . . . Well, the nation would be changed because of that too.

After the closing strains of the amen, Alice touched his arm and softly said, "She would be a good choice."

He glanced down at his sister. "I don't know what you mean."

"Yes, you do."

"She doesn't think much of me, Alice."

"You could change her mind."

He offered the crook of his arm. "I doubt it."

Alice glanced once more toward the organ. "Perhaps I can help. After all, she has agreed to spend a great deal of time with me and with Todd until . . . until she's no longer needed." She offered him a courageous smile.

It didn't remove the sting from her words, the reminder that she was dying and there was nothing he could do to change it.

Together they left the church, complimenting the reverend on his sermon as they passed him in the narthex. Then they made their way slowly up the hillside toward home. Todd raced on ahead of them, eager to get home to play with Nugget.

"Stay in sight," Alice called to him.

"I will, Ma."

The boy was obedient. Matthew had to give him that. But he couldn't fend for himself. He still needed looking after. Nine was young to be orphaned and living in a gold camp. He would need his uncle to make wise decisions regarding his care and upbringing. When Matthew returned to driving stage—and he would return to it—he'd have to know Todd was in good hands. If he was a wealthy man, he supposed he could send the boy off to a boarding school. But he wasn't wealthy. Wasn't likely to ever be wealthy. Which brought him right back to his sister's suggested solution: a wife.

When Shannon stepped outside the main doors of the church, she found Joe Burkette standing at the bottom of the steps. He smiled and tipped his hat when he saw her.

"Miss Adair."

"Mr. Burkette."

"A fine service. I told your father so already."

So he was waiting for her and not her father. Once again, she felt a rush of pleasure.

"Might I walk you home?" he asked.

This was the second time in two days that Joe had made this offer. Since her home was a mere stone's throw from the church, it wasn't as if she needed an escort, but it flattered her that he seemed intent on looking out for her.

"Civilization can come slowly to the camps," Joe said as she took his arm and they began walking. "A fine minister like your father will go a long way toward bringing that to pass in Grand Coeur."

Yesterday she'd cared only for the news he could share about what was happening in Virginia. But today she was growing more curious about the man. "What is it you do here, Mr. Burkette?"

"I own the livery stable." He smiled as he leaned closer, his voice lowering, as if sharing a secret. "It has been my observation that those who provide goods and services to miners become far richer than the miners themselves. Of course, that doesn't mean I don't hope to strike it rich on my own claim."

This surprised her. Mining for gold didn't seem a gentlemanly profession, and Joe Burkette seemed a gentleman. But then, society was quite different here in the West, a truth she had best accept.

"Perhaps I might take you for a buggy ride tomorrow afternoon. I'd like to show you my mining claim, if you're interested."

The image of Alice Jackson and her son—along with Matthew Dubois—popped into Shannon's mind. She'd seen them that morning, sitting in the last pew. That the effort to attend church had taken its toll upon Alice had been obvious to Shannon, as had Matthew's concern for his sister. She supposed a man could not be all bad if he could care so much for his family. Perhaps she'd judged him too harshly when they first met. Her father seemed to believe so.

"Miss Adair?"

She shook her head, returning her attention to Joe Burkette. "It's a kind invitation, sir, but I'm afraid I won't be able to accept." Reaching the parsonage, she released his arm. "You see, I'm helping to care for a member of our congregation who is ill. I shall be quite occupied most days with my nursing duties."

"Then perhaps another time." He sounded disgruntled, as if he wasn't used to being refused.

She smiled, hoping to soften her refusal. "Yes, perhaps another time."

Joe took a step back, tipped his hat again, and then wished her a good day before walking away.

How odd. She should have felt sharp disappointment that she couldn't accept his invitation. It was ages and ages since a handsome young man—with all of his limbs intact—had called upon her. And Mr. Burkette was certainly both handsome and young. It also wasn't as if she had no curiosity to see a mining claim. She did.

And yet she wasn't disappointed.

Nor was it Joe's image that lingered in her mind as she turned and entered the parsonage.

Dearest Katie,

I pray that you and your mother are doing well. I was informed yesterday that a major battle has taken place in Cold Harbor. I hope against hope that the news is wrong, that General Lee has not been pushed south as far as Spotsylvania. You promised you would write often, and I watch with anticipation for a letter from you so that I might know you are well and safe.

Father and I have been in Grand Coeur for two weeks. We have settled into the parsonage and have hired an Oriental woman, a Christian, to cook and clean for us. Her name is Sun Jie. Her husband, Wu Lok, owns the mercantile where we do most of our shopping. We were advised that he is the most honest merchant in town, and he seems to have the best prices as well. They live in a section of Grand Coeur known as Chinatown. I find myself quite fond of Sun Jie, and I am fascinated by her stories of China. In appearance, she looks to be no more than thirteen, but she is almost my own age.

In my last letter, I shared that I wasn't sure what I would do with my time and that I missed helping Dr. Crenshaw. It seems that God was watching as I wrote those words, for He has sent me to care for a woman who is, according to the local physician, dying. Her name is Alice Jackson, and she is a widow with a nine-year-old son. Mrs. Jackson came to Grand Coeur soon after our own arrival to live with her brother. She told me she expects us to become good friends, but I do not see how that would be possible. She is a Unionist. Her husband was killed fighting for the Yankees. If he had not died before Benjamin, it could have been her husband who shot my fiancé. How can there be friendship between two women who support such different causes?

I also took an instant dislike to her brother. Mr. Dubois stated in our first conversation that he does not care who wins the war, that it makes little difference to him. Can you imagine? But Father does not seem bothered by this man's point of view. In fact, I believe he thinks rather highly of Mr. Dubois. Heaven knows why.

A sudden image in her mind of Matthew caused Shannon to pause in her writing. It was tempting to describe him to her dear friend—tall, dark hair, blue eyes, firm jaw, broad shoulders, muscular arms, large hands. But why would she when he meant nothing to her? Better to think on someone who could mean something to her.

I have also made the acquaintance of a gentleman from North Carolina. His name is Joe Burkette, and he owns and operates the livery stable in Grand Coeur. His grandfather knew my grandparents. I believe he has taken an interest in me. Perhaps I shall write more about him in the future.

I will continue to watch for a letter from you. I pray that the tides will turn soon for the Confederacy.

Your devoted friend,
Shannon Adair

"You don't go wandering off today," Matthew said to Todd as the boy finished the last of the hotcakes on his plate.

"I won't."

"Let your ma rest and listen to Miss Adair."

"I will."

"And keep Nugget out from underfoot."

"All right."

His words were his sister's fault. Last week he'd been grateful for Shannon's offer to help care for Alice, but he hadn't worried if the boy would cause her any trouble. Now that the thought of marrying had taken hold of him, it seemed of paramount importance that Shannon like the boy, that she find him well behaved and obedient.

It might be better if Matthew worried more about her liking *him*.

A knock sounded at the front door.

"I'll open it," Todd said as he sprang up from his chair.

Matthew ran the fingers of one hand through his hair, then strode out of the kitchen at a slower pace than his nephew. Shannon was already standing in the entry hall when he got there. She didn't glance his way as she removed the lightweight shawl from her shoulders and draped it over the coatrack near the door.

"Good morning, Miss Adair."

Now she looked in his direction. "Good morning, Mr. Dubois." Then she leaned toward the boy, a smile bowing her mouth. "Good morning, Master Todd."

"Mornin'."

She straightened, her gaze returning to Matthew. "I hope Mrs. Jackson had a good night."

"She seems well rested," he answered. "And her appetite was better this morning."

"I'm glad to hear it." She set her reticule on a nearby table. "Any special instructions for me?"

He shook his head.

"Then I shall go up to her." She moved toward the staircase.

He tried to think of something more to say, but his mind had gone blank. He'd never given any thought to courting a woman before. He didn't know the first thing about wooing and winning a wife.

"Miss Adair?"

She glanced back at him.

"I hope you know how much we appreciate your offer to help. We would be lost without you."

In response, she gave him a brief nod. It would have been nice if she'd smiled at him the way she'd smiled at Todd.

Giving his head a mental shake, he set his hat on his head, said, "See you tonight," to the boy, and left the house.

The town was coming to life as he made his way down the hillside toward the Wells, Fargo office. Merchants were opening the shops.

Miners were heading up into the hills. Dogs without masters left their sleeping places and began searching for food wherever they could steal or beg for it. A freight wagon lumbered its way along Main Street. Several saddle horses stood near hitching posts, snoozing while swishing their tails. On a morning like this, it was hard to believe gunfire could erupt right in the center of town or that one miner could murder another over a gold claim. Grand Coeur seemed almost bucolic.

When Matthew entered the office a short while later, he saw William behind the counter, helping a customer. Matthew removed his hat and hung it on a hook on the wall.

"We'll get that telegram sent right away, Sheriff," William said.

Curious to see the man who represented law and order in this gold camp, Matthew remained where he was—and was taken by surprise when the sheriff turned around. "Dickson?"

"As I live and breathe. Matt Dubois. It *is* you. I heard there was a new Wells, Fargo agent, but I didn't believe it could be the same Dubois I knew. Had to come see for myself."

Matthew laughed as the old friends moved toward each other. He clasped the sheriff's upper arms. "And I can't believe it's you, Jack. I heard you were shot dead in Virginia City a couple years back."

"Shot." Jack mirrored Matthew's action, holding his arms tight. "But not dead."

"You don't know how glad I am to know it. And to find you here in Idaho Territory."

"What about you?" Jack cocked an eyebrow. "Never thought I'd see the day you'd give up driving."

"Makes two of us." He released his grip and took a step back. "It's just for the summer."

"Where are you staying?"

"The company's got a house up the hill." He pointed in the general direction. "My sister and nephew are with me, so I needed a place big enough for them."

"Full of surprises, aren't you, Matt? I never knew you had any family left."

Matthew shrugged. What could he say? That he was a poor excuse for a brother?

"I'd better get back to the jail. Had a bit of trouble at one of the saloons last night, and I've got more men in the cells than usual. But don't be a stranger. Stop by and we'll catch up."

"Why don't you come to supper some night? Alice would like to meet you, and I know the boy would think it special to have the sheriff of Grand Coeur sitting at the supper table. Let me find out what day would be best, and I'll let you know."

"Be my pleasure. I'm not one to turn down a home-cooked meal." Jack tugged his hat farther down on his forehead. "Right good to see you, Matt. Right good." He glanced toward the counter again. "Thanks, Bill. Let me know when you get an answer."

"I'll do that," William replied seconds before the door closed behind Jack.

Amazing how seeing his old friend improved Matthew's spirits. Maybe the time spent in Grand Coeur wouldn't be as bad as he'd once thought. And if he really hoped to get Miss Adair to marry him, he'd better be thankful Jack Dickson wasn't a churchgoing man or he might have some serious competition for her affections. Jack definitely had a way with the ladies.

Alice was having one of her good days. The kind of day that was too few and far between anymore. Her heart beat steadily, her breathing was unlabored, her stomach without pain. In fact, she felt well enough to come downstairs and eat lunch with Todd and Shannon at the dining room table.

"I think when we're done I'd like to go outside and sit on the porch," she said before taking another bite of her sandwich. "Oh, that is so good."

Shannon laughed softly. "That's the third time you've said so. I am quite certain it isn't *that* good."

"But it is. Still, you should know that I told my brother we can't have you go on caring for me *and* cooking. I've asked him to find us a cook. Although I'm certain we shall not find anyone who makes a sandwich as tasty as this. Or your fried chicken either. Especially since we can't pay very much for a servant."

"Father hired a Chinese girl to come in to cook and clean at the parsonage during the week. Her wages are quite reasonable, he said. Perhaps Sun Jie knows someone in her community who could cook for you. Would you like me to ask her?"

"Would you? That would be most helpful."

"I'll be happy to ask. Sun Jie and her husband are Christians, and she talks as if they know everyone in Chinatown. I'm sure she'll know of someone suitable."

There was something different about Shannon today, Alice thought. What was it? Then it came to her. There was a noticeable absence of underlying resentment. That's what it was. She seemed to have forgotten—at least temporarily—that Alice's husband had been a Union soldier. That Alice was related to "the enemy." That was good. Shannon wasn't simply doing her Christian duty or utilizing her training as a nurse. They were making progress toward becoming friends. And Alice so wanted that to be true before she died.

"I'll tell Matthew to speak to you about it." She pushed the now empty plate away from her.

Shannon rose from her chair and came around to Alice's side of the table. "Todd, would you fetch a blanket for your mother? We don't want her taking a chill while she's outdoors. And a pillow, please."

"Sure." Her son jumped to his feet and tossed a grin in Alice's direction. "I'll get 'em, Ma."

Shannon offered the crook of her arm to aid Alice to her feet, then the two women walked slowly out to the veranda and around to the sunny side where Alice sat on one of the wooden chairs waiting there. Soon Todd reappeared, blanket and pillow in his arms. First the pillow went behind Alice's back, and afterward Shannon tucked the blanket snugly around her legs.

Alice took a deep breath of the crisp mountain air. "Heavenly," she whispered.

"Todd," Shannon said, "will you stay with your mother while I take care of the dishes?"

"Sure." He sank to the floor of the porch.

"I won't be long," Shannon added before walking away.

Nugget scampered around the corner of the veranda and hopped onto Todd's lap. The puppy's paws hit her son's chest and his tongue swiped his face again and again. Todd laughed as he tried to escape the uninvited bath. Nugget's tail wagged back and forth like a metronome in a frenzy.

Watching them, Alice laughed too. It felt good to laugh, to feel an ordinary pleasure in life, to forget that there were too few of these kinds of moments left to her. Ah, but that thought was sad, and she didn't want to be sad today.

"Stop it, Nugget!" Todd protested, still laughing, proving he really didn't mind.

The puppy ignored him anyway.

"Here," Alice said. "Give him to me. Before long, he'll be too big to sit in anyone's lap. Look at those paws. When he grows into them, look out."

Todd stood, pup in arms, and placed Nugget in her lap. Alice pressed her face against the puppy's soft coat on the back of his neck and rubbed her forehead back and forth. The fur tickled her nose, and again she laughed, the sweetness of this day, this moment, bursting within her a second time.

Thank You, God. Thank You. Thank You.

From the corner of the house, Shannon observed Alice, Todd, and the puppy. Though the tenderness of the scene made her smile, at the same time unshed tears of sorrow caused the threesome to swim before her eyes.

There were things she, as someone who'd learned how to nurse the sick and dying, could do to ease the pain of Alice Jackson's moving from this life into the next, but there was nothing she or any physician could do to stop it from happening. She hated the helplessness she felt at such moments. Alice shouldn't have to die at such a young age. She shouldn't have to leave her son an orphan.

I've seen too much death already. Too much death.

God's will be done. That's what her father would tell her. And Shannon truly did want God's will. Only she would much prefer that

His will wasn't so difficult at times. She felt a twinge of guilt, realizing that what she wanted was for His will not to be difficult for *her. She'd* seen too much death.

Forgive me, Lord. I don't want to be selfish, to think only of myself. Help me to be more like Father, to serve and not want to be served.

"How is she?"

Her heart raced as she glanced over her shoulder, her prayer forgotten in an instant. Matthew stood mere inches away, and she was all too aware of his height and breadth. Though no later than one o'clock, there was already a shadow beneath the skin of his clean-shaven face. Would it feel rough beneath her fingertips if she touched it? An almost overwhelming desire to discover the answer swept over her. Swallowing hard, she turned toward Alice again, answering in a whisper, "She seems stronger today."

"Good. I'm glad you think so. I thought so too."

It seemed an eternity, but at last he moved a step or two away. Her breathing eased.

"I won't disturb her," he said in a way that caused a shiver to run up her spine.

She heard his footsteps carry him back into the house, and almost without conscious thought she followed after him. He looked surprised at the sight of her entering the kitchen. Feeling the need for a reason to be there, she hurried to explain, "Mr. Dubois, your sister mentioned that you want to find a cook."

"Yes."

She took a moment to tell him about Sun Jie and her husband. When he seemed unconcerned that she was recommending a servant from Chinatown, relief swept over her. Though why she should feel relieved was a puzzle to her.

"Maybe I could stop by and speak to Sun Jie on my way back to the office," Matthew suggested. "Would she be at the parsonage now?"

"Yes, she's there."

He set his hat over his dark hair. "Thanks. I'll talk to her." He paused, then added, "I appreciate all you're doing for Alice, Miss Adair."

"I'm glad I could be of service."

Wordlessly, he continued to look at her, something unspoken swirling in his eyes. Nerves tumbled in her belly.

"You've been a godsend," he said at last, sincerity in his gentle voice.

Unable to speak, she shook her head, the compliment making her uncomfortable for some reason. *He* made her uncomfortable for some reason.

"I'll see you tonight." He turned on his heel and left the house.

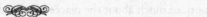

Matthew was halfway to the Wells, Fargo office before he remembered he'd intended to stop at the parsonage first. Something about Shannon's expression, about the green of her eyes, about the way she'd looked at him as she stood in the kitchen, had made him forget everything else. Including speaking to his sister about Jack Dickson joining them for supper later in the week. Couldn't do that without hiring a cook. Couldn't expect Shannon to prepare a meal for not only his family but a guest too. Besides, he'd just as soon Jack didn't meet Shannon Adair anytime soon.

A frown creased his brow at the return of that thought. He told himself it was only because he didn't want any competition as he sought to woo Miss Adair—and he only needed to woo her because of Todd, because the boy would need someone to mother him after Alice died.

He turned on his heel and walked back up the hill, turning aside on Gold Hill Road. A short while later, he rapped on the door of the parsonage. It was opened not by the expected servant, but by the reverend himself.

Matthew removed his hat. "Good afternoon, Reverend Adair."

A concerned expression crossed the pastor's face. "I trust nothing is amiss with your sister, Mr. Dubois."

"No, sir. Alice is doing better this week. I came to speak to Sun Jie. Your daughter thought she might know of someone we could hire as a cook."

"Oh, thank the Lord. Of course." The reverend stepped back from the door. "Come in."

Prior to coming to Grand Coeur and moving into the large home farther up the hillside, Matthew hadn't been the sort of man who noticed much about the places he stayed. Beyond the comfort of a bed and the quality of meals, nothing much mattered to him. Certainly not the size of a place or how a room was decorated or if there were enough windows to let in adequate sunlight.

But he noticed all of those things now, and he suspected the parsonage must feel a terrible comedown to Shannon Adair, who was unquestionably used to a home larger and finer than anything in Grand Coeur.

"Sun Jie," the reverend said, pulling Matthew from his thoughts. "Mr. Dubois has come to speak to you."

Like other Chinese women Matthew had seen in gold camps through the years, Sun Jie was petite. He doubted she tipped the scales at more than ninety pounds, if that. But she had inner strength. He saw it clearly in the dark gaze that met his for a brief moment before she gave him a respectful bow.

When he explained why he'd come to see her, she smiled and said, "My sister, she even better cook than Sun Jie. Sun Ling work for you, you want her to. I know. I bring tomorrow morning to your house."

Looked like Matthew could choose an evening to have Jack over to supper. Would that all of his problems were solved as easily as this one. He set his hat back on his head. "Agreed." His gaze shifted to the reverend. "Thank you, sir."

"Not at all. Not at all."

Matthew wondered if he should ask the man's permission to call upon his daughter. A part of him thought he should. Yet it felt dishonest somehow. He couldn't very well say that he was interested in marrying her so she could care for his nephew when Matthew went back to driving stagecoaches. No, he'd best concentrate on Shannon first and worry about her father later.

With the efficient Sun Ling in charge of the Dubois kitchen and Alice Jackson seeming to grow a little stronger each day that week, Shannon began to wonder if she was needed at all. At least not as a nurse, although Alice did seem to want her for a friend.

"Sit with me," Alice said to Shannon as she returned once again to a chair on the veranda on Thursday afternoon, this time on the north side of the house overlooking the small fenced yard where Todd played with his puppy. Alice's eyes rarely left him, a gentle smile upon her lips.

Shannon tucked the light blanket around Alice's legs before sitting on the chair beside her. Then she took up the embroidery work she'd brought with her from home.

"What are you making?"

"An altar cloth for Father's church."

"It's lovely," Alice said. "I was never much good with a needle. I did well enough for fixing a tear in my husband's shirt or for letting down the hem of Todd's trousers. But not for something as intricate and fine as that."

"My mother taught me to embroider. She didn't believe it was healthy for a woman to be idle, so when we were at home, we were embroidering or playing the piano or trying to perfect our painting. I suppose that's why I liked helping the doctors at the army hospital. It made me feel busy and useful, as if I could make some bit of difference in the world."

Of course, it was doubtful Adelyn Adair would have approved of her unmarried daughter tending to the needs of men who'd been shot or blown apart by cannon fire. Thankfully her father believed caring for others was of more importance than social conventions. "Mother's one exception in regard to idle hands was reading. She loved to read and she encouraged my love of books as well."

"I hope Todd will develop an appreciation for books and learning."

Shannon heard the longing in her voice, the fear that she wasn't going to be around to help Todd develop that appreciation.

"When I was little, Matt used to read to me at bedtime." Alice closed her eyes, and her expression seemed to indicate she could still hear that voice from her past. "And when there wasn't a book to read," she continued at last, "he made up stories for me. Oh, the tales he could spin." She laughed softly.

Shannon tried to imagine the scene in her mind. Alice as a little girl, looking up at her older brother, perhaps Matthew's arm around her shoulders.

Alice sighed as she opened her eyes again, her gaze immediately returning to Todd. "I don't suppose my brother has had time for reading much since leaving home. But perhaps now that he is here, with us . . ." She let the words drift into silence, the thought unfinished.

Shannon hadn't seen any books in the boy's room. They probably hadn't been able to bring much with them from Wisconsin. This the two women had in common. Shannon had left many things behind in Virginia, some of them quite dear to her. She took another careful stitch, trying *not* to remember those things she might never see again.

"Matt is going to make a wonderful father when he gets around to marrying and starting a family. He has such a huge capacity for love. Whoever he chooses for a wife will be such a lucky woman. I can only pray it will be someone worthy of him."

This comment drew Shannon's eyes back to the woman beside her. But Alice's gaze was now focused up the hillside, almost as if she were unaware of Shannon's presence.

Matthew Dubois marrying someone *worthy* of him? What a thing to say. Shannon had modified her initial opinion of him from their first meeting. He wasn't quite the ignorant, uninformed Yankee that she'd first thought him. He was kind to his sister and nephew, and he did seem to appreciate Shannon's help. He'd attended both church services since arriving in Grand Coeur—and as far as she knew would continue to do so. Thus she couldn't fault him there. But he was not a man of any social standing. No woman of good society would consider him a fine catch. And what sort of education could he have had, growing up in Oregon Territory and then striking out at an early age to work for an express company? It was surprising he'd learned to read.

"Whoever he chooses for a wife will be such a lucky woman. I can only pray it will be someone worthy of him."

She imagined that slow smile of Matthew's, the twinkle in his dark-blue eyes when he was amused. He was undeniably handsome. She could almost—

"Afternoon, ladies."

Snapped from the unwelcome direction of her thoughts, she would have been pleased to see anyone but Abraham Lincoln himself standing on the other side of the fence. Who she found was Joe Burkette, tipping his hat in her direction.

"Mr. Burkette." Shannon set aside her embroidery and rose from her chair, giving him a warm smile. "Won't you come and meet Mrs. Jackson?"

Joe opened the gate, but before he could take more than a couple of steps, Nugget raced over and jumped up, slapping Joe on the thighs with his oversize puppy paws. Joe brushed the dog aside with one hand. Not a mean gesture, and yet it caused Shannon to momentarily catch her breath.

Joe stepped onto the veranda, his hat in one hand. Shannon made the introductions, and Joe took Alice's fingers, bowing slightly. "A great pleasure to meet you, Mrs. Jackson. Joe Burkette at your service."

Alice nodded. "Thank you, Mr. Burkette. It's a pleasure to meet you too."

"I was wondering if I might speak with Miss Adair for a moment." Not waiting for permission, he turned toward Shannon. "Will you be occupied on Saturday? If not, I was hoping we might take that buggy ride I spoke to you about last Sunday."

There wasn't a reason in the world, as far as Shannon could tell, to refuse him. She wasn't needed at the Dubois house on Saturdays any longer. "I shall need to ask my father," she answered.

"Of course." Joe's return smile was confident, showing no doubt that the reverend would approve. "Shall we say one o'clock? I'll pick you up at the parsonage."

Delaney Adair set his few items on the mercantile counter and waited while Wu Lok tallied the purchases. Looking about, he saw that he

and the shopkeeper were alone in the store for the moment. Now would be a good time to broach the subject that had been on his heart for several days.

"I was wondering, Wu Lok, if there is anything I can do to be of assistance with your church in Chinatown." Although they'd spoken briefly with one another twice since Sun Jie had come to work at the parsonage, neither of them had brought up the matter of their shared faith until now.

Wu Lok was a quiet, unassuming sort, with a reputation in Grand Coeur for being honest. Not an easy reputation to acquire for a man whose race was almost universally despised by white miners.

Many a time in prayer, Delaney had asked God what could be done to stop that kind of hatred. Hatred for one color against another. Hatred for one religion against another. Hatred for one nationality against another. Even hatred for one brother against another. The only answer he'd received was the age-old one: as long as men were controlled by their sinful natures, they would find or create reasons to hate other men.

But this man—slight of build, with yellow skin and brown-black eyes—was Delaney's brother in Christ. They were to love one another, as the Scriptures commanded. *"By this shall all men know that ye are my disciples, if ye have love one to another."* Now if only Delaney could teach this to his congregation. If only he could make those who attended his church see the importance of loving all mankind, including those who were different.

"That very kind offer, Reverend Adair," Wu Lok answered, the slightest of smiles curving the corners of his mouth. "Only six of us, but God give patience."

Delaney suspected those six Chinese Christians knew more about commitment to God, to steadfastness of faith, than dozens upon dozens of the believers he'd pastored through the years. Untested faith was rarely strong. Deep, abiding faith was tempered through fire.

"Where do you meet for your services?"

"In our home. Someday maybe need building. Not yet. Someday."

"If you ever wish, you are welcome to use our building at a different hour of the day."

Surprise widened Wu Lok's eyes. "No. No. Thank you very much. Very kind. No. We meet in home."

Ah, the chasm between their two cultures was a wide one—made wider, no doubt, by cruel words and even crueler acts. But a bridge could be built, little by little by little. Delaney would not give up.

"Well, remember my offer, Wu Lok. And if ever you need anything, anything at all, you let me know." He paid for his purchases, gave the shopkeeper a brief nod, and left the mercantile.

Matthew wrote out the message coming across the telegraph wire. When he finished, he looked at William, who was adding numbers in a record book on his desk. "I've got a message for the sheriff."

There must have been something in his voice, for William looked up. "Trouble?"

"A shooting at the hot springs south of Idaho City. Two men dead and the gunman thought to be headed this way."

William gave a shake of his head as his gaze returned to the accounting.

Matthew put on his hat as he headed out the door.

The month of June had grown warmer with each passing day, and although mornings were still crisp, by this hour of the afternoon the sun beat down upon the town from a relentless sky. Dust rose beneath the feet of the men and horses who traversed the streets of Grand Coeur. From the saloon on the corner of Clark and Main, piano music—slightly out of tune—wafted through open doors, as if to greet Matthew as he passed by on his way to the sheriff's office.

Jack Dickson was there. Matthew handed him the telegram.

Jack read it, then swore beneath his breath as he lifted his eyes toward Matthew. "Politics," he said in disgust. "Too many men want to bring the war into these mountains. A Democrat shoots a Republican and gets help from the Rebs. A Republican shoots a Democrat and gets help from the Yanks. We're like a tinderbox up here, ready to explode into flames."

"Guess I didn't realize it was that bad." That wasn't true. Matthew hadn't *wanted* to know it was that bad. Just because *he* wanted to stay removed from the brutal civil war that had gripped the States for over three years didn't mean it wasn't in the minds and hearts of others around him. He'd become more aware of that reality in the weeks since he'd shared that breakfast table with Shannon Adair and her father.

Jack shook his head. "Gold camps are dangerous places even without the added complication of North versus South. We don't need any—" He broke off suddenly, shaking his head a second time. "No point borrowing trouble. But you'd best tell your drivers there could be difficulties on the roads. No telling what could happen next, especially if the fugitive escapes capture."

"I'll do it." Matthew took a step back. "You still coming for supper tonight?"

"Planning on it."

"Good. Alice and Todd are both eager to meet you."

The sheriff gave a half grin. "You do know I'll want your sister to tell me all about you as a kid. Right? Every little detail."

Matthew chuckled. He supposed he would do the same if he were to meet a member of Jack's family. The two men were similar in many ways, and they brought out the shared dry wit in each other whenever they were together. It had been thus from the beginning of their friendship. Although they hadn't spent long periods of time in the same towns over the years, they always fell back into an easy camaraderie when reunited.

But Jack's expression turned serious again. "You and William keep your eyes and ears open over at Wells, Fargo. No telling what you might learn that could help us keep the peace in Grand Coeur."

Matthew nodded.

His thoughts turned dark as he walked the two blocks back to the office. Maybe he should tell Miss Adair to make certain Todd stayed close to home until the gunman was found. No telling what a desperate man might do. Then again, it wasn't likely he would come into town even if he was escaping in the direction of Grand Coeur. He wouldn't want to risk running into another sheriff or his deputy.

Unless, of course, he had friends in these parts. Then there was no telling what the fugitive might do. And Matthew's gut told him that's what Jack meant when he'd said to keep eyes and ears open. Sheriff Dickson *was* afraid the gunman had friends in these parts.

Shannon saw the difference in her patient immediately on Friday morning. The good days were over, at least for now.

"Are you in pain?" she asked Alice as she placed the breakfast tray on the table beside the bed.

"No," the woman answered—but it was a lie. Her dark eyes gave her away.

"You've overdone." Shannon placed her hand on Alice's forehead and was thankful to find she wasn't feverish. "Did you stay up late last night with your supper guest?"

"No. Sheriff Dickson didn't stay long after we finished eating. And truly, we did nothing but sit at the table and eat and talk." She forced a smile. "And laugh. The sheriff is quite entertaining."

Shannon wasn't fooled. Talking and laughing could be exhausting to the infirm. She'd seen that in the hospital. She should have warned Matthew something like this could happen. She should have demanded that he not have guests in his home. But his sister had done so well these past few days, it had been easy for all of them, Alice included, to forget that she was dying. It had been easy to begin to believe her improved appearance and increased strength would last and last.

"Are you able to sit up and eat something?"

This time Alice didn't try to pretend. "I'm not hungry. Maybe a little later."

"You should take some laudanum. It will help you sleep."

"Not yet," she replied softly. "It muddles my head so. I think I would like to spend some time with Todd and his puppy instead. They always cheer me up."

Shannon wanted to refuse the request but found she couldn't. "For a short while. Then you must eat and rest."

It took only a few moments for Todd to answer Shannon's call. "Your mother wants to see you," she said when he appeared at the bottom of the staircase.

She didn't have to tell him to bring the puppy, for Nugget was right on the boy's heels as he came up the steps. The two of them were inseparable. Shannon understood that Todd had found comfort in the pet in a time of upheaval. So much had changed for him. His father was gone and would never return, killed on the battlefield. He was living in a strange house in a strange town, far from the place of his birth and all that was familiar. He was living with an uncle he'd never met before arriving in Grand Coeur, and—in a town where women were scarce and children even more so—he had no friends his own age to play with. On top of everything else, did he understand his mother was dying?

She watched from the doorway as Todd settled onto the chair next to the bed and took Nugget into his lap. The smile he'd worn as he'd darted up the stairs vanished, and in his eyes was the answer to Shannon's question. Yes, he knew his mother was dying. Even at his tender age, he could tell there'd been a change in how his mother felt.

And all of a sudden he went from being a playful boy to being solemn and careful. A little man, shouldering responsibilities he shouldn't have to shoulder.

"Tell me what mischief you and Nugget have been into this morning," Alice said softly.

Drawing a deep breath, Shannon turned away from the scene and went downstairs. She made note of the time. She would give them fifteen minutes together and then insist Alice eat and sleep. Or at the very least sleep.

For both their sakes.

Matthew was alone in the office when the two men entered and strode toward the counter. One of them was tall and fair and looked to be near about Matthew's age or a few years younger; he sported a thick mustache and looked too clean to be a miner. The other was shorter, older—in his forties, most likely—and had dark hair and beard.

"Can I help you gents?" Matthew asked as he rose from the chair behind the desk.

"Yes," the younger man answered. "How much to send a telegram to San Francisco?"

Matthew pushed paper and pencil across the counter. "It'll cost you a dollar, if you don't want to say much."

The two men exchanged a brief glance. Then the older fellow picked up the pencil and began to write while the younger dropped a couple of fifty-cent pieces onto the counter. Coins had become a rare commodity since the beginning of the war, and in towns like Grand Coeur gold dust was a more common way to pay. Matthew picked up the two half-dollars and rolled them over in the palm of his hand while waiting for the message to be written down.

It was a brief one, addressed to a Frank Thompson on California Street, San Francisco: *Conditions excellent. Encourage you and others to join us in Grand Coeur without delay. Advise of arrival date. Mack Patterson.*

"And when there's a reply," Matthew said, looking up from the paper, "where can I reach you, Mr. Patterson?"

"Best send that information to Mr. Burkette here. He runs the livery at the north end of Montgomery Street and can be found more readily than I can."

Joe Burkette? This must have been the man his sister had told him about. The one who'd invited Shannon to go on a buggy ride tomorrow. The man who, according to Alice, was competing with Matthew for Shannon's affections.

He felt an instant dislike for the good-looking fellow with the pale-gold hair and mustache. "I'll see that any reply goes to Mr. Burkette." He slid the pencil behind his ear.

Courting Miss Adair hadn't seemed an immediate priority to Matthew, what with Alice feeling so much better. But this was the second time in five days that he'd found himself concerned another man might win Shannon's interest before he could make a case for himself—first Jack Dickson and now Joe Burkette.

With a shake of his head he pushed away the troublesome thoughts. After sending the telegram, he returned to the desk to finish entering figures into a ledger—not his favorite task in the office, but he made sure it was done right. He and William Washburn were responsible for the shipments of treasure out of the Grand Coeur Wells, Fargo office, and he didn't want there to be any question about the accuracy of the records.

He'd just closed the cover on the accounts book when the door opened and William and Ray came through the doorway, returning from their early supper break.

"Still quiet in here, I see," William said.

"I sent a telegram." Matthew rose from the chair. "That's all the business there was while you were gone."

"Unusual."

"Least there hasn't been any of the trouble the sheriff was expecting."

"Not yet, anyways."

Matthew went for his hat. "Guess I'll head on home."

After nearly three weeks in Grand Coeur, folks in town had begun to know Matthew. He was greeted on the street by a merchant standing in a shop doorway; Mrs. Treehorn, who was hurrying home after closing her dress shop; and Jack's deputy, Horace Vale, riding down Main Street on horseback. He returned their greetings with a touch of his fingers to his hat brim, but his thoughts were once again on Shannon. He didn't have to worry about Jack going after the pretty daughter of the reverend because Jack hadn't met her yet—and wasn't likely to since he didn't attend church services. But this Burkette fellow . . . The Southerner was another matter. He was taking her for a buggy ride.

What would Matthew do if Shannon liked Burkette more than she liked him? Which wouldn't take a lot, to be honest. The two of them hadn't gotten off to the best of starts, although he believed matters had improved since she'd been looking after Alice and Todd.

Time to get serious, however. Beginning right now.

He opened the gate to the small yard and strode up to the front door. When he entered the house, he discovered Shannon standing at the bottom of the stairs. She looked especially pretty in the forest-green dress she wore today. It complemented the perfection of her pale skin and the fiery color of her hair. No wonder Joe Burkette wanted to take her for an afternoon drive in a buggy. Any red-blooded male would be attracted to her.

Well, two could play at that game.

He gave what he hoped was a charming smile. "Good evening, Miss Adair."

She didn't smile in return.

In an instant, he understood. "What's wrong?" His eyes darted toward the top of the staircase.

"Your sister's had a difficult day."

He looked back at Shannon. "Do I need to go for the doctor?"

"No." She shook her head. "He's already seen her."

"It's that bad? I should have been here. You should have sent for me."

"It was the doctor's day to visit, Mr. Dubois. I didn't send for him. And there was nothing you could do for her, even if you had been at home. She is weakened. That is all. It isn't . . . it isn't her time yet."

Her words were true enough, he supposed, but they did little to ease the guilt that washed over him. Guilt because he hadn't been there when she needed him, as had been the case for too many years.

"I'll go up."

Shannon lifted a hand as he moved toward her and the staircase. "Eat your supper first, Mr. Dubois. Alice is sleeping now." She glanced toward the kitchen. "I believe Todd is waiting for you."

Matthew didn't think he could eat at the moment, but Miss Adair probably knew better than he what was best for his sister. But Todd? Matthew wasn't sure he would *ever* know what the boy needed from him. He felt ill equipped to face him, to guide him, to raise him.

"Stay and dine with us," he said, desperation seeping into his voice.

"I'm not sure that I—"

"Please, Miss Adair."

"Well—" Uncertainty fluttered across her face, then disappeared. "I suppose it would be all right. I'll need to let Father know."

Relief was instant and strong. "I'll ask Sun Ling to stop by the parsonage on her way home." Not wanting to give Shannon a chance to change her mind, he strode toward the kitchen to speak to the cook.

Why on earth did I agree to stay?

It was all quite confusing. While she didn't dislike Matthew Dubois as she had when they'd first become acquainted, neither was he anyone she wanted to befriend. After all, they were much too different, if only because he had little sympathy for the cause of her beloved Virginia.

She'd come into this home to nurse Matthew's sister and to keep an eye on his nephew. It was a charitable act. Nothing more. She was performing her Christian duty while putting her nursing experience to good use. Compassion. That's what she felt toward Matthew Dubois. He was a man in need, and she'd responded to that need as God would have her. With compassion.

With her silent question answered to her own satisfaction, Shannon turned and climbed the stairs to check on her patient one more time. She found Alice sleeping, just as she'd told Matthew. She was glad of it too. Alice had resisted taking a dose of laudanum until late in the afternoon, and there'd been no doubt in Shannon's mind—or in the mind of the doctor—that her pain had been severe today.

For a moment, Shannon saw herself standing in the temporary army hospital some miles from Covington House. It seemed she could still smell the blood and the sweat and the fear that had surrounded her every day. She could hear the moans of those in pain, those for whom there had been too little laudanum—or, more often than not these days, none at all.

And with the memory came a sudden gratitude that her father had been called to the West and brought her with him. Perhaps she was terrible and selfish and shallow, but for the first time she realized she was glad to be far removed from the battlefields and the hungry and the wounded and the dying.

Matthew called her name softly from the bottom of the staircase. She took a step back from the doorway. "I'm coming, Mr. Dubois."

Those first minutes seated around the dining table felt awkward to Shannon. She wasn't sure why Matthew had pleaded with her to stay. But with the way he glanced at Todd again and again, worry in his eyes, and with the way Todd glanced toward the staircase again and again, fear in his eyes, she finally understood. Both of them, the boy and the man, needed to think of something besides the woman upstairs and how their lives would soon change when she was gone.

Shannon's heart went out to them, and she sent a quick prayer up to heaven, asking how she might help them.

Dearest Katie,

A full week has not yet passed since my last letter, but I am having trouble falling asleep and so I put pen to paper. I hope that this will reach you eventually, and I hope against hope that I will receive a reply from you soon.

My patient that I wrote you about last time, Mrs. Jackson, took a turn for the worse today. She was in pain and trying valiantly not to let her son or her brother see it. I suppose I thought this kind of bravery belonged only to the Confederate soldiers I once cared for, but I was wrong. Alice Jackson is every bit as courageous as the young men I tended in the army hospital.

I confess that I was also mistaken about Mr. Dubois. No man who cares so much about his sister can be all bad. Yes, he is misguided in his opinions about the war, but I suppose I cannot fault him for that. The fighting does feel far removed here in Idaho Territory. Even I sometimes find it possible to not think about the war for lengthy periods of time.

Above all, Mr. Dubois is a man out of his depth when it comes to his nephew. He has spent all of his adult life driving coaches for Wells, Fargo, never staying in one place for very long. Now he suddenly finds himself guardian to a young boy and is unsure of the future. I could see it in his eyes tonight as we ate supper.

I was determined to take his and young Todd's thoughts off of Mrs. Jackson, if only for an hour. You would have been proud of me, Katie. I entertained them with every story I could think of about our friends and neighbors in Virginia before the war began. Especially the funny stories. Like the one about Mrs. Samuels and the frog. (Remember what happened at their ball the year I turned eighteen?) I do believe I succeeded in my efforts, for they did laugh.

Tomorrow I am going for a buggy ride with Mr. Burkette. Without a chaperone. (Would Father have allowed it if we were still in Virginia and war had never come? Things are so very different now.) It will be my first opportunity to see the area beyond the town, including a mining claim. I am quite curious to see the gold that comes out of the waters in these mountains.

Please give my love to your mother.

Your devoted friend,
Shannon Adair

Joe Burkette, Shannon decided, had much to recommend him. Besides his Southern heritage, his looks, his age, and having all his limbs, he owned a profitable livery business and was ambitious for more. He was certainly most generous with his compliments and so very attentive.

And yet after they started back for Grand Coeur, Shannon found her thoughts turning to someone quite different from her escort. She and Joe had passed the Dubois house on their way out of town, and she'd wondered then how Matthew was faring today. The question had lingered throughout the drive into the mountains and the walk around Joe's mining claim. It lingered still: how was Matthew doing?

A twinge of guilt reminded her that there were two other people she should be concerned about: Alice and Todd. But naturally she hoped Alice was better and that Todd was dealing well with his mother's illness. It was just that Matthew—

"Miss Adair, I believe you've become bored with me."

She blinked, pulled abruptly to the present.

Joe was grinning, his head cocked to one side. "My feelings are quite crushed."

"I find that hard to believe, sir. Surely I could not wound you so easily."

His grin faded. "You're wrong, dear Shannon. I think you have the capacity to wound a man with a careless glance."

Although she laughed and waved away his words—including his rather presumptuous use of her given name—she suddenly wished they were back in town and she was no longer in his company. Which made no sense whatsoever. Hadn't she been listing his qualifications as a suitor just moments before?

"It's good that you aren't infected with gold fever," he said, the hint of a smile returning to his lips.

"Why is that, sir?"

"Because it's ruined many a good man. They taste a little success, find a little gold, and it takes over their lives. They become consumed by it."

"But *you're* hunting for gold."

"Only in passing, Miss Adair. It's the tradesmen in the gold camps who grow wealthy, not the miners themselves. At least not the majority of them. I would venture to say that Chinaman, Wu Lok, has stashed away a small fortune in the past two years."

"The man who owns the mercantile on Lewis Street? Sun Jie's husband?"

"Yeah, that's who I mean. Is he married? Afraid I didn't know that. Not that it matters." Joe clucked to the horse and slapped the reins against the gelding's rump.

Was Joe right about Wu Lok? Was he among the wealthiest in town? For some reason it bothered her that Joe had singled him out.

As if hearing her thoughts, her companion continued, "I get angry, thinking of all the gold and silver coming out of places like Grand Coeur, and most of it going into the Union coffers or making foreigners wealthy. Lincoln created this territory just so the Yankees could claim as much of the gold as possible. If I could find enough in that claim of mine, I'd use it to help the Confederacy win the war." He drew a deep breath and let it out before adding, "And even then it would take a miracle."

She heard the discouragement in his voice. "You think the Yankees are going to defeat us, don't you?"

"Miss Adair, the North has more guns and cannons and ammunition, more money, more men, more horses, more food, more of just about everything. The Confederacy has right on their side and not much else."

Do we have right on our side?

She stiffened at the unexpected thought and looked away so Joe wouldn't see the confusion in her eyes. When her father, in the first year of the war, had refused to join other Southern ministers in declaring that Almighty God was on the side of the Confederacy, she'd been angry with him and embarrassed for him. How could he not say it? How could he not *believe* it? Wasn't a great deal of the Old Testament about war and the side that God was on? Surely God *had* to be on the side of the Confederacy.

She could still see her father shaking his head. She could still hear him saying, "*If only it were always simple to know the will of God, Shannon. Have you considered that He is on the side of humanity and is more concerned with the war in our hearts than in who is victorious on the battlefields?*"

Her head was beginning to hurt. She disliked feeling uncertain. She used to be so confident of her own opinions. When had that changed?

Matthew sat at his sister's bedside, watching while she sipped a cup of broth. She was eating for his sake more than her own, and he knew it.

It surprised him, the depth of his feelings for his sister. He'd given her only passing thoughts through the years, had sent her only the occasional letter. But now . . . now he knew he would miss her when she was gone—and not just because he dreaded being the guardian of his nephew.

"Shannon told me there's to be a dance on the Fourth of July," Alice said as she placed the cup on the tray. "Did you know that?"

"Heard something about it."

"You should ask her to go with you, Matt."

"I'm not much of a dancer."

"That isn't true. I remember Ma teaching you how." She smiled and closed her eyes. "She would push the table and chairs aside and Pa would play his fiddle while the two of you danced around the center of the room."

He did remember. He remembered far more than he'd realized. Perhaps it was being with his sister again that made it all so vivid in his mind: the exciting adventure of the journey west on the Oregon Trail the year he was eleven, helping his father build their house out of logs in Oregon, carving the soil behind a team of oxen and a plow, harvesting the first crops, learning to shoot his pa's rifle and bagging his first deer, watching for Indians when news of danger reached them, family church on Sunday mornings until a minister came to the area. And the dancing. He remembered the dancing in their log house.

He shook his head. "That was a long time ago, Alice. I've forgotten everything Ma taught me."

His sister looked at him again, her expression sobering. "You need to ask Shannon to the dance before someone else does. She's out with that Mr. Burkette today. He may have already asked her."

The dislike Matthew felt for the livery owner was sharp.

"Shannon's so good with Todd. You should see them together while you're at work. I believe she loves him already."

"Alice—"

"It won't be much longer, Matt. You can't wait. There isn't enough time left."

He didn't have to ask what she meant.

Her voice now soft and wispy, Alice sounded far away, as if she already had one foot in another world. "I need to know Todd'll be all right after I'm gone."

"Okay. I'll ask her to the dance. I give you my word. I'll ask her the next time I see her." Feeling his throat tightening up, he rose and took the tray downstairs.

Joe Burkette had taken Shannon for a buggy ride. Matthew wouldn't be able to do the same without a horse. And he *should* own a horse. He'd be here for the next few months at the very least. It made sense to own a horse. Plus there was a small shed and corral on this property. Plenty of room for a horse or two. There wouldn't be the expense of stabling an animal.

Which brought his thoughts right back to Burkette.

He really didn't like the man. Something not quite trustworthy about his eyes or the set of his mouth or something. He was surprised the reverend hadn't thought the same thing.

From outside came Todd's shout. "Bring it here, Nugget. Bring it here."

Matthew moved to the open kitchen door and around the veranda to where he could see boy and dog playing in the yard. Nugget, it was clear, had no concept of the game of fetch. He attacked the stick his master had thrown, growling and barking and jumping about but never picking it up and carrying it to Todd.

"I believe she loves him already."

A sad smile curved his mouth as he remembered Shannon at the supper table the previous night. Alice was right. She did seem to be fond of the boy. And she'd taken pity on Matthew, too, entertaining him and Todd with amusing stories, taking their minds off the invalid upstairs for nearly an hour. He'd been surprised by the compassion she'd shown, although he supposed he shouldn't have been after the way she'd cared for Alice for the better part of two weeks. For certain the young woman with hair the color of burgundy wine and eyes the same green as the forest surrounding Grand Coeur wasn't the hot-house flower he'd once thought her.

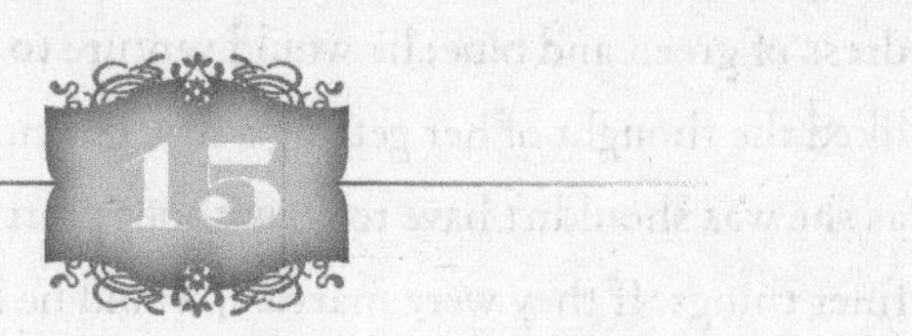

Delaney Adair's sermon that Sunday was taken from the twelfth chapter of Romans, the eighteenth verse: *"If it be possible, as much as lieth in you, live peaceably with all men."* He spoke of peace. He spoke of God's plan for the world and for nations. "'The Lord,'" he quoted from Proverbs, "'hath made all things for himself: yea, even the wicked for the day of evil.'" He promised that God's sovereign will would be accomplished, no matter what men planned.

Although the reverend never mentioned the war raging in the East, Matthew believed that was the underlying reason for his message. Did Delaney Adair realize a good percentage of his congregation was men who resented, even hated, the opposing percentage of his congregation? A message about living in peace with all men would surely fall on a few pairs of deaf ears.

Seated in the third pew, right side of the aisle, his nephew next to him, Matthew wondered for the first time about the minister's political leanings. He'd assumed Reverend Adair's feelings and beliefs about the

South and the war would be the same as his daughter's. But now? After this sermon, he wasn't so sure.

His gaze moved to Shannon. As she did every Sunday, she sat in an upholstered chair set near the organ. She looked very pretty in a dress of green and blue; he would venture to guess that it was new. He liked the thought of her getting a new gown. A young woman as lovely as she was shouldn't have to go without pretty clothes. She was used to finer things. If they were married, would he be able to—

Realizing how far his thoughts had strayed from the sermon, Matthew forced his attention back to the reverend in time to hear him say, "Let us pray." Matthew bowed his head and hoped he hadn't missed anything the good Lord had intended for him to hear.

After the prayer, the congregation rose to sing the final hymn, and although Matthew was aware of Shannon moving from her chair and onto the organ bench, he kept his attention focused on the reverend, not wanting his thoughts to wander a second time.

A short while later Matthew and Todd moved toward the narthex. He greeted many of the churchgoers by name. There was the sheriff's deputy; Mr. Rutherford, publisher of the *Grand Coeur Democrat*, and his wife; Dr. Featherhill and his wife; and Mack Patterson, manager of the Bank of Idaho at the corner of Main and Clark Streets, and his wife.

The wives.

There was no doubt about it. Married women civilized the gold camps and other communities. They influenced the culture of a town, even when those women were few in number. They caused even the coarsest of men to mind their speech and, on occasion, their hygiene.

Unable to help himself, he glanced over his shoulder toward the organ. As Shannon played the final chord, she lifted her eyes. Their gazes met and she smiled. It warmed him deep inside, in a place he hadn't realized was cold.

He looked toward the exit again in time to see Reverend Adair lean down to shake Todd's hand. "Good morning, Master Todd."

"Morning, sir."

"How are you?"

"Fine, sir."

"Good. I'm glad. And how is your mother?"

Todd's expression sobered. "Not too good."

"I am sorry." The reverend straightened, his gaze rising to Matthew. "Shannon told me Mrs. Jackson took a turn, but I'd hoped . . ." His words drifted into silence. They weren't needed.

Matthew nodded. "She insisted Todd and I come to church without her."

"Do you suppose she would like a visitor this afternoon?"

"She always enjoys seeing you, Reverend."

Delaney nodded. "Then I shall come. Shall we say three o'clock?"

Matthew nodded, told the reverend he'd enjoyed the sermon, and moved on out the doorway into the bright sunshine. Once at the bottom of the steps, he told Todd to run on home and keep an eye on his mother. "I just need a few words with Miss Adair. Tell Sun Ling I won't be long."

It was nearly noon. Sun Ling would have their dinner ready for them. The woman had agreed to stay at the house on Sundays until after the family returned from church and the dishes from the midday meal were washed. Then she would leave to attend her own church service that was held on Sunday evenings somewhere in Chinatown.

Todd didn't seem to mind his uncle's instructions. He set off at a run toward home.

He's a good kid. Matthew looked toward the entrance again. *And he deserves a loving woman to care for him.*

The congregation had mostly dispersed, although a few stragglers were still talking to the reverend. Hoping he looked as if he'd left something behind, Matthew reentered the church and made his way into the sanctuary.

Shannon had finished playing the organ and was now walking up the aisle in his direction. When she saw him, she stopped. "Mr. Dubois."

Matthew found himself suddenly nervous. He knew even less about courting a woman than he did about dancing with one.

"Was there something you needed?" she asked. Then her eyes grew worried. "Is it your sister? She hasn't—"

"No. It isn't Alice." He removed his hat, holding it by the crown in his right hand.

Relief swept across her face. "Thank the Lord."

"Yes. Thank the Lord." He drew a quick breath. "Miss Adair, I was wondering . . . I was hoping you might consent . . . I'd like you to go with me to the Fourth of July celebration."

This time it was surprise that flickered in her eyes. Surprise and something else, though he couldn't guess what.

He rushed on. "I've heard there'll be lots of food and good music and a dance too. And, of course, fireworks."

"A dance? With so few women in Grand Coeur?"

Matthew relaxed a little, seeing as how she hadn't refused him outright or announced she was already engaged for the evening with someone else. "Miners in these camps aren't a particular bunch, Miss Adair. If there aren't enough women to go around—which there never are—some men will take the part of the women so everybody can dance. I've seen them don an old crinoline for the occasion, but usually they just tie a colored string or a scarf around their arms." He touched his bicep.

"Surely you're joking."

"But I'm not."

"That doesn't sound very . . . very proper. Or dignified."

"Dignified?" He chuckled as he shook his head. He'd forgotten how sheltered Shannon was in many regards, how unused she was to life on this side of the Mississippi. "No, I don't reckon it's dignified. But these men have little enough fun in their lives. So they like to cut loose on occasion. In the camps, entertainment mostly comes down to drinking, gambling, and dancing. Everybody will want to dance on Independence Day, with or without a sufficient number of females in attendance."

A frown furrowed her brow. "I see."

"Some of the men who attend this church are part of the planning committee. I believe they mean to ask your father to join them."

That news seemed to ease her concerns a little. Something told him she was close to making her decision. He decided to press his case, saying with a smile, "I would much rather dance with you, Miss Adair, than with a man with a string tied around his arm."

Shannon couldn't help herself. She laughed aloud at the notion of Matthew Dubois twirling around a dance floor with another man. Of course, she shouldn't accept without talking to her father first.

"Will you do me the honor of allowing me to escort you?" Matthew asked, his smile vanishing.

Suddenly she didn't feel like smiling either. A cloud of butterflies took flight in her stomach. She didn't want to wait and talk to her father first. She wanted to be certain she got to step into this man's arms and whirl around a floor in time to the music. "I would be pleased to go with you, Mr. Dubois."

"I should warn you that I can't claim to be much of a dancer." The smile crept back into the corners of his mouth.

In response, a shudder of pleasure ran up Shannon's spine.

He set his hat back on his head. "I'd best go. Sun Ling will want to return to her home soon." As he turned, he added, "I'll see you in the morning, Miss Adair."

"Yes. In the morning."

She waited until he left the sanctuary before she stepped into the nearby pew and sat down. How unexpected. Matthew Dubois had asked her to a dance, and she'd *wanted* to go with him. She'd *agreed* to go with him. Gracious! What would her father say? She knew he personally liked Mr. Dubois. But would he consider him a proper escort for her?

Do I consider him a proper escort?

The image of Joe Burkette popped into her head—dashing and handsome . . . and Southern-born. She should want to go with him.

She didn't.

"Merciful heavens," she whispered, rising to her feet once again.

"Shannon? Are you ready to go home?"

"Yes, Father. I'm coming."

Todd lay on the bed beside Alice, her arm around his back, a children's storybook propped against a pillow on their laps. She listened to her son reading to her without actually hearing the words. It mattered little, for it was a story she knew by heart. Her own mother had read it to her from this very book when she was a child. Perhaps one day Todd would read from it to his son or daughter.

"One generation passeth away, and another generation cometh: but the earth abideth for ever."

Once the thought of dying had filled her with dread. How foolish that seemed now. God's presence had become ever so much more tangible to her in recent days. Heaven was ever so much more real to her. When she passed from this life into the next, she would be free of pain. And Edward and her parents and her grandparents would be waiting for her too.

Nevertheless, she was in no hurry to leave this earth that abided forever. There was comfort to be found in the knowledge that she would not die one moment too soon or one instant later than was in God's plan.

His ways are not our ways. His thoughts are not our thoughts.

Her eyes closed, she pressed the side of her face against Todd's thick, unruly hair and breathed in. He smelled of little-boy sweat and puppy-dog slobber, of pinecones and wood smoke. And suddenly she felt like crying, for she was certain she would miss these smells, even in heaven.

Forgive me, Father. I don't mean to cling to this world. It's only—

Her breath caught in her chest as the strangest of sensations swept over her. She would almost swear that someone had touched her hair, had breathed deeply of her scent. And an instant later an overwhelming sense of being loved swirled around her, a love so big it encompassed her son as well.

"Ma? You all right?"

She opened her eyes. "Yes, I'm all right, darling. I really am all right."

The Wells, Fargo changing station was located at the western end of Main Street, far from the center of Grand Coeur. Thankful for an excuse to be out of the stuffy office for a while, Matthew led the first pair of horses out of the traces and into the corral. Once there, he removed the last of the harness and set the two bay geldings free to slake their thirst at the watering trough and to fill their bellies with hay.

It wasn't until the four remaining horses were also in the corral that Clint Anderson, the driver, spoke to Matthew. "I was sorry to hear your sister's ailing, Matt. Is she doin' better?"

"No. Doctors don't give us much hope." *Any hope,* he amended silently.

"That's rough."

Matthew nodded.

"You going to return to driving eventually?"

"Eventually. But I've got my nephew to think of now."

Clint turned and leaned his back against the lodgepole rails of the corral. "I got a bad feeling about that shooting up in Idaho City. Nobody's caught the man who did it. He could be anywhere by this time."

He grunted agreement.

"Did you hear there was another attempt to hold up a stage comin' out of Virginia City? Confederates, they say."

Matthew wasn't surprised. Considering millions of dollars of treasure was carried into San Francisco by stage, only to sail out of its harbor every month, bound for the Union treasury, one couldn't expect Southern sympathizers to ignore those same coaches, ships, and steamers.

The previous year some Confederates had outfitted a ninety-ton schooner to use as a privateer. Their plans called for them to intercept bullion shipments on the high seas. The schooner, the *J. M. Chapman*, never cleared the bay. The Copperheads were arrested and charged with treason. Some were jailed, but others skipped bail to attempt to steal other gold shipments coming out of the mining camps.

"Company's hiring more guards to work the stage routes," Clint added.

"That's good. We could use them."

"It'll get worse before the war's over. Mark my words."

The war. It touched everybody's lives, even out here. He'd been a fool to think otherwise. The war had killed Edward Jackson, leaving Alice a widow and their son without a father. And if Todd had a father, Matthew wouldn't be in Grand Coeur today, wondering what he would do when Alice died.

Clint dusted the palms of his hands against his equally dusty trousers. "How 'bout joinin' me for a drink? I could use somethin' to wet my whistle."

"No, thanks. I need to get back to the office." No point reminding Clint that he was a teetotaler. He'd made that decision after he'd seen an innocent passerby get gunned down by a man who was three sheets to the wind. His ma had warned him more than once about the evils of drunkenness, and the best way to avoid it, he figured, was to avoid liquor altogether.

With a nod, Matthew bid the driver a good day and sauntered back along Main Street toward the center of town. But while he was still two blocks away from the Wells, Fargo office, he was hailed by Jack Dickson. He turned and crossed the street.

"Stage came in on time, I see," Jack said as Matthew stepped onto the boardwalk. "Any trouble?"

"No, but Clint seems to expect it eventually. He said the company's hiring more guards."

Jack nodded, his expression thoughtful.

Matthew had the feeling his friend had more to say. He waited, not bothered by the silence.

His gaze moving down the street, Jack finally spoke. "How's your sister?"

Surprised—he'd expected something about the gunman on the loose or about the war—Matthew answered, "Not good."

"Oh? I'm sorry to hear it. I was . . . sort of thinking about calling on her. If you wouldn't mind. I know your sister's a good Christian lady, and she probably wouldn't be interested in a man like me."

Strange. Matthew had been afraid Jack might take an interest in Shannon Adair. It hadn't occurred to him it might be Alice who caught his fancy.

"Never would've guessed you had a sister like her. Anyway, when she's feeling better, I'd like to—"

"Jack—" Matthew shook his head. "Alice isn't going to get well. She's dying."

That caused the lawman to take a step backward.

"I'm sorry, Jack. I thought you knew. I thought I told you."

"No, I didn't know. You didn't tell me. Are you sure? She didn't look that sick the other night. She—"

"The doctors are sure." Matthew rubbed his forehead. "Last week she seemed better for a few days, more rested, more energetic. But it didn't last long."

Jack removed his hat, stared at it for a few moments as if it might tell him what to say, then set it back on his head. "I'm sorry, Matt. Real sorry."

"Yeah."

He was going to have more of these conversations, Matthew realized, especially after Alice passed. People saying how sorry they were. People like Clint and like Jack who knew Matthew well but not his sister. People like the reverend and Shannon, who had become Alice's friends in a short period of time. People who were complete strangers. He would say "yeah" and "thanks" and "appreciate it." Some would pat him on his back a time or two, and there would be pity in their eyes.

He would hate it. All of it. He already did.

He jerked his head toward the east. "Bill'll be wondering where I am. Best be on my way."

"'Course. Didn't mean to keep you. Give my regards to your sister, please."

"I will." He started to turn, then stopped and looked back. When he spoke, his voice was low and earnest. "If circumstances were different, Jack, I'd have left it up to Alice whether or not she'd let you come courtin'. She's a woman who knows her own mind."

As the afternoon grew long, delicious odors—heavy with spices from the Orient—drifted up the stairs from the kitchen. Shannon's stomach growled in response, and that caused Alice to laugh, though the sound was weak.

"Between Sun Jie and Sun Ling, I shall grow as fat as my Aunt Claire," Shannon said, feigning petulance as she took the cup of tea from Alice's hands.

"I doubt that. But even fat, you would still be so very beautiful."

"If you think flattery will keep me from insisting you finish your tea, you are sadly mistaken. The doctor said you don't drink nearly enough liquids."

Alice's expression grew serious. "It wasn't flattery. I meant it. And you're not only beautiful but also kind. No wonder my brother is falling in love with you."

"Falling in—" Shannon felt heat rush to her cheeks. "How preposterous!"

"It isn't preposterous at all. It's the truth."

Shannon held out the cup. "Finish your tea."

"He likes to spend time with you, Shannon. Haven't you noticed? If it weren't for me . . ." Alice let her words drift away as she took the cup and raised it to her lips, sipping slowly.

"If it weren't for you, Alice, Mr. Dubois and I would scarcely know each other."

"Do you really believe that?" Resting against the pillow at her back, Alice shook her head. "I don't. Even if I was in the best of health, Matt would be in church every Sunday, seeing you play the organ and falling in love with you, just as he is now."

Why did Alice's words disturb her so? Shannon had been praised for her beauty by young boys and old men and more than the occasional mother of sons. She'd heard her share of declarations of love and devotion from the stronger sex.

But Matthew Dubois? She wouldn't want him to love her, even if Alice were right. Certainly she could never love him. They were too different.

Her heart fluttered, as if disputing her silent objection.

Matthew in love with her? It was ridiculous. Yes, he had asked to escort her to the celebration on the Fourth. But who else could he have asked? There wasn't an abundance of young, unmarried, respectable women to choose from in Grand Coeur. She'd simply been the obvious choice.

All the same, she remembered the crazy way she'd felt yesterday, knowing she wanted to dance with him, and the flush returned to her cheeks.

Not bothering to repeat her request for Alice to finish her tea, Shannon stood and left the bedroom. She hurried down the stairs and straight out the front door onto the veranda. Stopping at the railing, she closed her eyes and drew in a deep breath. There. That was better. How silly to be bothered by a sick woman's idle comments. Alice had taken a fancy into her head. Perhaps tomorrow they would laugh about it.

A sound caused her to open her eyes in time to see Matthew stride around the corner. He'd rolled up his shirtsleeves to his biceps, and his long strides ate up the ground beneath his boots. And when he saw her standing on the porch, he grinned.

"No wonder my brother is falling in love with you."

There went that quickening of her heart and that odd fluttering sensation in her stomach again.

"Miss Adair." He opened the gate and entered the yard. "I saw your father a short while ago, and he tells me you have a good eye for horses."

"Horses?" Her mind couldn't quite make sense of it. What had horses to do with falling in love?

"Yes." He climbed the steps onto the porch and stopped before her. "I've decided to buy a couple of horses. For me and the boy. Bill tells me the best place is a ranch about twenty miles south of here."

"Doesn't the livery have horses for sale?"

A slight frown furrowed his brows for a moment, then went away. "I'm told I'll like the stock down at the Crawford ranch better. More to choose from."

"Of course."

"I wondered if you might be willing to go with me and Todd tomorrow. Look at the horses with us. Give us your opinion. I've borrowed a horse and buggy to take us there."

"No wonder my brother is falling in love with you."

Oh dear. Oh my. Could it be true?

"Sun Ling can look after Alice for the afternoon," Matthew continued, unaware of Shannon's inner turmoil. "I already asked her. And your father said he would be happy to look in on Alice for a couple of hours. She won't even miss us."

Only two days had passed since Shannon had gone with Joe Burkette into the hills to the north. It would be nice to see more of the countryside. And surely, if her father thought it was all right to go with Mr. Dubois and his nephew, there was no polite way to refuse.

Even if she wanted to refuse.

And she didn't want to.

"Adelyn, I believe our daughter has some interest in Mr. Dubois." Delaney walked with his hands clasped behind his back, his eyes on the trail before him. "I wonder if you would approve of him. I confess I do. I like him a good deal. But is he wrong for her? They come from such different worlds."

It had surprised Delaney to learn that Matthew Dubois invited Shannon to go with him to the celebration on the Fourth. It had surprised him even more that his daughter wished to go with him. It wasn't, after all, a Confederate holiday, and Matthew had obviously different sympathies than Shannon. Such things mattered little to Delaney; it was people who mattered to him. But they mattered a great deal to his daughter. Or at least they'd mattered to her once. He thought distance and beginning to know folks who weren't born and raised in the South might be giving her a slightly different perspective. He hoped such was the case.

"I've prayed that she would give her devotion to the cause of mankind rather than politics, that she will find forgiveness for those who think differently than she does, that she will be a woman willing to not only bind up the wounds of soldiers but bind up the brokenhearted as well."

Delaney followed a familiar path, one he'd discovered two weeks before, far enough away from Grand Coeur that he was in the trees once again. Except for Sundays, he'd walked it every day since. Sometimes he saw men panning for gold in the creek that flowed in the deep canyon below the trail. At this time of day, there was no one else in sight. He liked the gentle sounds of the forest, the crunch of pine needles beneath his feet, the scurry of small animals running for cover.

"There is little, if anything, that is genteel in this place, Adelyn. But what is evil is not hidden as it often was in the life you and I knew together, where gentility could put a respectable cover over something wicked. What is evil here is visible to all. Flaunted, even. But good exists here too. Good people. Good intent. I'm needed here. Shannon is needed here as well."

He thought again of Matthew Dubois, of Alice Jackson and young Todd. He thought of the members of his congregation and other members of the community—men like the sheriff, who didn't attend the church. He thought of those whom the Pharisees would have shunned but with whom Christ would have broken bread—including the woman who had called to him nearly two weeks before from that second-story veranda in town. He thought of Sun Jie and Wu Lok and the fledgling church in Chinatown.

"Father, help me to make a difference for Thy kingdom. Protect my daughter and fill her heart and mind with all spiritual wisdom."

It was one of those perfect early summer afternoons. Warm but not hot. The sky was dotted with a few cotton-ball clouds; just enough to accent the expanse of blue. The rains of spring had spread a blanket of green underbrush through this mountain forest, and the scent of pine was strong in the air.

Matthew felt lighter in spirit than he had since the day the doctor told him Alice was going to die. This had been a good idea, asking Shannon to come with them to look at horses. While he spoke a little with her every weekday morning when she arrived and again each evening upon his return home, this would give him an opportunity to hopefully impress her a little.

"Woo her, Matt," Alice had said to him last night. "Show her some of your charm."

Charm? He wasn't sure he had any.

At the moment, Shannon and Todd were both eating some cookies she'd baked especially for this outing. Or so she'd told them when they'd arrived at the parsonage in the borrowed buggy. When Matthew looked over at her, there were crumbs in the corner of her mouth and on her chin. Swallowing a chuckle, Matthew brushed his own mouth and chin with his fingertips. The instant she realized his meaning, she blushed and turned away. When she turned back, the crumbs were gone. At first her expression was prim and unamused, but then she laughed, and soon Todd and Matthew joined in.

"Tell me, Todd," Shannon said, still smiling. "What color horse do you hope to find?"

The boy, who was seated behind Matthew and Shannon, leaned forward so his head was between their shoulders. "I don't know. Never owned a horse before."

"My favorite horse was a gold-colored mare with a flaxen mane and tail. My father gave her to me for my tenth birthday."

"I'm nine."

"Yes, I know."

"What was your horse's name, Miss Shannon?"

"Artemis."

When Matthew looked to his right again, he saw Todd wrinkle his nose. "What sorta name is that?" the boy asked.

"In Greek legends Artemis was the goddess of the hunt." She lifted her gaze to meet Matthew's. "Father didn't approve of the name. He thought it sounded too pagan for a minister's daughter. But I was studying Greek and Roman literature at the time, and he couldn't dissuade me. I was a very stubborn child."

He could believe that but wisely chose not to say so.

"I loved to ride her across the countryside, jumping hedges and fences. I wasn't supposed to go off by myself, but I did. All the time. I suppose I should be thankful I didn't break my fool neck."

"It would be a pity for such a pretty neck to get broken, Miss Adair."

Shannon's eyes widened.

Too late Matthew realized a gentleman wouldn't have said anything like that to a lady. Not one he'd known such a short while anyway. But what did he know of being a gentleman? What did he know about wooing and courting? Nothing. He was a Wells, Fargo stagecoach driver who'd grown up in the wilds of Oregon Territory, a man more familiar with horses and guns and rugged adventurers than the fairer sex. He'd never spent much time around people of culture or money or breeding. He'd spent even less with ladies of quality like Shannon.

He was thankful that he saw the turnoff at just that moment. It relieved him of trying to think of something to say to cover his gaffe. But if Shannon was offended by his words, she didn't say so. Instead she twisted on the buggy seat and paid close attention to the passing countryside.

"It would be a pity for such a pretty neck to get broken, Miss Adair."

Shannon enjoyed flattery as much as the next girl, she supposed. Benjamin used to pay her outrageous compliments. He'd had a silver tongue and had plied it with ease. He'd told her she was pretty in every way imaginable. But nothing he'd said had ever made her feel . . . *special* . . . the way she felt now over Matthew's silly comment. She tingled all the way down to her toes as the words echoed in her memory.

"Such a pretty neck."

"There's the ranch," Todd called, leaning forward once again, pointing with his arm.

The house was a single-level log building with a low roof. Not far from it was a barn, although not a large one, and beyond it were a number of corrals and some fenced land where horses grazed on shoots of grass. As they pulled into the barnyard, a grizzled fellow in a flannel shirt and coveralls came out of the barn and waited until the buggy halted before approaching them.

"Howdy," the man said. "What can I do for you folks?"

"Are you Mr. Crawford?"

"That I am."

"My name's Matthew Dubois, and this is Miss Adair and my nephew, Todd. Bill Washburn sent us to see you. I'm in the market for a couple of saddle horses." Matthew motioned with his head toward Todd. "For me and the boy. Bill said you've got the finest horses for sale in these parts."

"I do at that." His gaze shifted to Shannon. "No horse for the little lady?"

"No," Matthew began. "She—"

"I might want to buy one," Shannon blurted out. In truth, buying a horse hadn't crossed her mind until then. Why, she couldn't say, since she took great pleasure in riding. Perhaps it was because two years had passed since the last of the Adair horses had been taken for use by the Confederate Army, and she'd grown used to not owning one. But Virginia and the war were far away. Here in this rugged territory, men still bought and sold horses with ease. No soldiers were going to ride up and take them away.

She got out of the buggy without waiting for assistance, suddenly eager to look at the horses for her own sake, not Matthew's or Todd's.

The stubble on Lawrence Crawford's face had plenty of gray mixed in with the black, and Shannon guessed him to be in his fifties, although the way he walked as he led the way to the nearest corral made her think of a much older man. She suspected he'd been seriously injured in the past and wondered at the circumstance.

When they reached the corral, Crawford stepped onto the bottom rail of the fence and looked at the horses inside. "These here are mostly green broke. They're built good but they're young." He looked at Matthew. "I wouldn't recommend 'em for the boy or the lady, but one of 'em might do for you if you've a mind to finish trainin' yourself."

Shannon wanted to say that she could make up her own mind about what horse would suit her, but she'd learned that trying to correct such thinking in men was too often akin to spitting into the wind.

Crawford stepped down from the rail and led them toward one of the pastures. "These are the best saddle horses I've got on the ranch. Some I've trained myself. Some I've bought from men needing cash more than they needed their horses."

She supposed he meant miners who'd not done well on their claims.

Matthew slipped between the fence rails and strode out to the horses. Almost in unison, they raised their heads to watch his approach. Sensing no danger, they returned to grazing, all but the one he reached first. Matthew ran his hand over the horse's neck, withers, back, and hindquarters. Shannon heard him speaking softly to the sorrel and saw the horse's ears cock forward and back. The gelding had fine confirmation, although he was no more than fourteen hands tall, if that. He didn't seem large enough for Matthew, but he might suit Todd.

As for Shannon . . .

Her gaze was drawn to a bay mare with a long mane and tail, and her pulse quickened a little. That was the horse she wanted. She didn't have to look closer to know it. Now, if she could only convince Father to buy it for her. That could depend upon the price Mr. Crawford set. It would behoove her not to let the man know how much she already wanted the mare.

She returned her attention to Matthew and watched as he continued to inspect the animals. Even from where she stood she could tell he knew how to judge good horseflesh. It was in the way he looked at them, the way he touched them, the way he talked to them.

Another shiver whispered through her as she wondered what it might be like for him to look at her, touch her, talk to her in much the same way. Heat rose up her neck and into her cheeks.

What was wrong with her? She wouldn't truly want those things. He held no interest for her. None at all.

To which her heart whispered, *Liar.*

For some reason, the two horses now residing in the Dubois stable gave Alice another burst of energy. Perhaps it was because of the joy she saw on her son's face whenever he mentioned the sorrel gelding he'd named Dusty. He didn't seem to mind that he couldn't go riding often, with his uncle at work during the days and tending to Alice in the evenings. It seemed to be enough that Todd could brush and feed the horse and talk about him with his family—and with, as Todd called her, Miss Shannon.

The two women sat on the veranda on a Wednesday afternoon, both of them looking across the yard toward the small barn and corral. Todd was in view, brushing Dusty. The tall dappled gray that Matthew had purchased for himself stood in the shade of the barn, flicking at flies with his tail.

"I believe I've at last convinced Father to go look at Mr. Crawford's horses," Shannon said into the companionable silence. "I can't stop thinking or talking about that bay mare."

Alice swallowed a smile. How perfect. Perhaps the three of them—Matthew, Shannon, and Todd—would take rides together. Horses were a shared interest, and a shared interest was a good thing in a marriage and a family. They already shared faith in Christ, and both Matthew and Shannon were fond of Todd.

"Father says the price for the mare must be reasonable or he'll have to say no." Shannon sighed. "You'd think after three years of sacrificing that I wouldn't mind so much when I can't have what I want. Before the war . . ." She fell silent.

Alice looked at Shannon. "I know you'd like to buy that mare a great deal. I'll pray Mr. Crawford will set an unusually reasonable price for her."

"Thank you." Shannon met her gaze. "I never thought it could happen, you know."

"What couldn't happen?"

"Us becoming friends."

"Oh. That." Alice smiled. "Some things are simply meant to be."

"But we are so different, you and I."

"Not so very different. Not really."

Shannon's expression was thoughtful for a time before she answered, "No. I suppose you're right. Not so very different after all."

"Hey, Ma!" Todd called. "Look at me."

Her gaze returned to her son, and she was surprised to find him astride his horse, bareback. She felt a flutter of alarm in her chest, but she forced it to quiet. She mustn't be overprotective. She didn't want to make him afraid. The gelding was a calm animal. Her brother had assured her of that.

"Be careful," she called back to him.

"I will." He lay forward, hugging the horse's neck, his face hidden in the mane.

Alice felt a tiny catch in her chest. She wanted to remember every detail of this moment, of the way her son looked just now, the sun gilding his dark hair.

"He's a good boy, Alice."

"Yes," she whispered.

"You need not fear for him or his future."

Tears welled in her eyes. "I don't. Not really."

A little longer, Lord. Please give me a little longer. Just until I'm sure . . .

Raised, angry voices from the boardwalk outside drew Matthew to the window of the Wells, Fargo office. Across the street, outside of the saloon near the corner of Jefferson and Main, five men were gathered around a sixth, a man much smaller than the others. As they shouted, they gestured with their arms. One tapped the holster strapped to his thigh. Another shoved the one in the middle.

"There's trouble," he said to William as he moved toward the door. When he stepped outside, he saw something he hadn't noticed before. Against the encircled man's blue shirt hung a long, jet-black queue.

"We don't want your kind here," one of the men said loudly. "You need to get out." He swore, calling the man a derogatory name.

The Chinaman didn't look at the men. He kept his gaze downcast, whether out of fear or subservience or habit Matthew didn't know.

More people had gathered on the boardwalks by this time, but no one moved in the direction of the disturbance. Matthew wondered if anyone had gone for the sheriff. Maybe he should—

One of the assailants grabbed the black queue and pulled it upward, yanking the man two steps backward. The rest of the gang of thugs laughed. An ugly sound. Matthew drew a deep breath as he headed across the street. No time to go for Jack. If something wasn't done, this could turn deadly.

"You men have a problem?" he asked as he stopped near the hitching post.

They were a rough lot. Miners, from the look of them, but not very ambitious ones or they wouldn't be in town at this hour of the day. Their faces were unshaven, their clothes covered in dust and dirt.

"What if'n we do?" one of them—the largest of the group—snarled back at Matthew.

"Well, you see . . ." He stepped onto the boardwalk. "I was looking for my friend there. Need him to run an errand for the express office."

"Your friend?" The fellow's lip curled in derision.

The Chinaman lifted his gaze toward Matthew. Matthew didn't see fear and hoped what he saw instead was intelligence because they might both need to be quick thinking.

"He helps out sometimes," he added, his eyes returning to the larger man.

"We don't want his kind on this side of town, takin' our gold, takin' our jobs."

"Look." Matthew took a couple of steps closer, almost in reach of the Chinaman. Maybe he could just take him by the arm and lead him out of danger. "We don't want any trouble. The express office has work that needs done, and some of it isn't the sort of work any of you would be willing to do. So we hired this fella."

Was every lie a sin? He hoped not. All he wanted to do was avert a shooting or a lynching, and that's what this felt like it could become.

"You know what I think?" a second man said, a growl in his voice. "I think this ain't none of your business."

The next thing Matthew knew, someone shoved him. Then his left arm was grabbed. He threw a punch with his right, connecting with the man's jaw. Someone else slammed a fist into Matthew's midsection. Shouts erupted as he went down, taking one of the assailants with him. More punches were thrown before they rolled off the boardwalk and into the street. The hitching post stopped them from going too far. The other man raised up far enough to land a punch to Matthew's face. One, then a second. First to a corner of his mouth, next to his right eye. Pain shot to the top of his head and down his spine. He tasted blood and dust. His vision blurred.

"Break it up! That's enough. Break it up!"

Matthew'd never been so glad to hear Jack's voice before—although it was tempting to hit the man in the street with him one last time before they drew apart.

"Get back there."

Matthew got to his feet.

"Go on, folks. The show's over."

Matthew touched his mouth. His fingertips came away red. His head throbbed. To make matters worse, his eye was already beginning to swell shut.

"Matt, go back to the office," Jack said in a low voice. "My deputy and I can deal with this. I'll talk to you later."

Matthew gestured toward the Chinaman in the blue shirt. "He wasn't doing anything. You need to let him go."

Jack nodded. "He'll be fine. Go on. In fact, you probably should see the doctor. That cut above your eye might need a stitch or two."

"You sure? About him, I mean."

"I'm sure. I'll come see you later."

The pain behind his eye was bad enough now, he decided not to argue. He would trust Jack to sort things out.

Shannon was seated in the parlor, working on her embroidery while Alice napped on the settee and Todd played in his room upstairs. When she heard the front door open, her gaze darted to the clock on the mantel. It wasn't yet four o'clock. Much too early for Matthew to be home.

And yet it was Matthew who appeared in the doorway a few moments later—although he didn't look much like himself. His right eye had swollen shut. The skin was red and painful looking. It looked as if he had a cut above his eyebrow too. His lips were puffy and cracked.

"Mr. Dubois," she said softly, setting aside her sewing. "What on earth?"

"It's nothing."

Putting her finger to her lips and glancing toward the settee, she rose and walked across the parlor. "It isn't 'nothing.' That's obvious. Come with me."

Briskly she headed for the kitchen. Matthew followed right behind. Once there, she told him to sit in a chair, then went to retrieve some basic medical supplies. When she returned, she found Sun Ling studying the wound above his eye.

"He need stitches," Sun Ling said to Shannon.

"I know."

Matthew said, "I tried to see Dr. Featherhill on my way home. He wasn't in his office."

"No matter. I can stitch it."

"You?" Perhaps he raised his left eyebrow in surprise, but she couldn't be sure.

As with all female volunteers helping in wartime hospitals—and a few who served courageously on the battlefields—Shannon's eagerness to help care for the sick and wounded had been met with great resistance at the outbreak of hostilities. Many people thought women were a nuisance in the wards. Well-meaning, perhaps, but still just in the way of the doctors. Some feared the more delicate ladies would lose their moral stature. Even some of the wounded tried to object to a woman—one who wasn't a wife or mother or sister—caring for them. Shannon had learned to ignore objections, no matter from which quarter the complaints came.

"Sit still while I wash your eye and see how bad it is," she said, using her sternest voice.

Sun Ling delivered a bowl of warm water and a cloth, setting them both on the table near Matthew's left elbow.

"Thank you, Sun Ling." Shannon took up the cloth, dipped it in the water, and began to cleanse Matthew's wounds. When he winced and drew back, she said, "Hold still, Mr. Dubois. If you do this with the cleansing, what will you do when there is a needle in my hand?"

"It hurts."

"Of course it hurts. And it's going to hurt more before it gets better. What did you do, sir? Let a horse kick you in the head?"

"No." He tried to smile but the expression was more odd than amused, given the swollen nature of his mouth. "But it felt like it."

She continued washing.

"There was a fight across from the express office. I got in the middle of it."

"Fisticuffs on Main Street?" She *tsk-tsked* softly. "I thought you were smarter than that."

He winced again as she moved to the corner of his mouth. "Me too. But there was a little guy about to get beat up"—his good eye flicked toward Sun Ling—"and I reckoned somebody ought to step in and help him."

He didn't say the words as if bragging, as if wanting to be congratulated for doing something good to help another. She found herself liking him a great deal for it. She lightened her touch as she leaned a little closer, trying to be more careful.

His gaze met hers, and the kitchen seemed to tip to one side. Her breath caught in her throat as she straightened away from him. She felt too warm all of a sudden. Surely it was because Sun Ling was using the stove to cook supper.

"Are you going to take those stitches now?" Matthew asked in a low voice.

She swallowed. "Yes." The word cracked. She cleared her throat and added, "Yes, I'm going to do it now."

The next day, leaving her patient and Todd under the watchful eye of Sun Ling, Shannon and her father visited the Crawford ranch.

"Thank the Lord for such a beautiful afternoon," the reverend said, his eyes lifted heavenward.

He was right, of course. It was a beautiful day. The air was warm, the fresh scent of pine surrounding them as the buggy carried them south from Grand Coeur on their way to the Crawford ranch. It surprised Shannon a little, the way she felt about the passing countryside. She hadn't thought any of it nearly as pretty on the day the stage had delivered them into town over a month before. She'd found only things to criticize then.

"Look." Her father pointed toward the hillside on the opposite side of the creek that followed the road.

It took her a few moments to see the deer drinking at the water's edge. Camouflaged by the hillside, trees, and underbrush behind them, there were two spotted fawns, three doe, and a buck. The buck lifted his head to observe the Adairs pass, watchful but unalarmed.

Not so very long ago, there had been plenty of deer in her beloved Virginia, but they'd disappeared after three years of war. Eaten, she supposed, by Union and Confederate soldiers alike. She hoped none of the deer she saw now would ever be shot, even though she rather enjoyed a venison steak. She would rather think of them living free in these mountains.

Living free. She wanted to live free too. Was that why God had brought them to Idaho Territory, so they might be free? Free of war. Free of talk of war. Free of death and want and sorrow and regret. Free of—

"Is that the turnoff?" her father asked, drawing her attention to the road ahead.

"Yes, that's it."

He slowed the horse from a trot to a walk and guided him onto the narrow track that would take them to the Crawford ranch. Immediately she thought of the day last week when she and Matthew had followed this same road, Todd on the seat behind them, leaning forward with excitement when the ranch came into view. And thinking of those two, uncle and nephew, she realized she wished they were with her this time too.

Matthew had known she wanted the bay mare. She hadn't said a word to him about it. Hadn't entered the pasture to see the horse up close. Hadn't paid more attention to her than to the two geldings Matthew purchased that day. So how had he guessed she hoped to buy the bay? How had he been able to read her wishes so well? Was it because they were becoming friends?

Friends . . .

She was glad when the ranch house and barn came into view, for it helped focus her thoughts on the horse she wanted to buy and not on the man who was . . . who was becoming . . . her friend.

As had happened the previous week, Lawrence Crawford came

out of the barn upon their arrival. His jaw was still shadowed with the stubble of a beard, and he wore what appeared to be the same flannel shirt and the same pair of coveralls. He also wore a friendly grin.

"Well, Miss Adair. Good to see you again."

"Thank you, Mr. Crawford."

"Come to buy a horse for yourself this time?"

She ignored his question. "I'd like you to meet my father, the Reverend Adair."

"Reverend, eh?"

"Indeed, Mr. Crawford." Her father offered the man his hand. "A pleasure to meet you."

"Likewise." They shook hands.

"My daughter tells me you have many fine horses for sale."

"Glad she thinks so." He motioned with his hand. "Why don't you come have a look for yourself?"

Her father stepped down from the buggy, then helped Shannon do the same.

"That friend of your daughter's, Mr. Dubois, he chose probably the finest of the horses I've had for sale. A big gray. But I reckon Miss Adair can find one she likes."

Shannon imagined Matthew seated astride the big gray and felt something warm and wishful twist in her heart.

"That's quite the black eye, Matt." Jack leaned his forearms on the counter in the Wells, Fargo office.

Matthew grunted his acknowledgment. "Did you arrest the guy who gave it to me?"

"Sorry. Witnesses weren't clear on who started the fight."

"What do you mean? They accosted that man in the street. I stepped in to help. And I didn't throw the first punch."

"That may all be true, but there are some who say you did."

He grunted a second time.

Jack straightened. "That isn't why I came by. Wanted you to know they caught the suspected gunman in that shooting a couple of weeks ago up near Idaho City."

"That's good."

"Yeah." The sheriff rubbed the back of his neck. "I just wish it felt like I could relax now. But something keeps nagging at me. It seems like there's more strangers in town lately."

"Strangers?" That seemed an odd thing to say. Jack couldn't know every man in these mountains, not even by sight alone. The gold camps were filled with strangers.

"I mean the men who obviously aren't miners but who don't seem to be here on business either." Jack shrugged. "They make me nervous, especially if they're from the South."

"Not all Southerners are Confederate sympathizers." As he spoke, Matthew thought specifically of Reverend Adair. On the other hand, the reverend's daughter . . .

"Maybe not, but plenty of them are." Jack took a step back from the counter. "Let's just hope nothing happens to spoil the town's celebration on the Fourth. Maybe with a bit of fun, some of the tension will die down."

Or it could just make it worse.

The sheriff turned and walked to the door, but he stopped there and looked behind him. "Hope your sister's doing better."

"She's holdin' her own."

"Maybe I could call upon her."

Matthew nodded. "If you want to, I'm sure she'd take pleasure in seeing you again."

Delaney felt a catch in his heart as he watched Shannon stroke the neck of the mare while staring deeply into the horse's eyes. He'd seen his wife do the very same thing more than once during their marriage.

He gave silent thanks to God that the war hadn't ruined him financially as it had ruined others. He was not as wealthy as he once had been, but at least he could buy a horse for his daughter to enjoy.

Memories of the three of them—Delaney, Adelyn, and Shannon—riding together through the countryside surrounding Covington House filled his head. It seemed only yesterday. It seemed much too distant.

"She's beautiful, isn't she, Father?"

He looked at Shannon again. "She's a fine horse. Good conformation." He turned toward Lawrence Crawford. "How does she go?"

"I can saddle her up if you want to try her. Afraid I don't have a sidesaddle, though."

Shannon answered before Delaney could. "I'm able to ride astride if I must."

Crawford looked surprised at this bit of information.

Delaney said, "If you don't mind, yes, please put a saddle on her."

But he was certain his daughter had already made up her mind. They would return to Grand Coeur with the mare in tow.

The bay mare was hers!

Shannon felt far more excitement over the purchase than she'd anticipated. She'd loved riding from the time she was a little girl and had taken it for granted that she would always be able to walk to the stables and ride the horse of her choosing at a moment's notice. The past three years—after the Confederacy had taken the last of the Adair horses for use by the army—had taught her that nothing in life was guaranteed.

"I'll have to think of the perfect name for her," she said as she looked over her shoulder at the mare. "Oh, Father, thank you for buying her for me." She slipped her arm through his and gave it a squeeze, leaning her head on his shoulder at the same time.

He chuckled. "You're quite welcome, my dear girl. It gives me pleasure that I could do this for you." His voice took a more serious tone. "You've done without a great deal since the war began, and you've borne it without complaint."

Shannon felt a tug of shame. Had she done without horses or new dresses or her favorite foods or leaving Virginia without complaint? No. Perhaps she hadn't always put her feelings into words, but she'd complained in her thoughts and in the irritated looks she'd cast in her father's direction and in the heavy sighs she'd breathed in his company.

"I don't believe that's true, Father, and neither do you. I don't deserve your kind favor."

"Ah, but that's the very definition of grace, Shannon. Undeserved kindness and favor from God when what we rightly deserve is His judgment." He looked at her with a patient smile. "If the Lord God Almighty can show grace to me, however much more do I need to show it to others? Including to you, my daughter." He leaned close and kissed the tip of her nose. "I'm very blessed to have you with me. I know you might have chosen not to come to Idaho."

She let her gaze move over the passing countryside. "It isn't as bad as I thought at first."

"I'm glad that's what you've found."

Half an hour later, she watched as the bay mare—now christened Ginny, short for Virginia—was untied from the back of the rented buggy by Joe Burkette. As he led the horse toward a stall inside the large barn, he said, "If I'd known you were in the market for a saddle horse, Reverend Adair, I could have shown you a few." He jerked his head toward the corrals beyond the barn doors. "I've got some fine ones."

"My daughter had her heart set on this particular mare," her father replied.

Joe closed the stall door, then turned toward Shannon. "Then I understand. Who would not wish Miss Adair to have whatever she wants?"

Odd. She was certain he meant the words as a compliment. And yet they didn't feel like one. Or perhaps she simply didn't want anyone to give her a compliment other than one particular man with black hair and deep blue eyes.

"It would be a pity for such a pretty neck to get broken, Miss Adair."

"Well, you needn't worry about your horse," Joe said, intruding on her thoughts. "I'll see that she has the best of care."

"Thank you. And perhaps you could find a sidesaddle for me. I wasn't able to bring mine with me."

Joe gave his head a slow shake. "Not much call for a woman's saddle in these parts, but I'll see what I can do."

"I'm obliged."

He turned toward her father again. "Reverend, I understand you've been helping with the plans for the Independence Day celebration."

"Yes, I have."

"I trust you think it a suitable function for your daughter to attend?"

Her father glanced at her, then back at Joe. "Of course."

"Then I would like your permission to escort her."

It was Shannon who answered him. "I'm sorry, Mr. Burkette. I cannot accept your kind invitation."

Surprise filled his eyes.

"I have accepted a previous one," she added.

A flicker of annoyance replaced the surprise.

She could tell he wanted to inquire who'd asked her first. She was thankful he didn't. For some reason she didn't want him to know. Not because she was sorry she was going with Matthew. It had more to do with Joe's demeanor or that look in his eye or . . . or something she couldn't quite define.

"Well, Mr. Burkette," her father said, breaking into the taut silence, "we must be on our way. I have work still to be done, and my daughter must return to Mrs. Jackson."

Shannon sent a smile to Joe, hoping it looked genuine. "Please let me know when you find a saddle, Mr. Burkette."

He gave a curt nod.

She slipped her hand into the crook of her father's arm, and they walked out of the livery barn. When they'd cleared the doorway, she said, "Thank you again, Father. For buying Ginny."

"I'm glad I could do it for you, Shannon." He covered her hand with his free one. "I'm not unaware of the sacrifices you've made by coming with me to Idaho."

She felt a second twinge of guilt for the times she'd complained, by words or by actions. "We were doing without in Virginia, too, because of the war."

"Yes, but we were still in our own home. That made some hardships more tolerable." He pressed her hand. "I'm proud of you, my dear girl."

"You are?" She looked up to meet his gaze.

"Yes." He smiled, adding, "And I pray for you without ceasing." They turned the corner onto Clark Street and the parsonage came into view. After a few moments of silence, her father asked, "You aren't sorry you had to decline Mr. Burkette's invitation, are you?"

"No, I'm not sorry." She shook her head. "It surprises me a little that I'm not. I suppose I should want to go with him. He is from North Carolina, after all, and his family knew our family years ago."

Her father chuckled. "The heart wants what it wants, Shannon. And although the Bible warns us about the deceitfulness of our hearts, those hearts aren't always so. Not for the Christ follower. It's in our hearts that God resides and into them that He whispers His will."

"Oh, Father, it isn't my heart that wants—" She stopped, realizing what she'd been about to say was untrue. Her heart *did* know what it wanted. It wanted Matthew Dubois. She cared for him. Deeply cared for him.

"No wonder my brother is falling in love with you."

"Well, I declare," she whispered to herself. "Am I falling in love too?"

"What's that, my girl?"

"Nothing, Father." She smiled with determination. "Isn't it a glorious day?"

He chuckled again, as if he knew she'd changed the subject on purpose. "It is, indeed."

Matthew put his hat on his head and bid William a good night, then headed for home. With the sheriff's words still echoing in his mind, he found himself studying the faces of people he saw on the street. More than one stared back, but he figured that had more to do with the black-and-blue eye he sported than anything else.

And maybe Jack was right. Maybe there were more strangers in town. Thinking so left him with an uneasy feeling.

When he turned the corner, he saw Todd leap off the veranda and come running to meet him. That brought a small smile to his mouth. The boy's happiness over his horse had spread throughout the household. It was contagious. In some ways Alice was doing more than holding her own.

"Uncle Matt, guess what."

"What?"

"Miss Shannon got a horse today."

"Really?" He opened the gate. "The mare she was looking at last week?"

"Yep. That's the one."

He ruffled Todd's hair with his hand. "Maybe the three of us can go riding together sometime."

"That's what she said."

Matthew's smile grew a little wider. "She did?"

"Uh-huh."

It was a good sign, he figured, that Shannon was willing to spend more time with them—not just with the boy but with Matthew too. Maybe he wasn't as inept courting a woman as he'd feared. And after all, he didn't need her to fall in love with him. There were plenty of good marriages based on other things besides love—mutual respect, friendship, and necessity, to name only a few.

Matthew climbed the steps to the veranda. "Did you feed the horses already?" He didn't need to ask. He knew what the answer would be.

"Yep, and there's plenty of water in the trough too."

"You've taken the care of the animals seriously. Not just the horses but Nugget too. I'm proud of you."

Todd beamed in response.

Inside the house he was pleased to see his sister still downstairs at this hour, for the second day in a row. When he'd seen Dr. Featherhill earlier in the day, the physician had expressed surprise at the rally Alice had made in the past week, although he'd done his best to caution Matthew about expecting her strengthened condition to last.

Matthew walked to the settee where she was reclining, leaned down, and kissed her forehead.

She took his hand and squeezed his fingers. "Did you hear about Shannon's horse?"

"Todd told me."

Alice lowered her voice. "I think she's almost as excited about Ginny as Todd is about Dusty."

"Ginny?"

From the parlor doorway came Shannon's reply. "It's short for Virginia."

"Ah." He turned to look in her direction, silently wondering if she would ever be content away from the place she'd grown up. He could even sympathize a little. After all, he didn't want to give up driving stage either.

"I've asked Mr. Burkette to find me a sidesaddle."

Joe Burkette. Matthew didn't like the sound of his name. Didn't want him finding anything for Shannon. He supposed it couldn't be helped. The livery was the logical place for her to board her horse. Still . . .

"Hopefully he shall find one soon. I'm eager to ride her. I can ride astride if forced to, but I don't enjoy it as much."

Alice squeezed his fingers again before releasing his hand. Somehow he knew she wanted him to say something more.

He took a step forward. "Never could figure out how a woman manages to stay on a horse using one of those sidesaddle contraptions. Looks plenty uncomfortable. Sittin' atop a stage seems a far sight better to me."

"Then it's a good thing you weren't born a female, Mr. Dubois." She laughed softly.

Desire coiled through him at the sound. He thought there was a far greater reason he could be glad he hadn't been born female—and she was standing in the doorway to the parlor, grinning with amusement and looking prettier than he'd ever seen her.

Shannon was walking home on Saturday morning, her shopping basket on her arm, when the stagecoach barreled past her at the corner of Main and Jefferson. A cloud of dust followed in its wake, and Shannon had to cover her nose and mouth with her hand and turn her head to avoid getting dirt in her eyes. The stage came to a halt in front of the Wells, Fargo office, and before the dust could settle, Shannon heard shouts and saw men running toward the still-rocking coach.

Inquisitiveness drew her in that direction, too, although at a more restrained pace. She arrived in time to catch a glimpse of a man as he was lifted out of the coach; blood stained his shirt a bright red.

"Somebody get the doctor!" Although Shannon couldn't see him through the growing crowd, she knew the voice belonged to Matthew Dubois. "What happened, Clint?"

"Robbers, about seven or eight miles south of here. They wanted the treasure box. I told them there wasn't anything in it worth stealing, but the gentleman there . . . he pulled his gun and tried to prevent the robbery. That started the shootin'."

"Where's your guard?"

"Back in Boise City. He took sick at the last minute so we had to leave without him."

A man stopped at Shannon's side and in a low voice asked, "What happened, Miss Adair?" Joe Burkette.

In an equally soft voice she answered, "The stage was robbed. A passenger was shot."

"Did the thieves get away with anything?"

"I don't know. The driver said they were after the treasure box, but he didn't say they were successful."

A murmur in the crowd announced the arrival of the town's physician. Men moved aside to make way for Hiram Featherhill. Shannon had to stand on tiptoe and crane her neck to see him—hat on his head, black bag in his hand. When he knelt beside the wounded man, he disappeared from her view.

It wasn't long before the physician rose again. Then the patient was lifted from the ground by several men and carried toward the doctor's office. Afterward the crowd began to disperse. Next the green, wire-bound Wells, Fargo box—she assumed that meant the robbery had failed—was removed from the boot of the stagecoach and taken into the office by William Washburn, after which Matthew and the driver climbed up to the seat and drove the stage to the far end of town.

"I hope the passenger will be all right," Shannon said, at last looking at Joe.

"He was crazy to try to stop them. Besides, wouldn't have been anything of much value on a stage coming *into* Grand Coeur from the valley. Nothing to risk your life over." He shook his head. "Those thieves were fools. Time to rob a stage is when it's leaving a gold camp. That's when the box is full of treasure."

"You sound as if you know something about robbing a stagecoach, Mr. Burkette."

Her comment caused him to laugh. "Not hardly, Miss Adair. But I've lived in Grand Coeur long enough to know how the system works." He glanced down at the basket over her right forearm. "You've been shopping. Were you on your way home?"

"Yes."

"May I walk you?"

She inclined her head. "If you wish."

"You know, you really shouldn't go about town alone the way you do. It can be dangerous for a woman. Especially a woman as lovely as you."

"It would be a pity for such a pretty neck to get broken, Miss Adair."

She tried to ignore the memory of Matthew's words, especially when Joe was standing at her side, paying her pretty compliments. If only she wouldn't rather hear pretty compliments from Matthew instead.

"May I?" Joe reached for the basket.

She let him take it. Then they turned and headed in the direction of the parsonage.

"I have some good news," he said after a brief silence. "I've found a sidesaddle for you. I should have it next week."

"So soon?"

He grinned. "I thought you'd be pleased."

Maybe she'd been wrong about his reaction when she'd declined his invitation to go with him to the town celebration. Or else he'd forgotten his irritation with her.

"I am," she answered. "You can't know how very pleased I am."

"And perhaps you and I can ride together sometime soon."

Her father's voice echoed in her memory: *"The heart wants what it wants, Shannon."*

Her heart didn't want to go riding with Joe Burkette. Not sometime soon. Not ever. There was only one man whom she would wish to go riding with, and he would be seated on a tall dapple gray.

She made a noncommittal sound in her throat and quickened her pace in a hurry to get home.

It didn't make sense, trying to rob the stage *before* it reached Grand Coeur. While there might be things of value being shipped into the gold camp, mostly one would find legal documents and the like. It was far more profitable to rob a stage on the way out when the treasure box was full of gold.

Matthew knew it. So did Clint. So would the sheriff when he heard the news. But it seemed the thieves hadn't thought it through. Newcomers to the mining district perhaps. Or men made desperate by circumstances.

After the horses were changed out, Matthew made his way to the doctor's office. He found Hiram Featherhill at his desk. Jack was with him.

"How's the passenger, Doc?"

"He'll live. Just a flesh wound."

"Thank God for that."

"Yes," the doctor replied.

"I'd like to ask him a few questions. Is he up to it?"

"Maybe later. He's had a shock and needs a chance to recover from it." The doctor looked at the sheriff. "Jack here asked the same thing. Got the same answer. You'll both have to wait."

Jack turned toward Matthew. "The driver still at the stables?"

"Yeah, Clint's still there. He'll leave on the return trip in about an hour."

"Then I'll go talk to him now."

Matthew nodded to Dr. Featherhill before following Jack out the door. They both stopped on the boardwalk.

"Did you come to the same conclusion I did?" Jack asked.

"You mean robbing the stage on its way into town instead of out of it?"

"Doesn't add up."

"No, it doesn't."

Jack Dickson looked up at the sky. "There was another murder near Idaho City. A Confederate shot a Unionist for singing 'Battle Hymn of the Republic' and refusing to stop when he was told."

"Not much reason to kill a man."

Jack removed his hat and wiped his shirtsleeve across his forehead. As he set the hat back on his head, he said, "I'm sworn to uphold the law, and whether the men in these mountains like it or not, the law of this territory is set by the Union."

"I've got no quarrel with that, Jack."

"I know, Matt. I just wish there were more like you." He tugged down on the brim of his hat. "I'd best go talk to your driver."

Matthew remained on the boardwalk, watching as the sheriff headed toward the Wells, Fargo stables. There was more trouble coming, just like Jack said. Matthew could feel it in his bones.

After Joe bid Shannon a good day at the door of the parsonage, she left her shopping with Sun Jie and went to the church to tell her father what had happened in town. As she'd expected he would, he declared his intention to go to pray for the wounded man and to offer whatever assistance might be needed. Shannon went with him.

Tagging along had little to do with concern for the victim, however. The truth was she wanted to see Matthew again. All the way home, even with Mr. Burkette walking at her side, it had been Matthew whose face she'd seen in her mind. It had been her father's voice she'd heard in her head: *"The heart wants what it wants, Shannon."*

She hadn't thought she could befriend a Yankee, and yet she had become a friend to Alice and to Alice's son. As for Matthew . . . Well, she truly believed she'd come to feel something more for him than friendship. It seemed impossible that she could care for someone who didn't love the South as much as she did, but there it was. She did care.

Her father would say they could be friends with any Yankee. Those who trusted in Christ were all the same in the Lord's eyes, all part of God's family, grafted into the vine. Her father would say war could not divide them because they were brothers and sisters in the faith.

But when she thought of Matthew, it most certainly wasn't as a brother.

Heat climbed up her neck to flood her cheeks.

Thankfully, she and her father arrived at the doctor's office at that moment. Dr. Featherhill welcomed them, then took her father to see the patient in the examination room, leaving Shannon to cool her heels in the front office. She was still standing near the window when the door opened and a man wearing a badge entered.

When he saw her, he removed his hat. "Good afternoon, miss." He looked around the small office area. "Is the doctor here?"

"He's in the back with my father. With Reverend Adair."

"Ah. Good to hear the patient's up to having visitors. I'm Sheriff Dickson. Pleased to make your acquaintance, Miss Adair."

"And yours, Sheriff."

The door opened again. This time she didn't need an introduction.

"The heart wants what it wants, Shannon."

Matthew's smile was fleeting, but she felt its force all the same.

Sheriff Dickson said, "The doctor's in the back with the reverend."

"The patient must be doing better."

"Seems so."

"That's good." Matthew looked at Shannon again. "I guess you heard what happened."

"I didn't have to hear. I was there."

"You were? I didn't see you."

"I went to the store to purchase some groceries and was on my way home when the stagecoach came into town. I'm glad the passenger will be all right."

Matthew motioned toward the chairs near the desk. "Would you care to sit while we wait?"

She complied, hoping he would choose to sit in the chair next to her. But he didn't. Instead he moved toward the door to the examination room, then walked back to lean his shoulder against the wall near the entrance.

The sheriff took a couple of steps toward her. "I'm sorry I haven't had the pleasure of meeting you or your father before today, Miss Adair. Wish it was under different circumstances."

"You're most kind, Sheriff Dickson."

Matthew pushed off the wall and crossed the room to sit where Shannon had hoped he would moments before. "Been over to see Ginny today?"

It seemed rude, the way he changed the subject and pulled her gaze away from the sheriff. Not only that, his voice had a gruff edge to it.

"Not yet," she answered. "But I did receive some good news. Mr. Burkette has found a sidesaddle for me. He hopes to have it next week."

His brows drew a little closer together. He didn't look like he thought it good news at all. Which is why his next words were so unexpected. "After you get it, maybe you could go riding with Todd and me."

She forgot his scowl and the rough edge to his voice. It mattered only that he'd asked her to go riding with him. And unlike Joe Burkette's invitation, she had no desire to refuse Matthew.

"Thank you, Mr. Dubois." She felt the heat returning to her cheeks. "I should like to."

Shannon looked up from the book she was reading to see that her father had fallen asleep in his chair. Poor dear. Sundays never failed to leave him exhausted. Not wanting to wake him, she set her book aside, rose, and left the parlor, slipping out the front door and closing it behind her.

The day was warm, almost hot. Thankfully, the nights were still cool. There were other things to be thankful for as well. Church attendance had grown a little each week, and on this last Sunday in June, three new families—recent arrivals from California—had come to the service. And except for the occasional fistfight in one of the saloons, Grand Coeur had remained a relatively peaceful place.

At this moment the town seemed to be slumbering like her father, but she had no delusions. Many of the inhabitants of Grand Coeur held little reverence for Sundays. There would be plenty of noise coming from the saloons as the day grew long. But for now all appeared at rest.

But Shannon didn't feel like resting. A walk would suit her much better.

She heard the sound of hoofbeats on the road and turned to see who was coming down Gold Hill Road. When the rider came into view, she felt a sharp disappointment, only then realizing she'd hoped it would be Matthew on his tall dapple gray. Instead she recognized Joe Burkette.

When he saw her, he waved an arm as he nudged his horse into a trot and steered him toward the parsonage. "Miss Adair," he called as he drew closer. "I was hoping I would find you at home."

"You almost missed me, Mr. Burkette. I'm going for a walk."

"It's a fine day for it." He reined in and dismounted. "Please allow me to join you."

He was persistent. She could say that about him. And she couldn't think of a reason to refuse. So she nodded.

Joe tied his horse to the rail of the porch, then offered his hand to assist her down the few steps to the ground. Afterward he motioned for her to proceed, allowing her to determine the direction they would go.

Shannon lifted the hem of her skirt and walked up the hillside between the parsonage and the church building. When she reached Canyon Road, Joe at her side, she chose to go left, following the road into the mountains. Turning right would have led her toward the Dubois home. Would she have turned that way if she'd been alone?

Oh, she wished she could stop herself from thinking such things.

Determined to do so, she looked at her escort. "I didn't see you in church this morning, Mr. Burkette."

"I'm flattered you noticed." He smiled and winked at her.

Winked? The impertinence of the man. She looked straight ahead and quickened her pace.

"Have I upset you, Miss Adair?"

"Not at all."

"But I believe I have."

You flatter yourself, sir, she wanted to say. Only that was unfair. He had upset her. She didn't want him winking at her. It was rude and . . . and suggested something between them that didn't exist.

"Miss Adair, please." His hand closed around her upper arm and drew her to a stop. "Whatever I did, I offer you my sincerest apology."

Perhaps she was overreacting. Things were different in the West. Rules of etiquette were not so strictly observed in a place like Grand Coeur. Was a wink such a terrible breach? It wasn't his fault her heart continued to pull her in another direction—a direction she wasn't convinced she should go.

An old memory came suddenly to mind. She and her mother had been together in Shannon's bedroom, Adelyn Adair brushing her hair as they prepared to attend a ball. The conversation had turned to some of the young men who were vying for Shannon's favor. "*It is the character of a man that matters, Shannon. Remember, it is not so much what a man has as what he is on the inside. Do not be influenced by mere magnetism. You will rue it if you are.*"

Six months later her mother had passed away, and the sting of missing her almost overwhelmed Shannon. How she wished she could turn to her mother now for much-needed advice.

"Miss Adair?"

She blinked, shoving away the memory into a deep corner of her heart. "Your apology is accepted, Mr. Burkette. And please, don't trouble yourself. Let us walk." To show that she held no hard feelings, she slipped her hand into the crook of his arm as they continued along the road.

After church, at Alice's insistence, Matthew and Todd went for a ride on their horses. When they returned, they put the two geldings into the corral beside the stable and tossed hay into the manger. Matthew was pumping water into the trough when Jack Dickson strode into view.

"Matt," he said with a nod.

"Jack."

"You busy? Hate to intrude on your Sunday."

"It's all right. We're finished here."

"Uncle Matt," Todd said quietly, "I'm gonna go see what Ma's doin'."

"Okay." He watched as the boy ran to the house and disappeared inside.

Jack glanced toward the corral. "Couple of fine horses you got there. Got them from Lawrence Crawford, didn't you?"

"Yeah."

The sheriff bumped his hat up on his forehead with the knuckles of his right hand. "I wanted to talk to you about the trouble yesterday. Stopped by Washburn's place, but he wasn't at home."

Matthew motioned toward the house. "Let's have a seat and you can tell me what's on your mind."

They crossed the yard in silence, neither speaking until they'd settled onto the veranda chairs.

"Matt," Jack began, "you're a sharp thinker. You got good instincts." He leaned forward, forearms resting on his thighs. "My gut tells me that robbery yesterday wasn't a bungled job by some amateur thieves. It was something more. What do you think?"

Matthew nodded. "The same."

"And maybe it was no accident that guard who was supposed to be on the stage took sick at the last minute."

That thought had crossed Matthew's mind too.

"I'm riding down to Boise City in two or three days to talk to him. I'd like you to come along with me."

"Why me?"

"Because I trust you, and you might catch something I miss. You've been driving stagecoaches in and out of mining camps for Wells, Fargo a lot longer than I've been a sheriff."

"All right. If you think I can help."

"I do." Jack stood. "I'll let you know what day."

Matthew rose from his chair. "Sounds good."

Jack Dickson stepped off the porch and strode away.

Boise City was a bustling supply town, birthed near the intersection of the Oregon Trail and the main road connecting the Boise Basin and the Owyhee mining camps. Unlike Idaho City, the largest city in the Northwest, and other gold and silver towns in the mountains of the territory, the inhabitants of Boise City were, for the most part, strong supporters of the Union.

That was certainly true of Sumner Hill, the agent in charge of the Boise City Wells, Fargo office.

"I don't know where Cantrell went from here," he told Matthew and Jack when asked about the guard who should have been on the stage four days earlier, "but I reckon he's up to no good, wherever he is." He muttered an oath beneath his breath.

Matthew exchanged a look with Jack before asking, "What have you heard?"

"Nothing specific. Nothing we haven't been expecting. You heard of the Red Fox? He's been seen in this territory."

"The Confederate captain, in Idaho?" The name was well-known in California. Captain Ingram headed up a band of guerrillas who were modeled after the notorious Quantrill's Raiders. Bushwhackers, murderers, and thieves, in Matthew's opinion, disguised as soldiers. "And you think Cantrell is one of his men?"

"Yeah. That's what I think."

Sheriff Dickson spoke up. "Where was he last seen?"

"Captain Ingram? In Silver City a few weeks ago. But nobody knows for sure where he is now."

With all the gold coming out of the Boise Basin, Matthew would wager he knew where the captain and his men were. Somewhere in the mountains to the north, scouting out the best place and best way to get their hands on the treasure being shipped on the Wells, Fargo stagecoaches.

"The company's hiring more men to guard the stages going in and out of the Idaho mining camps," Sumner said. "And you can be sure I'll know where their sympathies lie before they're hired. Won't make the same mistake I made with Cantrell." He shook his head. "Never should've let that stage leave without a messenger riding guard."

"Anybody can make a mistake," Matthew replied—and then silently thanked God for sparing the passenger's life.

With their questions answered, Matthew and Jack thanked Sumner Hill for his help and went outside. They paused on the boardwalk, watching the activity in the town.

After a while Jack said, "We need to find out where Captain Ingram is."

"Yeah."

"Do you think he was behind that robbery attempt?"

Matthew shook his head. "I don't know. I've never heard of him attempting to hold up a stage that didn't have plenty of treasure on board."

Jack drew in a breath and let it out. "It feels like a test."

A test. Yeah, that's what it felt like. And it was Wells, Fargo they were testing. That made it personal for Matthew. He'd worked for the company for a lot of years. He felt a strong loyalty to Wells, Fargo, to the men who ran it, and to the ones who drove for them. He didn't want to see a stage coming in or going out of Grand Coeur robbed on his watch. He didn't want to see anyone else get shot either.

Jack looked at him. "Before we start back, I'd like to talk to the local sheriff. Want to join me?"

"I don't imagine I can be of any help to you there. If you don't mind, I think I'll check out the general store. See if there's anything I want to take back for my sister and nephew."

"Suit yourself. I'll meet you back here in an hour or so."

Matthew waited until Jack mounted his horse and rode down the street toward the sheriff's office before he turned and walked to the large general store a block away.

He found a pretty shawl to buy for Alice. She would tell him it was a waste of money, but he didn't care. He would buy it for her anyway. But what did a nine-year-old boy want when it came to toys or games? Todd and his mother had brought little with them from Wisconsin. Since Alice knew she was dying, she wouldn't have left behind anything of importance. Which must mean they hadn't owned much to begin with.

Lord, how little I knew about the life my own flesh and blood led before they came here.

Well, he could hope to make up for some of that neglect by taking care of Todd to the best of his ability. He moved slowly down the aisle, checking the items on the shelves to his left and his right.

"May I help you, sir?"

He looked up to find a matronly woman in a dark-brown dress

standing a few steps ahead of him. "Yes." He cleared his throat. "I'm looking for a gift for my nephew."

"How old is the boy?"

"Nine."

She nodded. "Are you looking for something practical like clothing or—"

"No. I want something fun."

"Ah." Her tone seemed disapproving. "Please follow me." She turned and led the way to the end of the aisle, then turned left and walked to the far wall. "We have a number of items that boys enjoy. Here's what you need for a game of battledore and shuttlecock." She gestured toward each item as she spoke. "And over here we have some cloth balls. Boys can find many different ways to entertain themselves with balls. And of course the rolling hoops are quite popular with children."

What should he choose? He'd spent most of his youth working the farm beside his father. There hadn't been much time for play. But things were different for Todd. He couldn't work beside his uncle, and while he now owned both a puppy and a horse, he couldn't spend all of his time with the animals.

Matthew made a snap decision. "I'll take one of each."

The look on the woman's face said she thought he was spoiling his nephew. She could be right. But there were few children in Grand Coeur, none close to Todd's age, and no balls or hoops or rackets in the town's general stores. Better to buy them while he was here. Who knew when he would come south into the valley next?

For a moment he wondered if he should look for something for Shannon. No. He supposed that wouldn't be appropriate just yet, even though it seemed to him that this courtship was moving in the right direction. Better he wait.

He paid for the items, and as he carried them out of the store, he said a quick prayer that his horse wouldn't be skittish about the hoop and battledores. At least the ball and shuttlecock could be stuffed into his saddlebags.

Shannon could scarcely believe it when her father brought the letter to the Dubois home. A letter from Virginia that had somehow avoided battlefields and enemy lines and found its way into a mail pouch bound for the Idaho Territory.

"You can tell me what it says when you come home," her father told her.

After he spoke briefly to Alice, he left, and Shannon went out onto the veranda and sat in the shade to read the precious letter.

Dear Shannon,

I pray this letter will find its way through the lines and to Idaho Territory. I have not heard from you yet. I do not know if that is because you have not written or because your letters have been unable to reach me.

Things in our county have grown much worse since your departure. The fighting has come almost to our front door more than once. Mother and I have been quite frightened by it. Our own soldiers have stripped our garden bare. And even if we had enough money, there is no food to buy.

You must have heard in your travels that General Jeb Stuart was mortally wounded at Yellow Tavern, Virginia. The news of President Abraham Lincoln's nomination by the Republican party for a second term reached us. Young boys and old men swore and swaggered and promised to defeat Mr. Lincoln. Will we fight until there is not a man left alive or whole in all of Virginia?

I hope this letter finds you well, Shannon. Please pray for us. I sometimes wonder if we can make it through another month of fighting, and even those men who swear they will defeat Mr. Lincoln no longer boast they will do so before this summer is over. Perhaps that is because they are too tired and hungry to believe in that outcome.

Tell your father that Mother and I are praying for his work in Grand Coeur.

With great affection,
Katie Davis

Shannon wept, a tear splashing on the paper in her hands, causing the ink to smudge. Katie and her mother, hungry and in want. In physical danger with the war on their doorstep. How could God allow this to happen to the people she knew and loved? She longed to demand an answer from her father, but she knew what he would say. He would say that God worked in mysterious ways, His wonders to perform. He would say that man could not know the mind of God, for His thoughts were greater than their thoughts, His ways greater than their ways.

She didn't want to hear that kind of answer. She wanted to help her friends and loved ones who were still in Virginia. But what could she do from Idaho? Nothing. She couldn't even be certain her letters would ever reach them, if only to provide a few words of encouragement.

Her gaze went toward the church where her father was having another meeting about the Independence Day celebration. Didn't it seem wrong to celebrate that particular holiday when their friends, who wanted independence from the Union, were in so much trouble? She almost wished she'd refused to go with Matthew.

Only . . . only she wanted to go with him.

Alice stood near the doorway to the kitchen, watching as Shannon read the letter a second time. Although her friend's face was in profile, Alice could still tell she was upset by whatever the missive contained.

"Bad news?" she asked softly as she moved toward the open chair.

Shannon gave a humorless laugh. "Does any other kind come when people are at war?"

Ah, the war. "No. Even in victory, people die."

"It's from my friend Katie." Shannon touched the paper in her lap. "Until Father brought me here, Katie and I lived near one another our entire lives. If only I could help her, but there is nothing I can do." She shook her head. "Even if I was there, I wouldn't be of any help to her, I'm afraid. Not with things as they are."

"I'm sorry, Shannon."

"I know." She drew a deep breath and released it on a sigh. Then she looked toward the town. "Your brother should be back from Boise soon."

"Yes. Before supper, he thought."

"Do you suppose he and the sheriff will learn anything about the thieves?"

"I hope so," Alice answered.

In the days since the robbery attempt, worry had weighed upon Matthew's shoulders. He felt responsible in some strange way, as if he believed no one would have been shot if he'd held the reins. And he also feared more trouble would come.

Softly she said, "'Take therefore no thought for the morrow: for the morrow shall take thought for the things of itself. Sufficient unto the day is the evil thereof.'"

The two women fell silent then, both of them lost in thoughts of their own.

Shannon was unable to follow the advice of Scripture. She continued the remainder of the day to feel restless and frustrated by her inability to change things for her dearest friend in the world. After supper with her father, she decided to go to the livery to visit Ginny. It was too late for a ride, even if her sidesaddle had arrived—oh, how she hoped it had—but perhaps it would soothe her frazzled thoughts if she spent a short while with the mare, brushing her coat and talking to her.

There must be something I can do for Katie. There has to be something.

The livery was only one short block and one long block from the parsonage, so if there was a solution to be found in her head, it had no time to surface before she arrived at her destination. No one else was in the barn when she entered, so she went straight to the stall and led Ginny out of it. She tied the lead to a post near the open side door and began brushing her.

"You're very beautiful, you know," she said in a gentle tone. "I think you're the finest horse in all of Grand Coeur."

Although Matthew's gray is rather fine too.

No. She didn't want to think about Matthew. Thinking about him seemed to only confuse her more, and that wasn't what she wanted. She needed to think about Katie.

"Maybe we could send money so she and Mrs. Davis could join us here. Do you suppose they would do that, Ginny, if we could send them the money? Would they leave Virginia and come to stay with us?"

The mare snorted and bobbed her head, as if in answer to the question.

But that probably wasn't possible. Katie and her mother had shown no inclination to leave their home in Virginia. And even if they wanted to come and she asked her father to send them money for passage and he agreed, how could they get the money to Katie? It would probably be stolen before it made it across enemy lines.

She leaned her forehead against Ginny's neck. *Please, God. Isn't there something I can do?*

The sound of male voices in a muffled conversation caused her to look around. She'd thought she was alone in the barn.

"Two weeks. Three at the most." One voice became more distinct.

The men weren't in the barn but outside of it. Closer to her than moments before.

"You're sure?"

"I'm sure."

"We're all tired of waiting."

That was Joe Burkette. She recognized his voice now. And the two men sounded as if they were just outside the barn doorway now. Uncertainty formed a knot in her belly. She didn't want to be caught eavesdropping on their conversation. She moved to Ginny's other side and continued brushing the horse's dark-red coat.

"Miss Adair? Is that you?"

Swallowing hard, she straightened and looked over the mare's back. Joe stood framed by the doorway. "Hello, Mr. Burkette. I thought you must have gone home for the night."

"No." A slight frown creased his forehead. "Have you been here long?"

"Not long. At least I don't think so. I'm afraid I've been talking to Ginny and paying no attention to how much time has passed." She forced a smile. "You must think me very silly. Talking to a horse and being so lost in my own thoughts I have no idea of the time."

"I don't think you're at all silly, Miss Adair." His frown disappeared, and he moved forward, stopping on Ginny's other side. "What exactly do you find to say to your horse?"

"I was telling her about my friend Katie. I received a letter from her today. Things are going very hard on the people of Virginia."

"They're hard for people all over the South." His expression was as good as a curse.

"If I knew how, I would bring Katie and her mother to Idaho Territory." She resumed brushing Ginny's coat. "I don't even know if they would be allowed to leave Virginia. Father had his position with the church awaiting him, but that wouldn't be true of them. And I suppose it is costly to travel all this way. I never thought to ask Father about that."

Joe's smile seemed almost sly. "Perhaps the Yankees could pay their fare."

"Whatever do you mean? Why would the Yankees pay for two women to escape Virginia and come to this territory?"

"Allow me to think about that, Miss Adair. It's possible I might find a way to make it happen."

Was he jesting with her? He must be. His suggestion made no sense.

"But if I could help bring your friends to Idaho"—Joe leaned closer, his arms on Ginny's back—"you'd be grateful, wouldn't you?"

His words made her feel more than a little uncomfortable, though she refused to show it. "Of course I would be grateful. I should be the most wretched of creatures if I wasn't grateful for something like that."

"And I can be very determined, Miss Adair. Very, very determined."

On Saturday, Matthew carried the smaller saddle from the stable and set it on the sorrel's back. "Did you eat something?" he asked Todd, who stood near the horse's head.

"Yes."

"We won't be back for at least a couple of hours. Don't want you getting hungry while we're up on the trail."

"I won't. How 'bout you? Did you eat?"

Matthew chuckled. "Sun Ling made me a big breakfast."

"I'm glad Miss Shannon's saddle came so she can go with us."

"Me too." He reached over and ruffled the kid's hair. "You need your hat."

He smiled to himself as he cinched the saddle, remembering what had happened the previous evening. Todd had given him a rather good thrashing in a game of battledore and shuttlecock. Of course Matthew hadn't tried as hard as he could have to master the game, but he'd taken pleasure in watching the boy enjoy himself so much. That's when the realization had hit him. He and Todd and Alice had become a family.

He'd learned to genuinely care for the boy. In fact, it surprised him how strong his emotions toward his nephew were.

He'd never expected to have a family. Never thought it was something he wanted. Settling down, living in one place, hadn't appealed to him. He'd liked being on the move all the time. He'd liked being considered by many as one of the best stagecoach drivers west of the Mississippi. Still liked it. And yet maybe settling down wasn't such a bad thing. There were routes he could drive and still be home most nights. And he could make a good home for Todd with the right woman by his side.

With Shannon by his side.

"Uncle Matt, here."

Caught woolgathering, he turned from the sorrel to find Todd right behind him, holding his uncle's saddle in his arms, leaning slightly backward under the size and weight of it.

"Let me have that." He took the saddle from Todd and walked over to the gray, moving more briskly now. Why think about Shannon when he could be with her instead?

Clad in her riding habit—attire that had gone unused for several years—Shannon led the bay mare out of the livery barn and looked up the street to the east. No sign of Mr. Dubois and Todd yet. Where were they? Should she ride to meet them or wait here as agreed?

The sound of footsteps drew her gaze in the opposite direction. Joe Burkette walked toward her.

"Good morning, Miss Adair."

"Good morning, Mr. Burkette."

"Off for a ride, I see."

"Yes."

"Nice morning for it. It would give me great pleasure to join you."

"Well, I—" She glanced once more to the east and felt a rush of relief when she saw Matthew and Todd ride into view. "I'm already part of a riding party," she added, turning back toward Joe. "And here they come now."

It was his turn to look down the street. A frown furrowed his brow. "Mr. Dubois is that someone, I take it."

"Yes. And his nephew."

Joe stepped closer and took hold of the mare's reins. "Allow me to assist you into the saddle."

Strange how unwelcome his offer was. She was able to mount on her own. Or she could wait for Matthew to help her. But it would be rude to decline Joe's offer. She nodded. "Thank you, Mr. Burkette. You are kind."

Shannon was securely seated on her sidesaddle by the time Matthew and Todd arrived in front of the livery, and Joe was once more holding on to the bay's reins close to the bit.

"Mr. Burkette," Matthew said with a nod.

"Mr. Dubois," Joe answered.

The air felt thick.

Matthew looked at her and this time he smiled. "Miss Adair. Fine horse you picked for yourself."

"Thank you, Mr. Dubois." She took the reins in hand and backed the mare away from Joe, forcing him to let go. "Good morning, Todd. How's your mother this morning?"

"She's good. She said we're to have a pleasant time. I'm glad you're coming with us."

"Me too." She smiled at the boy as she nudged the bay toward the street.

"Enjoy your ride," Joe called after them.

Shannon chose not to respond.

"Uncle Matt's right," Todd said. "You got a good horse. I remember her from when we got ours. I'm glad you went back to buy her. Ma says it's good for us to get out of the house. You too."

Matthew, riding on the other side of Todd, turned his head to look at her and smiled.

Something unfamiliar unfurled in her chest.

"Where are we riding today, Uncle Matt?"

"I thought we'd take the main road north."

"I'll lead." The boy nudged the gelding into a jog, moving out ahead of Shannon and Matthew.

Grand Coeur had disappeared from view before Matthew broke the silence. "You look at home in the saddle, Miss Adair."

"I *feel* at home. You can't possibly know how much I've missed riding. I'm not sure even I knew how much I missed it." She looked from one side of the road to the other, mountains rising to the east and the west, the road following the snaking creek off to their right. "Of course the countryside was quite different where I used to ride."

"I reckon so. One thing I've learned driving stage, America's got something for everybody when it comes to land. Great deserts. Tall mountains. Crystal-clear lakes full of fish. Deep and muddy rivers. Land that's good for not much more than mountain goats. Land that's made for farmers, with soil that's rich for growing things."

"Creeks that are rich with gold."

He nodded. "Yeah, plenty of wealth in places like this, but not many make their fortunes. Not from what I've seen over the last decade."

"You never felt like trying to find gold for yourself?"

"No. That's not the kind of life for me." He motioned with his head toward the boy riding up ahead of them. "Not the sort of life for him either."

How very wrong she'd been about him when they first met. How very—

Ginny stumbled, jerking Shannon's attention away from the man riding next to her. She pulled in on the reins.

"Something wrong, Miss Adair?"

"I think Ginny's limping."

Matthew stopped his horse.

"I'd better check. She may have picked up a pebble." Shannon unhooked her knee and slipped to the ground.

Before she could lift the mare's left front hoof, Matthew had dismounted too. "Allow me," he said, stepping close.

She looked up and her breath caught in her chest. She'd stood near him before, but this time he felt taller, his shoulders broader, his eyes bluer. It was impossible to look away from him.

Matthew hadn't planned it. Hadn't even considered it a possibility. Not this soon and not this way.

But in that moment, standing so close to Shannon, seeing her beautiful eyes staring up at him, her generous mouth slightly parted, her chest rising and falling, only one thought existed—he wanted to kiss her. Wanted it more than anything he'd wanted in a long, long while.

She seemed to sway, first backward, then forward. His hands closed around her upper arms to steady her—and then to draw her to him. His head lowered, his gaze never breaking away from hers. Not until her image blurred because of her nearness. Only then did he close his eyes.

Her lips were soft. She tasted sweet. She went utterly still, not even seeming to breathe. A fire of wanting ignited within him.

"Uncle Matt!"

Matthew drew back from Shannon, releasing his grip on her arms. Her eyes opened and went wide. Her hand flew to her mouth.

"Yes," he called to Todd without looking toward the boy.

"What's keepin' you?"

"Miss Shannon's horse picked up a rock."

Todd trotted his horse back in their direction. Matthew took another step away from the lady he wished he could keep on holding.

"I'll check her hooves," he said.

"Please do." Her reply was a mere whisper. Then she turned and disappeared around the mare's rump. Hiding from him. Getting as far away from him as she could without running for home and leaving her horse behind.

He wanted to call himself all kinds of a fool. For all of her friendliness toward him and his family, she wasn't used to men like him grabbing and kissing her on a public road.

He lifted Ginny's front left hoof. No stone. He repeated the motion with the hind left hoof. Nothing there either. He went around the back of the mare to repeat the procedure. At the same time, Shannon moved around the mare's head.

Still hiding from him.

He stepped to the mare's head and looked to where Shannon stood, her right hand resting on the seat of the saddle, her eyes lowered toward the ground. "I don't see anything," he said.

"Maybe I should lead her back to the livery. If she's lame—"

He took a step toward her. Her head came up and her gaze met his.

"Please, Miss Adair," he responded quickly. "Don't go back.

Ride with us. Your horse isn't lame. I'm sure she isn't. Try her again."

Splashes of pink rose in Shannon's cheeks, and the color of her eyes seemed to go a shade deeper.

Matthew lowered his voice so Todd couldn't hear. "I ask your forgiveness, Miss Adair. I shouldn't have done that."

The surprising thing was Shannon didn't want his apologies. She wanted to be back in his arms with his lips upon hers. She wanted him to go on kissing her until she fainted for lack of oxygen.

Benjamin had kissed her on the mouth the day they'd become engaged. It hadn't been anything like this. Brief and pleasant, as she recalled, and she'd felt fondly toward him afterward.

It wasn't fondness she felt toward Matthew Dubois. It was more than that. Much more.

"Will you forgive me, Shannon?"

Her given name sounded sweet from his lips. She wished him to always use it. "Yes, Mr. Dubois. I forgive you. And I shall ride with you as long as Ginny is all right."

"Thank you. I hadn't given up hope that you would."

Trying to take control of her emotions, she gave her head a slight toss. "I fear you think me entirely predictable."

"You're wrong," he answered, eyes and voice serious. "I may think you many things, but never predictable."

Was that a compliment or a criticism? She wasn't sure. In truth, she didn't care.

"Mornin', Mrs. Jackson."

Alice stirred in the chair on the veranda.

"I'm sorry, ma'am. Didn't realize you were asleep."

"It's all right." She blinked away the slumber and forced her eyes to focus on the man standing on the steps. "Oh, Sheriff Dickson. Hello."

"I was hoping to speak to Matt, if he's got a minute to spare me."

"He isn't here at present. He's gone riding with my son and Miss Adair."

Jack glanced toward the road that went past the house. "Miss Adair, huh? Mighty pretty woman."

And one who isn't available to you, sir. Her brother had warned her that Jack had a way with the ladies.

"Mind if I sit?" he asked.

His question took her by surprise. "If you wish." She motioned to the chair beside her.

"Matt told me you haven't been feeling well." He removed his hat as he looked at her.

Alice was quite certain Matthew hadn't said it that way. He would have told his good friend the truth, that his sister was not expected to live long. But apparently he had done so after Jack had come for supper at the Dubois home rather than before. She liked Jack Dickson and decided to be candid with him.

"My time is short, Mr. Dickson." And perhaps this was the best opportunity to make certain he knew that his attentions toward Shannon would not be welcomed. "But it's good to know Todd will have the love of Matthew and Miss Adair when I'm gone."

Jack said nothing.

"My brother intends to ask Shannon to marry him."

This caused an instant wide-eyed reaction. "Matt, married?"

"When my brother returns to driving stages, he'll need a wife to watch over Todd, and Shannon has grown very fond of my son while she's been helping care for me."

"Ah. I see."

She wished she could say Matthew and Shannon loved each other, but she supposed that was wanting too much too soon. "They will do well together." And love would come. She believed it in her heart. Both were loving people. Both tried to honor and serve God. How could love not grow between them?

Jack spun his hat on an index finger. "Mrs. Jackson. I was wondering, are you feeling up to attending the town's festivities on Monday? If you are, I hoped you'd consider going with me."

It was her turn to look surprised.

"It sure would be my pleasure to be your escort," he added quickly. "And your boy, too, of course. We wouldn't stay longer than you wanted. If you got tired or started feeling poorly, I'd bring you straight home."

"That's very kind of you, Sheriff. I hadn't considered going, but now that you mention it . . ."

She felt a spark of excitement. It would be fun, and if she went with Jack Dickson, she wouldn't be in the way of Matthew and Shannon. Her brother could concentrate on courting and not on caring for either Alice or Todd. And, if she was completely honest, it was nice to have the sheriff want to escort her. It had been a long time since a man had seen her as a woman.

"Yes, Mr. Dickson. I will go with you."

Jack grinned. "Well, all right, then. I'll come for you about six o'clock." He rose, set his hat back on his head. "Tell your brother I was by. Nothing urgent. I'll catch up with him another time."

It was difficult for Shannon to decide what to wear to the town's celebration of the Fourth of July. Her ball gowns wouldn't be appropriate for this occasion, and Matthew had seen her in all of her best day dresses. Oh, what she wouldn't give to be able to go to Mrs. Treehorn's shop. But her father had already bought Ginny for her. Another new gown would be asking too much. She would do well to practice being content with what she had, as the Bible instructed.

Having made her decision—a dress with a white bodice and a red skirt, the yards of fabric filled out by a number of petticoats—she sat at the dressing table and brushed her hair. Before long, her image in the mirror blurred as her thoughts returned to Matthew and the kiss they'd shared on their ride two days before. A kiss that had shaken her to her core and left her wanting more of the same.

Matthew.

Who would have thought it, that she would find herself missing this man whenever they weren't together? He was nothing like Benjamin Bluecher Hood or any of the other young men of Virginia who had sought her affections. None of those boys—for that's what they'd been, mere boys—had made her feel the way this man made her feel.

Were his feelings the same? Did he long to be with her? Was he even now counting the minutes until he would be in her company? Did he think her beautiful?

If her mother were still alive, Adelyn Adair would warn Shannon not to concentrate on her outward appearance but on the inward. "Clothe yourself with the garments of modesty and virtue," her mother had often told her. "Those are qualities that a proper gentleman will seek in a wife. A man who wants only physical beauty is not worth catching. Remember that, my dear."

Tears pooled suddenly in Shannon's eyes. How she missed her mother. If only she could be with her now. She wished she could know what her mother might think of Matthew if she met him. Would she approve? Her father seemed to like Matthew, but her father was more interested in Shannon discovering her own feelings than in expressing his. His advice was often subtle and couched in questions to be explored. Her mother, on the other hand, hadn't been the sort to mince words, although they had always been gently spoken.

How simple her life had been before the loss of her mother. Shannon's world had revolved around church and balls and horseback riding and dinners with friends and innocent flirtations. The future hadn't been confusing or frightening. She had known exactly what it looked like. She would become engaged and marry a man of whom her parents approved. She would make a home somewhere in Virginia for her husband and the children who would be born. She would host parties and be a valued partner in her husband's business affairs, just as her mother had been a valued partner in her father's. And other wives and young women would look to Shannon for advice.

What a difference nine years—and a war—had made.

But if we never came to Idaho, I wouldn't know Matthew.

She blinked away the tears and stared at her reflection once again. To never have met Matthew Dubois. That was too terrible a circumstance to contemplate. He had become important to her. She cared for him. She shouldn't, she supposed. He was nothing like the boys who had won her affections in the past. And yet—

"Shannon," her father said from the other side of her bedroom door. "Mr. Dubois is here."

Her stomach fluttered. Her pulse quickened. "I'll be just a moment more, Father."

She hastened to finish dressing her hair, ending with a bejeweled decoration that had belonged to her mother. Then she rose, drew in a deep breath, and left the bedroom.

In Matthew's opinion, Shannon had never looked prettier than she did that evening. Her fiery hair was captured in a white net and sparkled with jewelry of some kind. The scooped neckline of her gown was low enough to reveal her pale throat and collarbone, high enough to be proper for a pastor's daughter.

Before Matthew could speak, Todd beat him to it. "You sure look pretty, Miss Adair."

"Why, thank you, Todd." Her eyes flicked to Matthew, a question in them.

He guessed what she was wondering and answered her. "Alice and Jack Dickson are waiting outside. Todd'll spend the evening with them." He took a step forward. "Are you ready to leave?"

"Yes." Her smile seemed to curl around his heart.

He offered her the crook of his arm, and she moved toward him to take it.

"Good evening, sir," he said to the reverend without taking his eyes off of Shannon.

If they'd had far to go, Matthew would have borrowed a buggy for the occasion, but Alice had insisted that it wasn't too far for her to walk as long as they weren't in a hurry. The dance was being held outdoors in a vacant lot on the east end of Main Street. Bad weather would have ruined everything, but that hadn't happened. The night was balmy, the skies clear.

Last week, Matthew had been part of a group of men who'd built a dance floor. Since then, others had strung lanterns on ropes stretched between buildings. In the soft light of this summer evening, the location had taken on a magical appearance. The plain, unpainted buildings seemed to fade from view, even before night fell.

Jack announced he was taking Alice and Todd to see what foods would tempt them. Matthew nodded, watching as the threesome walked away, uncertain how he felt about the sheriff bringing his sister to the festivities.

As if reading his thoughts, Shannon said, "Alice has been looking forward to this all day."

"I don't want her to overdo."

"I think she likes Mr. Dickson."

"It's not hard to like Jack. Everybody does, unless they're on the wrong side of the law. But things being as they are . . ."

Shannon laid her free hand on his forearm. "Mr. Dubois, your sister is still among the living. She deserves to feel that way."

For someone of her years and sheltered experience, there was a lot of wisdom in her words. He decided to let Alice enjoy the night the way she wished and concentrate instead on the woman by his side.

Matthew's explanation to Shannon about men dancing with men proved true, and as they stopped on the street they saw a number of such couples spinning around the makeshift dance floor in time to the music. But there were some women in attendance, wives of merchants for the most part, and they would be in high demand as dance partners throughout the evening.

Matthew would not be happy to see Shannon dancing with other men. If he could, he would keep her entirely to himself throughout the evening. But even a stagecoach driver who grew up in the wilds of Oregon, even one with a limited education, knew that would be selfish. By heaven, though, he would be the *first* to dance with her tonight.

The music came to a halt, and laughter and conversations rose to fill its place. Couples moved off the floor. More couples walked onto it. A Virginia reel was announced, which pleased Matthew to no end. This was one dance he'd mastered.

"Miss Adair?" he said, looking at her.

She smiled and nodded.

He escorted her onto the floor, where they joined two lines of six or seven couples. With the shortage of women, the lines were not always compiled of mixed pairs. Matthew knew the lead couple, though—Henry and Ruth Ann Rutherford. Henry was an elder at the church, his wife the self-appointed leader of Grand Coeur society. Or at least that's what Matthew had heard.

The music began. Ruth Ann Rutherford and the man at the foot of the line advanced diagonally toward each other. She curtsied while he bowed, then they retired to their places.

It would be awhile before anything was expected of Matthew and his partner, positioned as they were in the middle of the lines. Thus he allowed himself to simply watch Shannon, to enjoy the way the light played upon the jewels in her hair, to take pleasure in the lovely bow of her lips as she laughed her enjoyment.

Was he crazy to think she would consider marrying him? She could have her pick of a thousand or more men in these mountains. She could find a man from the South. She could find a wealthier man. She could find a man who was handsomer or older or younger or better educated. She could find a man without a nephew to raise.

Shannon looked toward him, found him watching her, and her smile broadened. The look took his breath away.

Look at her, Adelyn. Look at our daughter.

Delaney stood with other onlookers at the edge of the dance floor, watching Shannon as she waited her turn.

She's in love with him. Do you suppose she realizes it? She's said nothing to me. Not yet.

His gaze shifted to Matthew.

I like him, Adelyn. I think you would too. There's something solid about him. And look at the way he looks at Shannon. Here is a man who will cherish her. I believe it with all that is in me. But they'll be equals too. We were equals, Adelyn. Weren't we? Though you were always wiser than I, more patient than I, a better judge of people. I miss hearing your voice of wisdom, my dear.

"I'll wager you never seen anything like this back in Virginia. Did you, Reverend?"

Delaney looked to his left to find William Washburn standing beside him. "You would be correct, Mr. Washburn."

"Glad you put your stamp of approval on the festivities. You may not have been here long, but folks already look up to you. Even those who don't go to church."

Delaney gave the man a nod, acknowledging his words, before turning his eyes back toward the dancers.

If that is true, Father, grant me favor with those who oppose the coming of faith into this community. Give me wisdom and show me what I'm to do.

He saw Shannon spin in Matthew's arms. Her laughter drifted to him, causing happiness to blossom in his chest.

And if Matthew is the man for her, Lord God, show them both that it is Thy will. Speak to their hearts and help them walk in Thy ways.

It had been years since Shannon had enjoyed herself this much. The music. The dancing. The food. The laughter. The fireworks. And Matthew.

Matthew . . . How could she have ever thought him anything less than wonderful? He was more than wonderful. He was . . . perfect.

It was late as the pair left the heart of town and headed toward the parsonage. The sky overhead twinkled with stars, no moon in sight. The air was soft upon the bare skin of her arms.

"It was a fun night," he said, breaking the silence that had grown between them.

"A great deal of fun." She looked at him, though she couldn't see his face well. "But you lied to me, Mr. Dubois."

"Lied to you? About what?"

"You said you weren't much of a dancer."

"It wasn't a lie."

"But it was. You're a very good dancer."

He chuckled, the sound warm and inviting. "I reckon you're being kind."

"Not at all, Mr. Dubois."

In a pool of light spilling through the window of the Wells, Fargo office, he drew her to a stop, then turned her toward him with his light grasp on her arm. "Do you think you might get to the place where you could call me Matthew or Matt?"

The world seemed to narrow until it consisted only of him. Her breathing grew shallow. Her pulse pounded in her ears. She moistened her lips with the tip of her tongue.

His voice grew husky. "Do you think you could get to that place?"

"Yes," she whispered. "I think I could. Matthew."

Go on. Kiss me . . . kiss me . . . kiss me. Please kiss me.

Did she have the slightest idea what she did to a man with her eyes? It was all Matthew could do not to pull her close and kiss her until they were both breathless. But he'd made the mistake of acting on a similar desire once before and had nearly scared her away. He wouldn't make the same mistake twice. He might be inexperienced with courting a woman, but he was learning. He would proceed slowly and with care. He wouldn't get swept up with desire. He wouldn't act recklessly. He needed her to want to marry him. That was enough.

"Maybe we'd better continue walking, Miss Adair." His voice broke like a schoolboy's.

She stared at him a few moments longer before nodding.

But he didn't move. Neither did she.

The kiss, he supposed, was inevitable, and there was no doubt about her willing participation this time. As he gathered her close, her arms reached up to twine around his neck. He felt her rise on tiptoe to meet his lips.

It came to him then, the realization that his feelings for Shannon Adair were deeper and more complicated than he'd first thought. This wasn't only about her being the kind of woman a man wanted to help raise an orphaned nephew. This was about much more than that.

What that was, he couldn't yet be sure.

On Tuesday morning, Matthew stared at his reflection in the mirror over the bureau. His cheeks and jaw were freshly shaved. His hair was clean, trimmed, and brushed back from his face. Now if there was something he could do about the nerves playing havoc with his gut . . .

Last night's kiss had convinced him the time was right. What doubts had remained were swept away by the look in Alice's eyes when he'd checked on her earlier this morning. Her pain was back.

Lord, if this is what You want, would You clear the way? I think Shannon's willing, and it doesn't look to me like there's any other way. Maybe I wouldn't even want there to be another way.

He turned away from the mirror and went downstairs. After a quick look around, he found Todd in the parlor, playing with Nugget. The pup had grown a lot, although his head and paws signified how much more he still had to grow before reaching full size. They'd be lucky if the dog didn't eat them out of house and home.

"Todd, I need you to run an errand for me."

"Sure, Uncle Matt." He hopped to his feet. Staying up late last night to see the fireworks hadn't tired him.

"Run down to the Wells, Fargo office and tell Mr. Washburn I've got something to do this morning and I'll be a bit late to work. When you've talked to him, come straight home and sit with your ma." He wasn't sure that was the best thing for Alice, but he knew more time with her son was what she would want, nonetheless.

"Can I take Nugget with me?"

"Yes, but you'd better put the leash on him. Don't want him getting into trouble in town."

Todd hurried off to obey, Nugget on his heels.

As soon as Sun Ling arrived, Matthew left the house. He was glad Shannon hadn't come yet. He needed to talk to her father before he saw her again. And just to be sure he wouldn't run into her, he took the upper road to the parsonage.

Sun Jie answered the door at his knock.

"Good morning, Sun Jie."

She gave a slight bow of greeting.

"I'd like to speak with the reverend."

"He go to church."

"So early?" Apparently the town's celebration hadn't wearied the man any more than it had Todd.

When he entered the narthex a few minutes later, he heard the reverend's voice. "And what does freedom mean to the person who trusts in Christ?"

Matthew moved to the entrance to the sanctuary. Delaney Adair was pacing back and forth across the front of the room, his hands clasped behind his back, his eyes downcast.

"Could you, like Paul, raise your voice in praise and thanksgiving if you were in chains, locked up in a prison?"

Matthew cleared his throat.

The reverend stopped and looked in his direction. His frown of concentration changed to a smile. "Mr. Dubois. It's good to see you."

"Sorry to interrupt."

"Not at all. Not at all. Just putting together my thoughts for Sunday's sermon. Come in." He waved him forward with his hand.

Matthew walked down the center aisle. "Sounds like we're in for another good one."

"God willing."

"Would you like to sit?"

"Sure."

The reverend moved to the front pew, and Matthew followed his lead.

"What can I do for you?"

A flurry of nerves erupted again. Never in his adult life had he imagined this particular situation. He had no idea how a man was supposed to go about it. If there was a proper way, he hadn't learned it while driving stage for Wells, Fargo.

He drew a deep breath and began. "It's about your daughter, sir."

"Yes?"

"Well . . . You see . . . I'd like your permission to . . . to ask her to marry me."

The reverend's eyes widened a little. "Marry?"

"Yes, sir. I've learned to . . . to care for her these past weeks."

"Young man, that's been obvious to me. I believe she cares for you as well. But I hadn't expected you would ask for her hand so soon. No one should rush into marriage. It's a serious step."

Matthew nodded but said, "I'm not rushing, sir."

Delaney looked toward the altar, his expression pensive.

"If she'll have me, Reverend, I'll be good to her. She'll never do without. I don't know that we'll always have a house as nice as the one I live in now, but I'll do my best to provide for her."

Shannon's father looked at him again. "I believe that, Matthew. But I have one question for you."

"Sir?"

"When we talked that morning in Polly's Restaurant, that morning after we all arrived in Grand Coeur, you said you had no intention of settling down. That you would be returning to driving stage when you were no longer needed here. Has that changed?"

What should he say? He didn't want to lie to the reverend, but he didn't want to admit that he intended to return to driving stage. He would have to if he wanted to provide well for Shannon and Todd, as he'd just promised. He cleared his throat. "I didn't know Alice was dying when I said that. And I hadn't come to care for your daughter."

Delaney was silent for another long spell. When he spoke at last, there was the slightest of smiles on his lips. "You have my permission to ask for my daughter's hand. If I'd had any objection to you, I would have raised the issue with her before this. But I will remind you: Shannon has a mind and will of her own. I believe she cares for you, but only she knows if it is enough for marriage."

Relief whooshed through Matthew. It seemed God had answered his prayer to clear the way. Now to convince Shannon. He would ask her tonight, just as soon as he was off work.

While Alice napped late that afternoon, Shannon wrote to Katie. She gave only a brief description of the previous night's festivities and hoped that what she wrote wouldn't make Katie see her circumstances in even worse light. Of the kiss she said nothing. She wasn't ready to share that with anyone else yet. She wanted to savor it, to treasure it in her heart. And even if she wanted to share, how could she tell her dearest friend that she'd fallen in love with a man who had no allegiance to Virginia? If Katie could meet him, she would understand. But with thousands of miles between them . . .

Guilt wrapped around her heart. She'd been so angry with her father for accepting this pastorate in Idaho Territory. She'd declared she would never be happy anywhere but Virginia. She'd been determined to change his mind and eventually convince him to go home, whether or not the war still raged.

But now? Hard though it was to admit, she would rather be near Matthew than back home at Covington House.

She heard the front door open. Her eyes darted toward the mantel clock. It wasn't yet time for Matthew to be home. Perhaps it was Todd. Only there was no sound of puppy paws on the wood floor.

Matthew appeared in the parlor doorway.

Her heart skittered at the sight of him. "You're earlier than usual, Mr. Dubois." She rose from the chair.

"I was hoping we might have time to talk before you go home."

"Of course."

"How is Alice?"

She hated to answer the question. "She didn't have a good day."

"I was afraid she wouldn't. She never should have gone to the dance last night. It was too much for her, and she stayed out too long."

Compassion welled in her chest. "I do not believe staying home would have made any difference. Even not feeling well today, she kept saying what a special time she had last night. It's good she could have that."

"I suppose you're right." He motioned with his head toward the door. "Might we take a walk while we talk?"

"Of course. If you wish."

A short while later they set off on foot, up the hillside, heading away from town. Matthew shortened his long stride to accommodate hers. Neither of them spoke for what seemed to Shannon a very long time. She was tempted to fill the silence with mindless chatter. Katie had once declared that no one could keep a conversation going as well and with as little effort as Shannon Adair. And yet something kept her silent now. Waiting. But waiting for what? Why had he wanted to talk? And if he wanted to talk, why didn't he?

The memory of the kiss they'd shared last night rushed into her mind, and with her entire being she hoped he would stop, take her into his arms, and do it again.

Alice had heard the deep hum of her brother's voice when he'd arrived home, although she hadn't been able to make out his words from up in her room. *It's time,* she'd wanted to call out to him.

Time for what?

Time for him to ask Shannon to marry him.

Time for Alice to die.

It was time.

How good You have been to me, Father. I never expected to have all these weeks with Matt. I never expected to be cared for so tenderly by the woman I believe will mother Todd and love him when I can't be here to do it. Thank You for letting me know her.

It was time. But she would so like to know that everything was in place.

Not mine, but Thy will be done.

How should he begin?

Matthew thought it might be easier to face an Indian war party than to fumble his way through a proposal of marriage. He knew something about arrows and gunfire. But when it came to asking Shannon to marry him . . . Well, it wouldn't get any easier with continued silence.

He stopped walking. She took an extra step, then turned toward him. There was something swirling in her eyes, an emotion that he didn't understand. When she moistened her lips with the tip of her tongue, the same way she had last night, words wouldn't form in his mind. All he could think of was that he wanted to hold her and kiss her and—

He stopped the direction of his thoughts. This wasn't about desire. This was about doing what was right for Todd. He had to remain focused on that.

He cleared his throat. "Miss Adair, I went to see your father this morning. I wanted . . . I went to ask his permission for your hand in marriage. Which he gave."

There was no doubt what he read in her eyes now—complete surprise.

"Will you do me the honor of becoming my wife?"

She didn't answer with words. Instead, she nodded. A shallow nod, but a nod all the same. He felt his whole body relax, not until then knowing just how afraid he'd been that she would refuse. And if she'd refused . . . That didn't bear thinking about.

It seemed natural, then, to lean down to bestow a kiss. To seal the contract between them, he supposed. When they parted, he said, "We must go home and tell Alice. She'll want to know at once."

Again Shannon nodded.

They would do well, the two of them, and he would do all in his power to see that she was never sorry for accepting his proposal.

Dearest Katie,

Finally, I have received a letter from you. I wish it could have been full of better news. I want to help you, and I am helpless to do so. All I can do is pray for you and write letters and hope to be of some encouragement.

I wrote to you earlier today, but something more happened this afternoon that caused me to tear up that letter and write a new one. I hope my news will bring you joy, even if you will find it hard to believe. I can scarcely believe it myself.

Mr. Dubois has proposed and I have accepted. We are to be married. His sister, Alice, has asked that we not delay. She wants to be with us when we wed, and although she has seemed so much better in recent weeks, that is no longer true. We have settled on a date less than two weeks from now. July 17 at three o'clock in the afternoon. Alice expressed a wish that we wed even sooner, but there is much to do in a short period of time. How dear a sister Alice has become to me as I've spent time with her and cared for her. I wish you could have known her.

Father approves of Mr. Dubois. His Christian name is Matthew. Have I told you that before? I suppose I should get used to saying it aloud. Matthew Dubois. Matthew, darling. My dear Matthew. His friends and sister call him Matt, but I prefer the longer version. My beloved Matthew.

I can hear you laugh as you read those words. Oh, how I wish you could be with me at my wedding. As much as I care for Alice, you are the truest and dearest sister of my heart. How I wish you could stand with me as I exchange vows with my intended.

The wedding shall not be a large affair. We shall have the ceremony at Matthew's home because that will be less taxing on his sister. I do not believe she would have the strength to go to the church. Also the Dubois home has a lovely parlor while the one at the parsonage is small and dark. I will have a new dress, but it shall not be ornate, in keeping with the simplicity of our plans.

I wish I could be certain of your receipt of this letter. I so want you to know that I have found happiness, even though I am far from home. I was certain that would not be true, as you well know, and I made poor Father suffer with my moodiness. You know him, so you also know that he has forgiven my willfulness. Still, I wish that I had been more charitable to him. And now that I have found love, it seems to me that coming here was the best of all blessings.

Please share this news with all of our friends in the county. Tell them that Father is well and that he is serving the Lord with those he meets in Grand Coeur. His faith is strong.

Your devoted friend,
Shannon Adair

The second-story bedroom felt uncomfortably warm to Matthew when he checked on his sister before retiring for the night. "Maybe we should move you downstairs," he told Alice. "It's a little cooler there."

"I'm fine where I am. I don't want to be any extra trouble. Not now."

He settled onto the chair beside the bed and took hold of her hand. "You haven't been any trouble at all."

"Liar." She smiled weakly.

He returned it with no more conviction.

"I'll be ready to go whenever the Lord's ready to take me."

The words were painful to hear, for he didn't think he would ever be ready for her to leave. They continued to surprise him, these strong emotions that being with his sister had brought to life.

"'For to me to live is Christ, and to die is gain.' It's true, you know. I will be with the Lord. How could that not be gain?"

"Your faith is lots stronger than mine, Alice."

Again she gave him a weak smile, this time adding a slight shake of her head. "No, Matt. It's not. If it seems so, it's only because of God's grace."

"You're young yet. You shouldn't—"

"Hush." She squeezed his hand. "There isn't anything that can take me home to heaven any sooner than the Lord wills. I'm content with that."

Matthew was glad she was content, but what he wanted to do was argue with God.

"Help Todd to know God's love and to love Him in return. Don't ever let him be bitter about losing his ma and pa so young. Tell him how God collects his tears and knows every hair on his head. Tell him God's always near."

"You know I will."

"Matt, God brought you and me and Todd here so we could meet Shannon. See how much the Lord cared about us? Isn't it amazing? Only He could have worked it out so she and her father would come all that way from Virginia so we could meet her. Now you'll have a wife and Todd'll have a mother. All because of God's loving plan."

Something stirred in Matthew's spirit at the truth in her words. Perhaps he'd felt his faith begin to grow, to be more like his sister's. He hoped so.

The next days sped by in a blur of activities.

Shannon visited Gladys Treehorn's shop and ordered her bridal gown. She chose a lovely light-green silk organza, so pale it was almost white. It would have a three-tiered skirt and a ruffled off-the-shoulder neckline. The shoulders and center point would be accented with handmade satin roses. Mrs. Treehorn assured Shannon it would be ready before the seventeenth.

Suits were ordered from a tailor in Chinatown for the groom and his young nephew.

Sun Ling and Sun Jie set about giving the Dubois home a detailed scrubbing.

Three women from the church volunteered flowers from their gardens for the wedding day.

The reverend prepared his address to the couple.

Happiness pervaded the parsonage and the Dubois home alike. Even though Alice was once again confined to her bed, she wanted to talk of little else besides the wedding. She never failed to mention several times each day—to whomever sat beside her bed—how glad she was that Shannon and Matthew would soon be married, how happy their plans had made her.

Matthew didn't go to church on Sunday morning, one week before his wedding day. When he visited his sister's bedroom before leaving for the service, he found her struggling to draw breath and sent Todd for Dr. Featherhill. After the physician arrived, Matthew and the boy waited in the hallway. He tried his best to look calm for Todd's sake, but in his heart he feared the worst.

The creak of the bedroom door drew his attention. Dr. Featherhill's expression was grim as he gave his head the slightest of shakes. "She's asking for you, Mr. Dubois." The doctor then looked at Todd. "Young man, she wants to see you, too, but would like to speak to your uncle alone first."

She was dying. She was dying soon—and the knowledge hit Matthew like a brick between the eyes. He'd known loss before. Their parents had died during a cholera outbreak. A friend who'd ridden for the Pony Express had died after a fall from a horse. He'd known two other men killed by Indians while manning swing stations on the overland trail. But this felt worse than all of them put together.

Drawing a breath to steady himself, he moved into the bedroom and walked to the bed. The curtains were drawn against the bright sunlight, a lamp on the bedside table providing what illumination there was.

Alice seemed to have shrunk until her body scarcely made a ripple in the blankets on the bed. When she saw him, she lifted a hand, though it dropped to her side again before he reached her.

"Alice," he whispered as he sank onto the chair beside the bed. He took hold of her hand and folded it within both of his.

She smiled for a moment. "Remember what . . . we talked . . . about. Teach . . . Todd . . . to love . . . God."

"I will."

"Remind him . . . often . . . how much . . . his mother . . . loved him."

Matthew nodded.

"I'm . . . going to . . . a . . . better place."

A lump formed in his throat, making an answer impossible. Listening to her labored speech made his own chest ache.

"I'm . . . sorry."

"For what?" The question sounded raspy in his ears.

"For . . . not seeing . . . you sooner . . . I . . . love you . . . Matt."

He leaned closer. "I love you, too, Alice. Wish I'd let you know it more."

"I . . . knew it." The smile returned to her lips. "I . . . always . . . knew."

Her image swam before his eyes. The last time he'd cried had been when their mother died, only hours after their father. He blinked back the tears, unwilling to let them fall. He wanted to be strong for Alice.

"Be good . . . to Shannon."

"I will."

"Help Todd to love her as . . . she loves him."

"Alice . . ."

"Don't change . . . your wedding plans. Todd will . . . need her . . . more than ever." She drew a breath but it took great effort. "You need her . . . Matt. You . . . need her love."

His own breathing was labored, as if he were trying to breathe for her. "I know. We won't change our plans. But don't give up, Alice. Stay and be with us on our wedding day."

Sadness filled her eyes as she shook her head. "Bring . . . Todd in . . . please."

"Sure." He released her hand, stood, and returned to the door. Opening it, he said, "Your ma wants you, Todd."

The boy was past him in an instant. Matthew stayed by the door, watching as Alice drew her son's head down to her chest and stroked his hair. He couldn't make out her words from where he stood. They were spoken too softly. But he heard Todd begin to cry.

It was only moments, though it felt like hours, before Alice lifted her eyes to meet his. The lump returned to his throat, and he pushed off from the wall at his back. When he reached the bedside, he put his hands on the boy's shoulders. "Time to let your ma rest," he said.

"No." Todd straightened, looking up at him, then back at his mother. "Not yet."

"It's . . . all right . . . Todd," she whispered. "You go with your . . . Uncle Matt."

Matthew drew the boy back from the bed.

Alice closed her eyes. "I'll . . . see you . . . both . . . again."

Matthew believed it. Had always believed in the promise of heaven. But at the moment, the belief didn't bring much comfort. "Let's go, Todd." He turned the boy and propelled him toward the bedroom door. To the doctor, he mouthed the words, *I'll be back*. Then he and Todd went down the stairs to find Sun Ling.

Shannon and her father were just leaving the church when Sun Ling met them at the bottom of the steps. "So sorry. Mr. Dubois needs reverend."

"Is it Alice?" Shannon said softly. That explained Matthew's and

Todd's absence from church that morning. It's what she'd suspected, but she'd hoped she was wrong. It seemed she wasn't.

Sun Ling nodded.

"We'll come at once," her father said.

The three of them set off, the two women almost having to run to keep up with the reverend.

As they entered the house, Shannon felt the pall of death hanging over it, and she knew in an instant they were too late to bid Matthew's sister good-bye. Then she heard choked sobs coming from the parlor. She touched her father's arm, letting him know where she was going.

Todd was seated on the floor near the hearth, his knees pulled up to his chest, his face hidden in his folded arms. She hurried to him, sinking to the floor in a puddle of skirt and petticoats.

"Todd," she said softly.

He looked up, his face wet with tears. "My ma," he croaked out.

She opened her arms and he tumbled into them. "It's all right." That was a lie and they both knew it. It was never all right when one's mother died. But what else could she say to a lad so young? "It's all right. *Shh.* It's all right."

His sobbing slowed, then fell silent, though his body continued to quiver and shudder in her arms.

Shannon remembered the night her mother had passed into glory. She remembered the empty feeling that had swirled around and through her. Her mother had suffered a great deal in the weeks leading up to her death, and many friends and acquaintances had said to Shannon that she should be thankful her mother was in a better place, thankful she was free from pain at last. But being free from pain and in a better place hadn't mattered to Shannon. At the time she couldn't be thankful for either. Right or wrong, she'd wanted her mother on earth, not in heaven.

She stroked Todd's head, much as her father had stroked her head nine years ago. "It's all right," she repeated in a whisper.

A whimper drew her gaze toward the sofa. Beneath it, Nugget lay with his head on his paws, watching the two of them with sad eyes, as if he, too, understood what had happened, what it was like to lose a mother.

She kissed the air a couple of times and held out a hand to call him closer. After a hesitation, he came. "Nugget's worried about you, Todd."

The boy lifted his head from her chest and drew the puppy into the sad little circle.

Matthew was thankful for the reverend's presence, grateful for both his silence and his prayers. By the time the two men descended the stairs, he felt more ready to face his nephew's grief, as well as his own.

It was the sound of Shannon's soft voice that drew him toward the parlor, Delaney Adair right behind him. Matthew stopped in the doorway, taking in the woman, boy, and puppy on the floor, Shannon's skirts pooled around them. He wished he could join them there, wished he could gather all of them close, giving and receiving comfort.

Todd looked up, and Matthew saw a world of pain in the boy's eyes. He held out a hand in his nephew's direction. Todd jumped to his feet and came running. Another lump formed in Matthew's throat, making speech impossible. All he could do was draw the boy close and hold him there.

Across the room, Shannon raised her eyes to his. In that moment she seemed to represent all that was right in a world that had gone horribly wrong, and he was thankful she was there. She'd cared tenderly for his sister's needs as her body failed her. She'd been kind to Todd—and to Matthew too.

Shannon rose to her feet with a rustle of fabric. Then she moved toward him. "I'm so very sorry, Matthew."

He swallowed hard as he nodded.

"Is there something I could do to help?"

He cupped her face with his left hand, wishing he could put his feelings into words. She helped simply by being there. He hoped she would understand that despite the absence of words.

"Don't change . . . your wedding plans. Todd will . . . need her . . . more than ever. You need her . . . Matt."

Maybe he couldn't put it into words now, but someday, somehow, he would tell her.

As if knowing there was to be a funeral, Tuesday arrived with skies turned the color of sorrow, a deep slate gray that wept throughout the day.

It was late morning when Matthew, holding an umbrella to shield himself and his nephew from the light but steady rain, followed the wagon carrying his sister's remains up the winding road to the cemetery. There were only a few people with them—Reverend Adair and Shannon, William Washburn, Jack Dickson, Dr. Featherhill, and, bringing up the rear, Sun Ling and her sister and brother-in-law.

Once at the cemetery, the four men who'd been hired by the undertaker carried the wooden casket from the wagon to the grave, then used ropes to lower it into the ground. Afterward they stepped back out of the way while the reverend spoke a few words of comfort, read a few verses of Scripture, and said a brief prayer for the dearly departed. And with that, Alice Jackson was laid to rest.

Todd's shoulder pressed close against Matthew's thigh, but the boy didn't cry. Matthew understood Todd was doing his best to be strong. The boy understood death, even at his young age. Death meant his pa wouldn't come home from the war. Now it meant he wouldn't see his ma again either.

Matthew shook the reverend's hand and thanked him. He nodded to Shannon, wanting to ask her to stay with him but for some reason unable to do so. He received William's and Jack's and the doctor's condolences. He returned the respectful bows of the Sun sisters and Wu Lok. And finally, several minutes after the others had walked away, he and his nephew turned and made their way down the road from the cemetery and up the hillside to the silent, empty house that awaited them.

It was surprising how desolate it felt with Alice gone. Surprising because she had lived in the home less than two months, and much of that time she'd been bedridden. And yet her absence was keenly felt throughout.

Standing in the kitchen, Matthew looked with disappointment at the coffeepot that had been washed and dried and set to the back of the stove. Sun Ling must have washed it before they left for the funeral. Should he make another pot? Probably not. Besides, the stuff was expensive, and it wasn't as easy to get as it had been before the war.

Well, if not coffee, then food. "Are you hungry, Todd?" He turned to look at the boy who'd followed him into the kitchen.

"No."

"Well, sit down at the table. We need to eat whether we feel like it or not."

Ignoring his uncle, Todd picked up Nugget and buried his face in his soft coat.

A weight pressed on Matthew's chest. He wasn't up to this task. What did he know about raising a boy? He'd never been around kids much. Not even when he was a kid himself. Even with Shannon's help, he wasn't going to make much of a father for Todd. Maybe it was just as well he would return to driving coach.

He closed his eyes for a moment and drew in a deep breath, letting it out slowly, clearing his mind, trying not to worry about things he couldn't change. Better to concentrate on today. Right now he needed to get Todd to eat something. Even a lousy father understood that much.

There was cold beef and a bottle of milk in the icebox and, beneath a cloth on the counter, a plate of bread rolls. He cut open a couple of rolls and put sliced beef into the center of each. Then he poured milk into two glasses. He didn't much care for milk, but he figured it was part of setting a good example for the boy.

He motioned with his head toward the table and said, "Put Nugget down."

Todd obeyed, but he did so with a sorrowful look.

Moments later, their lunch on the table and both of them seated, Matthew blessed the food and then picked up his sandwich to take a bite.

Todd sat with his eyes downcast, unmoving.

"Eat your lunch."

"I'm not hungry, Uncle Matt."

"Eat it anyway. Can't let good food go to waste."

The boy glanced up. There were tears in his eyes.

Matthew felt like a bully. Speaking in what he hoped was a gentler tone, he said, "Come on, Todd. You need to eat. You didn't have breakfast. You need to eat something now."

"Okay." Todd sniffed, wiped his nose on his shirtsleeve, and picked up the sandwich with both hands.

Matthew's sandwich tasted like sawdust, but he ate it all and downed every last drop of the milk in his glass. Then he waited while Todd did the same at a much slower pace.

Shannon didn't need an excuse to go to the Dubois home. She was, after all, engaged to marry Matthew in less than a week. Still, she prepared a basket of food to take with her. Her father offered to go along, but he seemed to understand her wish to see Matthew alone. They'd barely been able to exchange three words in the past two days.

As she walked, she prayed that God would give her the words to help comfort Matthew and Todd. And she asked for comfort for herself, for she had lost a friend.

"I'm sorry, Miss Adair. I'm sorry you've had to experience the same kind of pain that so many other women are feeling because of the war. We shall be friends, you and I."

Sweet Alice. At least she had no more pain. At least she was with her beloved husband again. But her passing had left a large hole in the lives of those who'd loved her. Especially in her son's life.

"Poor Todd," she whispered.

When she married Matthew on Sunday, Shannon would acquire not only a husband but custody of a nephew too. She would have to fill the role of mother, even if Todd never called her that. She'd known this, of course. Alice and Shannon had talked about it several times in the days immediately following Matthew's proposal. But it hadn't seemed real or imminent. It had seemed a distant possibility, despite Alice's failing health. It was distant no more. She loved the boy already. But was love enough to make her a good mother to him?

She wondered then if Matthew had the same fears she did. Yes, he probably did.

"I will be his helpmeet. Together we will learn to be good parents to Todd. And to the children I will bear him."

Saying those last words aloud caused her cheeks to grow warm with embarrassment, even though no one was around to hear. Unlike many unmarried young women of her acquaintance, Shannon knew somewhat more about anatomy and the union of a man and a woman that led to childbearing, thanks to her work in the army hospital and some medical books she'd read as she sought to become a better nurse.

The sound of hoofbeats approaching from behind her caused her to move closer to the shoulder of the street.

"Miss Adair."

She stopped at the sound of her name and turned.

Joe Burkette slowed his mount as he drew closer. "You haven't been to the livery for the past week. I was concerned. Have you been unwell?"

What was it about this man that bothered her so? She wanted to like him. Truly she did. But she couldn't. "No, Mr. Burkette. I have not been unwell. Only busy."

"I'm relieved to hear it." He dismounted, and as he stepped closer he sniffed the air. "Mmm. Fried chicken if I'm not mistaken."

"Yes."

"Did you cook it yourself, Miss Adair?" He raised an eyebrow. "You do surprise me."

She inclined her head as a reply.

"I've been hoping for another opportunity to ask you to go riding with me."

"I'm sorry, Mr. Burkette. I couldn't do that."

"Why not?" He gave her a slow smile. "You must know I would like to know you better, Shannon. I think you beautiful and I—"

"I'm engaged to be married, sir."

There was a long silence before he said, a hard edge in his voice, "Not to that Dubois fellow."

"Yes." She tilted her chin. "As a matter of fact, it is Mr. Dubois I'm going to marry. We plan to wed on Sunday."

Joe's eyes narrowed. "I wouldn't have expected a true daughter of the Old Dominion to marry a Yankee."

She pressed her lips together to stifle a retort. What business was it of his whom she married? None at all, and he presumed too much to think he had a right to say anything.

"Some would call you a traitor for it."

Shannon's resolve not to answer him evaporated. "Mr. Burkette, I have learned a great deal since leaving Virginia. One of the lessons I've learned is that my father is right: we must do all that we can—short of disobeying God—to live at peace with others. I will no longer judge someone based upon where they were born or where they were raised or whether or not they have taken up arms for or against the Confederacy. We are all sinners who have earned God's wrath instead of His grace." With a toss of her head, she started walking again. "Good day, sir."

The gall of the man. How could she have ever thought she should like him? That she should prefer him over Matthew? There was nothing remotely appealing about him, and simply because his birthplace was in the South and his family had known hers two generations ago did not make him a gentleman. He was less gentlemanly than Matthew by far, no matter how highly he valued himself.

She would have to move Ginny from the livery. At once. Surely there was room for the mare in the stable behind Matthew's house.

She would speak to him about it. Today wasn't the best time, of course, but she couldn't abide the thought of running into Joe Burkette again. Insufferable man!

Perhaps she didn't have the passion for the Confederate cause she'd once had. Perhaps she no longer believed a victory on her side was what mattered most. Perhaps more of her father's beliefs and opinions—about peace, about slavery, about a united nation—had taken root in her heart and mind as never before. And perhaps that was because of Alice and Matthew and Todd.

A fine sheen of perspiration had formed on her forehead by the time she reached the Dubois home. She knocked and waited for the door to be answered. It was Todd who did so, Nugget right behind him, and seeing him, she forgot her encounter on the road for the moment. The boy's eyes, so much like his mother's, revealed such sorrow Shannon feared she might burst out crying. The pup, on the other hand, jumped up in welcome.

Swallowing her tears, Shannon said, "Hello, Todd." She held up the basket. "I brought fried chicken. You told me it was your favorite. Remember?"

He nodded.

"May I come in?"

He nodded again before turning and walking away.

As she entered, Matthew appeared in the parlor doorway. Although his expression didn't change much, she thought he looked glad to see her.

"I brought fried chicken," she repeated.

"Thanks."

"I hope Sun Ling hasn't already begun preparing your supper."

"She isn't here."

"Oh?" Shannon looked toward the kitchen.

"I . . . I gave her the day off." After a few moments of silence, he added, "I'm glad you came."

Love surged in her chest. She longed to go to Matthew, to hold him, to comfort him, but she couldn't. A woman must wait for the man to speak first, to move first. It's what she had been taught by her mother from the time she was a little girl.

She held up the basket. "I should put this in the kitchen."

"Here. Let me take it." He stepped toward her and reached out with one hand.

Shannon gave the basket to him, then followed him into the kitchen.

"Would you like to eat with us?" he asked, his back toward her.

"Father expects me home before supper."

"Of course." He faced her again. "I reckon he wants as much time with you as possible before the wedding."

Nerves fluttered in her stomach. "I suppose that is true, though it isn't as if he won't see me as often as he wishes. This house is not so very far from the church."

"Guess you're right." He cleared his throat. "One of the last things Alice said to me was that we weren't to change our wedding plans. She was plum set on it, even as she was dying."

Tears welled in Shannon's eyes. "I loved her too," she whispered.

"I know you did."

She thought of Joe Burkette saying she was a traitor because she was going to marry this man. Hadn't she believed much the same thing about friendship with Alice Jackson? How silly, to hang a name on someone and hate them for it—Yankee, Rebel, white, black, yellow, red.

She had much to repent of, it seemed.

Matthew awakened as the first fingers of dawn began to reach across the ceiling of his bedroom. As full consciousness arrived, he realized he was so close to the edge of the mattress he was in danger of falling off. A moment later he knew the reason. His nephew was in bed with him, and the boy's bony knees were planted firmly in the small of Matthew's back.

The nightmare. Sometime in the middle of the night, Todd had had a bad dream and awakened with a scream. No matter what Matthew had said, no matter what he'd tried, the boy hadn't been comforted. At last he'd let him crawl into bed with him.

Matthew wasn't cut out to be a guardian to the kid. They would both be better off when he was back on a stage, leather laced between his fingers. He couldn't do Todd any harm there. No telling what he might do wrong here.

Shannon's image drifted into his thoughts. God knew he'd come to care for her more than he thought he would. That first morning in Grand Coeur, he'd thought her spoiled and silly. That first Sunday in town, he'd thought her conceited and given to putting on airs. He'd misjudged her. More than once. He was sorry for that.

He wondered what she felt for him. Was it love? Perhaps. Perhaps not. But she did love Todd. That's all that mattered for now.

Carefully, hoping to let his nephew sleep as long as possible, he got out of bed, washed, and dressed. He went downstairs, built up the fire in the stove, and put the coffeepot on to boil. Then he went outside to feed the horses. Shannon's mare was the first to nicker as he walked toward the corral.

"Hey, girl." He patted the bay's sleek neck before giving her a small shove back from the gate so he could enter the corral.

When Shannon had asked yesterday if she could move Ginny out of the livery and to this corral behind his house, Matthew hadn't thought to ask for a reason. But now he wondered about it. Wondered if it had anything to do with Burkette.

He didn't like the man. Something about him rubbed Matthew the wrong way. Couldn't be just because Burkette was a Southerner and, according to Jack, a known Confederate sympathizer. If that's all it took, Matthew would be at odds with the better share of inhabitants of this gold rush town—his fiancée included. Shannon had never tried to hide where her allegiance lay.

Though she has mellowed a bit.

He figured his sister got some of the credit for the change. Alice had won Shannon's affections with her strength of character and her sweet smile and her joy of life even as she faced death. The sting of loss pierced his chest afresh. No wonder Todd was having bad dreams. Matthew hadn't had all that much time with his sister, and even his heart felt broken by her death.

After tossing hay to the horses, he pumped fresh water into the trough. Then he returned to the house, met by the scent of brewed coffee and the sight of Sun Ling tying an apron around her waist.

"Good morning, Mr. Dubois." She bowed.

"Morning, Sun Ling."

"You sleep good?"

"Not very," he answered honestly.

"I make you good breakfast."

He set a large cup on the counter near the stove and filled it with coffee. "Thanks. I'd appreciate it."

Delaney Adair waited in the front of the dress shop, wishing his daughter would hurry. He'd never been comfortable in this sort of setting, surrounded by ribbons and baubles and lace. But when she stepped through the curtain separating the front from the back of the small shop, his heart nearly stopped. Never had she looked more beautiful. Never had she looked more like his dearly departed wife. So much so that he almost spoke Adelyn's name aloud.

"What do you think, Father?" Shannon turned slowly.

He rose from the chair. "You look exquisite, my dear."

"It isn't too . . . joyful, is it? Alice will have been gone only a week." She looked toward the full-length mirror. "I should have chosen a darker color, but I thought . . ." She allowed the words to fade into silence.

Delaney moved to stand behind his daughter and put his hands on her shoulders. "It's to be a small ceremony with only a few present. No one will think ill of you for wearing the bridal gown you commissioned before Mrs. Jackson died." In her reflection in the mirror, he saw tears pooling in her eyes. "What's wrong?"

"I love Matthew, Father, and I'm so very happy he asked me to marry him. I'm sure it must be a horrible sin to be so happy when he and Todd are so sorrowful."

"Oh, my dear girl." He turned her to face him, then gathered her into a close embrace. "It is no sin to be happy over a marriage to a good man."

"He is good," she said softly against Delaney's chest. "He's very good. I didn't think so at first, but I was wrong."

"Yes, he is good. He's a man of strong faith and convictions or I would never have given my permission for him to ask for your hand."

Shannon sniffed as she drew back. A tremulous smile played across her lips. "I had better remove the dress before it gets spotted with my tears." She turned toward the curtain to the back of the shop. "I won't be long."

Delaney drew in a breath and let it out as he sank once more onto the chair.

So what do you think, Adelyn? I wish you were here. A girl needs her mother on her wedding day. I am a poor substitute, I fear. She does love him. I don't doubt that for a moment. But I wonder if she fully understands all the challenges that marriage brings.

He shook his head slowly.

No. Of course she doesn't fully understand. None of us do beforehand. You and I surely didn't. But God made us one, and our love grew and thrived. May their marriage be as blessed as ours, Adelyn. May it be as blessed as ours.

After leaving the dress shop, Shannon's father returned to the parsonage while she went to shop for a few more items—flour and sugar and coffee for the parsonage, a new hat to wear with her bridal gown, a gift of some sort for her groom. For the latter, she stopped in at a clock shop, located in a small building squeezed between a bank and a boardinghouse.

As far as she knew, Matthew didn't own a pocket watch. At least she'd never seen him with one. Not even on Sundays. She wished she could give him something fine, something gold filled and bejeweled, but she would have to settle for gold plated.

At Shannon's request, the shop owner removed several watches from the glass display case and laid them out before her. She picked each one up in turn, fingering the small details on each case, examining the faces. She pictured Matthew, wearing his Sunday suit, standing beside the fireplace mantel in the parlor of his home, taking the watch from his pocket and checking the time. She imagined him smiling at her as they both remembered the day she'd given him the gift.

"I'll take this one," she said at last.

"A very good choice. It's well made and reasonably priced. Your husband will be pleased."

My husband. Nerves fluttered in her chest. *In just four more days, he'll be my husband.*

Once before she'd been engaged. Once before she'd planned a wedding. But she'd known Benjamin and his family for nearly as far back as she could remember. She would have known how to be the proper wife of a tobacco planter because she'd seen examples everywhere. Would she know how to be a proper wife to Matthew Dubois, express agent and uncle to an orphaned boy? With resolve, she shoved away the doubts. Of course she would know how. Love would show her the way.

She paid for the pocket watch and tucked the small box inside her reticule. Moments later she set off down the boardwalk, walking quickly. She'd taken far too long in the clock shop, and Sun Jie needed the flour for her supper preparations.

Shannon was passing the newspaper office when Jack Dickson stepped through the doorway and into her path. She stopped mere seconds before she would have collided with him.

Jack's hands shot out to grasp her upper arms and steady her. "Whoa!" he said, laughter in his voice. "Looks like you're in quite a hurry, Miss Adair."

"I am sorry, Sheriff Dickson. I wasn't paying attention."

"I imagine there's plenty running through that pretty head of yours, what with the wedding and all." He stepped back, then held out a hand for the basket. "Please, allow me."

"Oh, but that isn't necessary, Sheriff. I wouldn't want—"

"Please. I insist. I wouldn't be a very good friend to Matt if I left his fiancée to carry a heavy basket by herself."

Releasing another small laugh, she handed him her shopping basket—which wasn't all that heavy.

Jack turned, positioning himself between her and the street, and the two began walking. "How's Matt doing?"

Her amusement was forgotten. "I haven't seen him today." She drew a deep breath. "He's very sad."

"I liked his sister. Didn't know her long, of course, but I got the feeling she was a special lady."

"She was. Very special."

"She was mighty keen on Matt marrying you, Miss Adair. You should know that. And I reckon it allowed her to die in peace, knowing you'd be there to care for the boy after she was gone. Matt's lucky you agreed to marry him without delay. Not every woman wants a ready-made family, especially not when Matt'll be away so much, driving coach."

Shannon glanced in the sheriff's direction. What did he mean? Did Matthew intend to return to driving stagecoaches soon? He'd never said so to her. Perhaps Jack was only surmising those were Matthew's plans. And anyway, would she mind if he did? Surely he wouldn't be away all that much.

No, there was something else that bothered her. Something she couldn't quite grasp in her mind as she walked beside Jack toward home. And a small seed of doubt took root in her heart.

He's never said he loves me.

Shannon came awake with that thought in the forefront of her mind.

But surely he does. Surely he wouldn't have asked me to marry him unless he loved me.

She got out of bed, pulling a light shawl over her shoulders as she headed for the door. Her bedroom was too warm and she longed for a cool breeze.

I haven't told him I love him either, but I do. He must know that I do.

A nearly full moon, hanging low in the western sky, illuminated her white nightgown as she stepped onto the small front porch. Although there was no cool breeze, she pulled the shawl closer as she sank onto one of the chairs. Grand Coeur was silent at this wee hour before dawn. Even the saloons and dance halls were closed, proprietors and customers having taken to their beds at last.

Of course he loves me. The way he kissed me . . .

Oh, how she loved his kisses. How she wished he would kiss her more often. But that would soon change. Look at all that had happened since his proposal. There'd been wedding plans to make that had occupied so much of Shannon's time. And then Alice had died and there'd been the funeral to get through and the grief to deal with.

What if he doesn't love me? Would I still marry him if he doesn't?

The question frightened her. She didn't think she wanted to find the answer.

Somewhere on the far side of town, a dog barked. From the west, she heard the nicker of a horse. Neither sound was close. They carried easily in the night air.

Is Sheriff Dickson right? Does Matthew intend to return to driving a stagecoach soon? How much will he be away?

Married but alone. Well, not alone. She would have Todd with her.

"I reckon it allowed her to die in peace, knowing you'd be there to care for the boy after she was gone . . . Matt's lucky . . . Not every woman wants a ready-made family . . ."

Her head began to ache, and a shiver—despite the warmth of the night—ran up her spine.

Father God, whatever is wrong with me? Am I ill?

No, not ill. Anxious. Agitated. Troubled. But why? Why, when she had so many reasons to be happy? It wasn't as if she hadn't known Matthew liked driving a stagecoach and that he planned to return to it. He'd said so plainly enough in the restaurant their first morning in town. "*I'm not the kind of man to stay too long in one place.*" Those had been his very words. "*I'll be back to driving the coach. I don't reckon that'll be too long.*"

No, it wasn't the notion that he would return to driving coach that troubled her. What troubled her was not knowing *why* he wanted to marry her. She needed him to tell her why. She needed him to love her.

After Alice died, William had told Matthew to take the rest of the week off. "You've got enough to deal with," he'd said. "Come back to work after the wedding."

It had seemed like a good idea at the time, but there'd been moments during the week when Matthew hadn't been too sure. He had too much time on his hands. Too much time to think, to dwell on his concerns about Todd, to wonder if he would make a decent guardian for the boy and a decent husband to Shannon.

Shannon . . .

He hadn't seen her at all yesterday, the day after the funeral, and the truth was he'd missed her. She'd become a part of his life. A necessary part of his life. Not just because she'd cared for Alice and for Todd. Her presence was necessary to him too. For his contentment.

Contentment? Yes. Contentment. Matthew had found contentment. The realization surprised him. Despite the sorrow over his sister's death, he wasn't longing for his old way of life as he had in those first weeks in Grand Coeur. He didn't seem to mind the hours he spent in the express office because he knew when he came home he would see Shannon.

There was no question about it any longer. He didn't just like Shannon Adair. He wasn't merely fond of her. It wasn't only desire he felt for her, and it wasn't because of Todd that he wanted to marry her. He couldn't imagine his life without her in it—because he'd fallen in love with her.

The discovery was still fresh in Matthew's mind when he answered a knock at the door to find Shannon standing on the veranda. He smiled, glad to see her, but she didn't smile in return.

"May I speak with you, Matthew?"

"Of course." He motioned for her to come in.

"Alone?"

"Sun Ling isn't here right now and Todd fell asleep in the parlor. He's been having bad dreams at night."

"Oh," she said, "I'm sorry to hear that." But she didn't step inside the house.

After waiting a few moments in silence, Matthew was the one to move out onto the veranda.

Shannon turned and walked to the railing, her eyes trained on the three horses in the corral.

He had the feeling she didn't want him standing too close. "What's wrong, Shannon?"

"I need . . . I need to ask you something."

He moved to stand at the railing as well but kept a respectful distance.

She turned her head to look at him. "Why do you want to marry me? Why did you propose?"

"Why? Well, I—"

"Was it because of Todd? So there would be a woman to look after him while you were away?"

Put in those words, it sounded bad. But there were plenty of marriages in the world that had begun for worse reasons.

Her face grew pale. "Is that the only reason?" she asked, her voice cracking.

"Shannon, I—"

"You plan to return to driving again, don't you?"

"I don't know. I used to want to, but . . . but things are different now."

"Things are different now," she echoed in a whisper. "You never said you loved me. I should have known it was only because of Todd."

He took a step toward her. "It's not. I *do* love you."

"No." She shook her head as she matched his movement by taking a step back. "Don't lie to me just so I'll marry you. Just so I'll be there to look after Todd. At least be kind in that regard."

"I'm not lying."

"It's all so painfully clear. I don't know why I didn't see it before. Alice wanted me to marry you because of Todd. You wanted me to marry you because of Todd. That's why you proposed. That's why the wedding needed to take place so quickly. Because Alice was about to die and Todd would need a new mother. A wife is preferable to a governess, I'm sure."

Matthew didn't know what to say. Shannon was right. She was right about all of it. Everything except for the part about him not loving her, and he'd only begun to understand his true feelings this very day.

"You must think me a fool," she said softly.

"No, I don't."

"Or perhaps you think me desperate for a husband."

"Of course not." His voice rose in frustration. If she would just give him a chance to explain.

She headed for the steps. "I'll send Father for Ginny. You needn't take care of her any longer. Not now that we've broken our engagement."

"Broken our . . . ? Shannon, wait. Please."

He reached for her arm but she pulled away. Then she was off and running, out of the yard, down the street, and around the corner, taking herself from his view.

Hot tears burned Shannon's throat and eyes. Blinded by them, it was a wonder she didn't stumble and fall headlong into the street. Halfway to the parsonage, she stopped and wiped the tears away.

What was she to do now? She wasn't ready to tell her father what had happened. She wasn't ready to tell him that she couldn't marry Matthew. *Wouldn't* marry Matthew.

"I do *love you.*" His voice in her head caused the tears to flow again.

Lifting her skirt, she turned and headed away from the parsonage, following the road into the mountains, up into the trees where she'd gone riding with Matthew and Todd, to the place where Matthew had kissed her the first time. Pain knifed through her chest at the memory.

So this was what a broken heart felt like.

She'd grieved the loss of her mother. She'd mourned the death of Benjamin. But this was different somehow.

I should have known. I should have known he didn't love me. I should have known I needed him to love me.

If only she could hate him. She wanted to hate him. She wanted once again to think him a foolish, ignorant man—if for no other reason than he wasn't a Confederate sympathizer. She wanted to believe him beneath her contempt. Just as she'd thought him that first morning in Grand Coeur. But it wasn't in her to hate him, and she knew him too well now to think him foolish or ignorant. He'd loved his sister and he loved his nephew. He'd tried to do right by them. He was still trying to do right by Todd. She was the one who'd read more into his proposal than was there. She was the foolish, ignorant one.

She was the one he didn't love.

She left the narrow, dusty road and sank to the ground under a tall pine. Leaning her back against its trunk, she covered her face with both hands and gave in to the tears. She didn't try to hold back the sobs. Who would hear her? She cried until she had no more tears left. Until she was spent and her breaths came in tiny gasps. Until at last she fell as silent as the forest surrounding her.

Conscious thought left her. There was only the silence . . . and the emptiness of her heart.

Matthew and Todd went looking for Shannon, first at the parsonage, then at the church. The reverend was in the latter location, but he hadn't seen his daughter since breakfast.

"What's wrong, Matthew?" her father asked.

"I'm afraid I've hurt her, Reverend Adair."

"Hurt her?"

Matthew glanced toward the doorway, wanting to resume his search. "She's broken our engagement." He looked again at the reverend.

Delaney Adair's expression made it obvious Shannon hadn't spoken to her father before going to see Matthew.

"Reverend, would it be all right if Todd stayed with you for a while? I need to find Shannon. I need to explain and I . . . I think it would be better if we could talk in private."

"Of course. Of course." Reverend Adair motioned for Todd to come stand beside him. "God go with you, Matthew."

"Thank you, sir."

When Matthew stepped outside a few moments later, he said a quick prayer. Where had Shannon gone, if not home? Into town? He didn't think it likely. To call upon a woman friend perhaps? Who would that be? Alice had been her closest—and perhaps only—friend in Grand Coeur. To the dress shop to cancel her wedding gown? Even that seemed improbable.

His gaze was drawn to the north. She would want to be alone. At least he would if he were in her shoes. He set off, following the road out of town and into the mountains.

Help me find her, Lord. Help me explain.

Explain? He wasn't sure an explanation would help anything. He had to convince her of his true feelings, the ones he hadn't been smart enough to recognize until it was too late.

Almost too late, he amended silently. He wasn't giving up yet. *Almost too late.*

With long strides, he followed the road until he reached the trees. Only then did he slow his pace. He wanted to shout her name, but he was afraid she wouldn't answer him if he did. Worse, she might try to hide herself. He couldn't risk it. He had to find her, had to convince her of his love. For the more he thought about it, the more he realized he couldn't imagine life without her by his side.

Alice knew. He stopped for a moment, mulling this new revelation. *Alice knew I loved Shannon.*

No wonder his sister had urged him to propose. It hadn't been for the sake of her son alone. It had been for Matthew's sake as well. Just like she'd said.

He moved on, raking the forest with his gaze. If Shannon had come into the mountains, if he'd chosen the right road, he could still miss her. Her dress, as he recalled, was the same color as the mule deer that populated these mountains, a perfect shade for blending in with nature.

And then he saw her, sitting on the ground about ten or fifteen yards above the road, her back against a tree. Her knees were drawn up to her chest beneath her gown, and she hugged her legs with her arms, her face buried in the folds of her skirt at her knees.

I'm the cause of her sadness.

He moved up the incline toward her. When a twig snapped beneath his boot, he heard a small gasp of surprise as she raised her head. There was no welcome in her eyes when she saw who it was.

He stopped. "Shannon, we need to talk."

"Please go away." She scrambled to her feet.

"We can't leave things like this."

"Of course we can." She looked around, as if she thought she might find a way of escape, a place where he could not follow.

She wouldn't find such a place. He'd follow her to hell and back if that's what it took to convince her he wanted her as his wife, convince her of his love.

"Please go away," she repeated. She headed for the road, giving him a wide berth.

Matthew turned and followed. "Look, Shannon. Maybe you're right about why I proposed in the first place. But only because I hadn't had a chance to recognize what I felt for you. How could I? Alice was sick and I had a new job and I've never felt anything like this before."

She didn't reply except to quicken her pace.

"Shannon, please."

Up ahead of them, a horse and buggy trotted into view from the other side of a small rise in the road.

Shannon raised her right arm and called out, "Wait!" Then she broke into a run. "Mr. Burkette! Wait!"

Recognizing the driver of the buggy at the same time Shannon called his name, Matthew came to a halt, a curse word rising in his throat. He swallowed it back.

Joe Burkette stopped the horse and waited for Shannon to reach him. Matthew couldn't hear what she said, but Burkette nodded and gave her a hand into the buggy. Then he turned the horse around and headed back in the direction of Grand Coeur.

Matthew could learn to hate that man.

Once again, Delaney Adair found himself praying on behalf of his only child. In the course of the past twenty-five years, he had come to believe that God gave people children equally as much for what the children would teach their parents as for what the parents would teach their children. And being a father had certainly kept Delaney on his knees, depending upon God's help and guidance.

No matter how many times or how many ways he'd asked Shannon to tell him what happened between her and Matthew, she only shook her head, refusing to answer.

"Lord, was I wrong to give my consent to Matthew? Is he not the man I thought him?"

That was difficult to believe. No, Delaney was quite sure Matthew was a decent man and that his daughter loved him. He was also certain Matthew was trying to mend whatever rift had torn the two young people apart. He'd come to the parsonage on three separate occasions, asking to see Shannon. She'd refused to see him every time.

"She can be stubborn, Lord." He released a humorless chuckle. "As can I."

If Adelyn were still alive, she would be able to find a way to make Shannon open up to her. Alas, she wasn't still alive. Delaney would have to try harder, pray more, listen better.

"I'm not giving up," Matthew said to Jack. "I'm going to change her mind about marrying me if it takes a month of Sundays to do it."

The sheriff leaned back in his desk chair and clasped his hands behind his head. "I believe you will."

"If she'd just listen to me. If she'd just give me five minutes."

"Never pictured you the sort to moon over a woman."

"Never pictured it myself."

"You know what you need? A few days away. Give her a chance to realize she misses you."

Matthew grunted. What good would going away do? She wasn't missing him now.

"Did you know there's a big shipment of treasure going down to Boise City on Monday?"

"No." He shook his head. "Hadn't heard. I haven't been into the office this week."

"Well, it isn't general knowledge. Good to know the word hasn't gotten out. The stage is due in tomorrow night from Idaho City, then it'll head south on Monday morning."

Matthew waited. His friend wasn't given to talk for talk's sake, so there had to be a point to telling him this.

"Bill Washburn asked me yesterday if my deputy could ride along.

Wells, Fargo has a messenger riding along, of course, but Bill's anxious about it. I can't spare Horace right now. Tempers have been rising right along with the temperatures, and it seems like more troublemakers arrive in Grand Coeur every week." He motioned with his head toward the jail in the back of the sheriff's office. "Our cells are full up this morning."

Matthew nodded.

"Maybe you could go along on Monday as an extra guard."

"You're forgetting my nephew. I can't just take off the way I used to."

"You'd be back Tuesday morning. You could find someone to look after the boy until then. What about that gal you've got cooking for you?"

"Sun Ling? She's already doing more than I hired her to do."

"He could stay with Bill for a night."

"I don't know. Bill's never been much on kids." Matthew rubbed the back of his neck. It might be good to go. Take his mind off his troubles with Shannon. Maybe give him a fresh perspective.

"Or what about the reverend and Miss Adair? She might be mad at you, but sure as shootin' she still cares about that boy."

Matthew sat straighter in his chair. His friend might have hit upon something there. Might be the best thing in the world, leaving his nephew in Shannon's care. Maybe God would use Todd to bring Matthew and Shannon back together.

He stood. "I'll see what I can arrange, Jack. I'll let you know."

He left the sheriff's office feeling more hopeful than he'd felt since Shannon broke their engagement. His feet carried him straight to the express office. Fortunately, no customers were there when he arrived, so he and William could talk plainly. "Jack told me about the special shipment coming in tomorrow."

"Yeah, and I don't figure I'll draw a decent breath until they get here from Idaho City, and then I'll feel the same way after they leave the next morning."

"How about if I go along as an extra guard for the trip down to Boise?" Matthew said.

"You? Messengin' again?"

"Why not? I'm almost as good pointing a rifle and shotgun as I am holding the reins."

"What about the boy?"

"I think I can arrange for someone to keep Todd for one trip."

"If you can, maybe I could relax a little."

Dearest Katie,

The wedding is off. I have broken my engagement to Matthew Dubois. It seems he only wanted a woman to care for his nephew, and he thought I was the best choice.

I know you would tell me that many a good marriage has begun for similar reasons—a widower needing someone to care for his children—and that many of those marriages turn into happy ones. Maybe I am silly and selfish. But I want to be loved the way that I love. Is that so very wrong, my dear friend?

I've told myself a thousand times that I no longer love Matthew, but that isn't true. I do love him. I can't stop loving him, and my heart is breaking. Today I wanted to plead with Father to take me back to Virginia. I thought I could be happy here, but I cannot. Not now. Sometimes I think I will never be happy again.

Matthew has asked Father and me to keep Todd while he takes a stagecoach down to Boise City on Monday morning. Father agreed to do it without asking my opinion. I would have refused. I don't think I can bear the reminder of what was to be.

Oh, Katie. Whatever am I to do? How I wish I could see you and talk to you and ask your thoughts. My heart was wounded when Benjamin was killed on the battlefield. But this is worse. Much worse.

Your devoted friend,
Shannon Adair

Shannon folded the letter to her friend and was slipping it into the envelope when a soft rap sounded on her bedroom door. "Yes, Father," she said, twisting on the chair.

The door opened a few inches. "May I come in?"

"Of course."

"Don't you think it's time you told me what's caused the trouble between you and Matthew?"

She shook her head. "I can't."

"Wounds exposed to the light heal more quickly."

"I'm sorry, Father." She looked down at the envelope on the writing desk. "I'm not ready to talk about it."

"I have the feeling he will keep trying to see you, Shannon. He doesn't seem inclined to give up easily."

"I hope you're wrong."

"Do you, my girl? I'm not convinced. Whatever he said or did, he seems determined to make it up to you. If what he's done is a matter of integrity, then that's one thing. But if it's merely your hurt pride that is keeping you from hearing him out, that is keeping you from healing the rift between you, that is something else again. Pride is cold comfort, dear girl."

She nodded, fighting tears, and was glad when she heard him take a step back and close the door.

The driver of the stage, Levi Jefferson, was about ten years older than Matthew, a man with leathered skin and a smile that revealed two missing teeth. Although they'd never met before, they knew each other by reputation. What Matthew had heard about Levi, he liked. And when he learned that the stage was carrying 250 pounds of gold bullion out of Idaho City—at the current rate of exchange, the treasure was valued at over a million dollars—he was even more glad for a seasoned driver holding the reins. No wonder the transport had been kept secret. No wonder William had been nervous and anxious for another guard.

Matthew would have liked it better if they could have made the trip down to Boise City without passengers. But if they hadn't allowed passengers, it might have drawn attention. Better not to do that. Wells, Fargo had announced this as a route change, nothing more. The stage shouldn't be at any more risk than any other coach leaving one of the gold camps—and that risk had been high for a long time.

Matthew stood back and watched as six paying passengers climbed into the coach for the journey down to the capital of the territory. Next, the messenger, Barclay Jones—a lad of about eighteen or twenty who looked like his smooth skin had yet to feel a blade scraping off facial hair—climbed onto the roof of the coach, leaving the seat next to Levi for Matthew.

Had he ever been as green as that kid looked? he wondered as he settled into place.

"All right, folks," Levi called to the passengers. "Hold tight."

With his left hand, Matthew gripped the double-barreled shotgun that rested on his thighs as Levi slapped the reins against the horses' backsides. The coach jerked forward. Levi kept the horses to a jog until they were out of town. Then he asked for speed, and they gave it. Dust rose in a cloud from the bone-dry road. The coach rocked and bucked, familiar and strange at the same time.

"I heard you were gettin' married," Levi said in a loud voice.

"I'm planning to." *If I can change the bride's mind.*

"Gonna give up drivin' coach altogether?"

He rolled the question over in his mind, examining it from every side before answering, "Yeah, I reckon I will."

"Don't think I could stay in one place for long. I like my freedom. Unfettered."

"That's what I thought when I took the agent position for the summer." He looked at the driver. "Being unfettered doesn't seem all that important to me anymore. I discovered I like being part of a family."

He recalled coming home from the express office and sitting down to supper with Alice and Todd—and sometimes with Shannon. It had been good. He'd liked it. Home. Family. Wife. Kids. They'd always seemed right for others but not for him.

He couldn't have been more wrong.

Shannon pressed her face against Ginny's neck and fought another wave of tears, determined not to cry in front of Todd, who waited for her outside the livery stall.

"Shannon, we need to talk."

How she longed to talk to Matthew. How she missed the sound of his voice.

"We can't leave things like this."

Had she been wrong to walk away? To run away? No, he should have told her he didn't love her when he proposed. He should have admitted that it was a marriage of convenience, for the sake of his nephew.

"I do love you."

She couldn't stop the tears now. They tracked down her cheeks and dampened the bay's coat.

"I hadn't had a chance to recognize what I felt for you . . . I've never felt anything like this before."

"Neither have I," she whispered.

Ginny nickered softly.

"I do love you . . . Shannon, please."

Her pulse quickened.

"I do love you . . . Shannon, please."

The memory of her father's words replaced Matthew's. *"But if it's merely your hurt pride that is keeping you from hearing him out, that is keeping you from healing the rift between you, that is something else again."*

But it wasn't only hurt pride . . . Was it?

"Pride is cold comfort, dear girl."

She straightened away from the horse. "What have I done? Why didn't I listen to Matthew?"

Pride. Oh, her cursed pride. Her father was right. If only—

"What are you doing, boy?" Joe Burkette's voice cut into her private thoughts, the tone sharp and demanding. "Get that dog out of here."

Shannon wiped away her tears before stepping out of the stall. "Todd and Nugget are with me, Mr. Burkette."

A smile replaced his scowl. "Miss Adair. I didn't know it was you." If he noticed she'd been crying, he didn't let on.

Joe had come to her rescue the previous week when she'd needed to escape Matthew, but that hadn't made her like him any more than before. Still, as long as she needed to board her horse in his stables, she would have to get used to seeing him.

"There is good news out of Richmond," he said. "Have you heard?"

She shook her head.

"Last week, General Early broke through the Union forces southeast of Frederick, Maryland, and his troops entered the District of Columbia. They had to withdraw the next night, but I predict the general will go on harassing the Yankees for some time to come."

Why didn't the news make her happy? It was obvious Joe thought it should. And he was right. It should. It would have not all that long ago. Now all she could think about was that people were suffering, many were dying, on both sides of the conflict.

Joe took a step closer, lowering his voice, implying his words were confidential. "There should be more good news for the Confederacy today. Money, and lots of it. Gold for guns and ammunition and food. It could help turn the tide of the war."

Shannon felt a flutter of nerves in her stomach—and once again wondered why what Joe had said didn't bring her pleasure.

"We should know soon enough." He glanced toward the main entrance into the stables. "Shouldn't be long."

Shannon reached with one hand to close the stall door, then held out her other hand toward the boy. "We'd best go, Todd. Father will be wondering what's keeping us so long." Glancing again at Joe, she said, "Good day, Mr. Burkette."

They walked outside, into the bright morning light. Already the July sun was hot. At the parsonage, a shady spot on the porch awaited them. But instead of setting off in the direction of the church, she continued down Montgomery Street into the heart of town.

"I thought we were goin' to your house," Todd said.

"We are. I just . . . I just need to see someone first."

"Who?"

Who, indeed. But that niggling feeling wouldn't leave her, and she realized she wanted—*needed*—to see Matthew.

She quickened her pace, pulling Todd along with her.

The stage slowed as it approached the sharp bend in the road, rocking to the left as they began the turn. A moment later, one of the lead horses gave a cry of alarm, and Levi braced his feet as he pulled back on the reins. The coach ground to a halt. A half dozen men on horseback, neckerchiefs covering the lower half of their faces, blocked the road. Their guns and rifles were leveled directly at Levi and Matthew.

"Morning, gentlemen," one of the masked men said as he nudged his horse forward. "I believe you should throw down the bullion so we can all be on our way and no one will get hurt."

"Perhaps you should come and get it," Levi replied, a snarl in his voice.

One of the passengers leaned out the window. "What's going on?"

Matthew barked an order. "Stay inside."

The leader of the band of thieves chuckled. "Very good advice. Now about that bullion."

Levi looked at Matthew, as if hoping he had another alternative. Unfortunately, he didn't.

The leader raised his voice, presumably so the passengers could hear him equally as well as the men atop the stage. "Gentlemen, we are not thieves. We are Confederate soldiers, and all we want is to relieve you of the treasure being carried by Wells, Fargo & Company as an agent of the Union government. The gold will assist us in recruiting for the Confederate Army."

If Matthew wasn't mistaken, the speech was almost identical to one the notorious Red Fox—a Confederate captain by the name of Rufus Henry Ingram—had given two months earlier during the robbery of a stage coming out of Virginia City carrying silver bullion from the Comstock. The newspapers had dubbed him "the gentlemanly robber" and his compatriots had been referred to as "Jeff Davis men." After shooting a sheriff and deputy, he'd escaped capture in California. Looked like the rumors of his coming to Idaho rather than hightailing it back to Missouri were true.

The six men were well armed, and Matthew could be certain the Red Fox and his band of thieves wouldn't hesitate to use their weapons if provoked. "Better give them what they want," he said to Levi, his gaze never leaving Captain Ingram.

Muttering something unintelligible, Levi wrapped the reins around the brake handle before reaching into the boot for the first heavy bag.

From behind Matthew, Barclay Jones whispered, "I think I can take him."

Matthew had forgotten the kid was there. He opened his mouth to tell the young messenger not to do anything stupid, but before he could speak, gunfire exploded near his left ear.

Horses reared and whinnied. The stagecoach bucked and jerked. More guns fired. Something hit Matthew, something that sent him flying off the driver's seat. He hit the ground hard, his ears ringing, the air knocked from his lungs.

I'm shot. The realization was accompanied by a feeling of surprise, though it shouldn't have surprised him. It wasn't the first time he'd faced thieves or been fired upon, though it was the first time anyone had hit his target.

He struggled to drag in a breath of air. Then the road seemed to give way beneath him, and he was tumbling down the hillside.

"Sorry, Miss Adair," William Washburn said to Shannon. "Stage left more'n an hour ago."

Of course. Of course he was already gone. Why had she thought he would still be here?

The young clerk who worked in the express office cleared his throat. "Excuse me, Mr. Washburn."

William looked over his shoulder. "What is it, Ray? Can't you see I'm busy with Miss Adair?"

"Yessir. But I think you'd better have a look at this telegram. It's for the sheriff."

William released a sound of frustration as he turned away from the counter. "What is it?" He took the paper from the clerk's hand, began to read, then glanced up, his expression altered. "I'll be back," he said to Shannon before skirting the counter and heading for the door.

"What on earth?" Shannon looked at Ray. "What was that about?"

"News from Idaho City. The sheriff there got word a gang of Confederate robbers might be after the treasure that left here this morning."

"We should know soon enough." Joe Burkette's words echoed in Shannon's mind. He had known about the Confederate plan to rob the stage. That was what he'd meant when he'd said it shouldn't be long. And even as that realization swept over her, she remembered the conversation she'd overheard in the livery stables several weeks before. *"We're all tired of waiting,"* Joe had said then. This was what he'd been waiting for. She was sure of it.

Another memory pushed the others from her head. The image of another robbery attempt and the bloodied, wounded passenger as he was carried to the doctor's office.

"Oh, Matthew," she whispered, spinning toward the door. "Be careful. Dear God, don't let anything happen to him."

Matthew returned to consciousness—and wished himself back into oblivion at once. Pain radiated from somewhere on the left side of his body. He couldn't be sure where he'd been hit, wasn't sure he wanted to look.

He opened his eyes. The sky was pale blue, the sun relentless, baking the ground around him. He turned his head slightly to one side, feeling as if the grit of the hillside was grinding into his skull.

He seemed to recall that his tumble down from the road had been steep and taken a long time to end. So much for trusted recollection when a man got shot. He wasn't much more than three or four yards down a slight incline.

What surprised him more was that the stagecoach was nowhere in sight. How long had he been out? Where had they gone?

He tried to sit up, and pain detonated in his body afresh. He cried out and fell back, squeezing his eyes shut.

But it wasn't physical pain he was trying to shut out. It was knowing that Levi Jefferson never would have left Matthew behind. Not as long as he was still alive. And what about the kid? Barclay. Was he dead too?

He should have been more vigilant. He should have been prepared at every turn in the winding road south for a band of robbers. Wasn't this exactly what William had worried would happen?

He thought about trying to move again. He should at least see how bad the bleeding was. Not that he could do much about it. He opened his eyes once more, gritted his teeth, and lifted his head off the ground enough to explore. The left side of his shirt had turned a maroon color as the blood dried. It looked like God had been watching out for him. A few more inches to the right, and the bullet would have pierced his heart.

His tumble down the hillside had been stopped by a clump of prickly shrubs. He needed to get away from them. He needed to get up to the road. He had to try . . .

A wave of dizziness washed over him, and he closed his eyes, waiting for it to pass. Instead, blackness enveloped him once again.

Shannon promised God a host of things as she galloped Ginny along the road toward Boise. It didn't matter that her father had taught her from the time she was a small child that one doesn't bargain with the Almighty as one would barter with a street vendor. *"We ask because of His mercy, Shannon,"* he'd said. *"We trust because we know He loves us. Does a father give a child a stone when he asks for bread?"*

But the lifelong lessons were lost on Shannon now. She would do anything, promise anything, that might allow her to find Matthew and tell him she loved him and wanted to be with him for the rest of her life.

It seemed as if she'd been riding for an eternity. She'd left Grand Coeur as soon as was humanly possible after the stage thundered back into town with the news of the shooting and robbery.

Please let me find him. Please let me find him.

The young express messenger—wounded and bleeding—had managed to bring the stage back to Grand Coeur as the driver lay dying beside him. He was the one who'd told her Matthew had fallen at a sharp bend in the road.

A bend in the road. A sharp bend. But there are so many of them. Help me, God. Please help me.

How far ahead of her were the sheriff and his posse? Might they have seen Matthew, stopped to help him? But Jack Dickson had left town soon after the telegram from Idaho City was received. Even if the posse had met the coach on its return, they might not know about Matthew. They were after the gang of Confederate thieves, not a wounded employee of Wells, Fargo & Company.

Let me find him, God. Let me help him.

How far behind were others from Grand Coeur who would join in the search for Matthew? Would the doctor be with them?

Please let the doctor be with them.

Because of the months she'd worked in the army hospital in Virginia, Shannon knew a great deal about gunshot wounds. She could write a long list of things that could go wrong with a patient who'd been shot. And all of those things that could go wrong swirled in her mind in time with the pounding of Ginny's hooves on the dirt road.

Then she saw a bend up ahead. A *sharp* bend. That had to be it. That had to be it.

"Matthew!" she cried. "Matthew, can you hear me?"

She pulled back on the reins and dismounted before the mare had come to a complete stop. She stumbled and nearly fell, caught herself, and hurried on to the edge of the road, her eyes scanning the hillside that fell away to the creek below.

"Matthew!"

Panic threatened to overwhelm her. Where was he? Was she mistaken? Wasn't this the bend the messenger had told her about? Had she already passed the place where Matthew had fallen? Or was it farther south from here? Should she go back or ride on?

"Matthew!"

And then she heard it. A groan? A gasp? A sigh? So soft she couldn't be sure she'd heard it at all. No, she was sure. She moved along the edge of the road until she saw him. Her heart skittered crazily in her chest as she rushed, slipped, and slid down the loose dirt and shale until she reached him.

Dropping to her knees, she spoke his name again, softly this time. "Matthew."

He looked up at her, pain and confusion mingling together in their blue depths. "Shannon?"

"Yes, it's me." She wanted to cry but refused to let herself give in to tears. Not when he was in need of her care. "Don't move. Help is coming. You're going to be all right." *Make it true, God. Please make it true.* "I love you," she added, needing him to know her feelings before he drifted back into unconsciousness—or worse.

Matthew wasn't sure if he was living or dead because some of the people he saw in this dimly lit place—was it a room? was it a cave? was it heaven?—were living and some were dead. Alice was there, looking pale but happy. Todd was there, tearful and scared but trying not to show it. The reverend was there, praying for him, encouraging him. His parents were there, smiling but never speaking. The doctor was there, telling him to lie still.

And Shannon was there. Shannon was always there. Holding his hand. Wiping his brow with a cool cloth. Giving him sips of water. Whispering that she loved him.

He must be dead. He could hardly believe she would say those words if he were alive.

Shannon had stopped trying to make deals with God and, throughout the rest of the day and the long night that followed, had instead thanked the Lord time and again for sparing Matthew's life. Now, as pink and golden ribbons of daylight began to wiggle and stretch across this room, she felt a great need for the Almighty's forgiveness and for the power from His Holy Spirit to change.

Lord, forgive me for my willfulness. Forgive me for being so quick to judge others. Forgive my foolish, foolish temper. Forgive my pride.

"Shannon."

At the sound of Matthew's voice, she straightened in the chair, her eyes flying open. "Matthew." She took his right hand between both of hers.

"Where am I?"

"At the parsonage. In Father's room. We wanted to take care of you, and Father thought it best that we bring you here."

Matthew grimaced and a soft groan escaped his lips. Then, after a long pause, he said, "The driver?"

"Mr. Jefferson died."

He nodded, as if he'd expected that would be her answer. "What about the kid?"

"Do you mean Barclay Jones?"

"Yeah."

"He's fine. He was wounded, too, but not terribly. It was Mr. Jones who drove the stage back to Grand Coeur."

"And the passengers?"

She leaned closer. "We can talk about all this later. You should rest."

"The passengers," he said, determination in his tone.

"No one else was hurt."

He closed his eyes for a short while, and she wondered if he'd slipped off to sleep again. But he soon opened them, this time asking, "Did the robbers get away with all the gold?"

"No." She gave him a little smile as she pressed his hand between hers. "They didn't get away with it. The sheriff and his posse ran them to ground. One robber was shot and killed. Three more were captured, along with the treasure. The leader and another man escaped, but not with any of the gold shipment." She could tell him later about Joe Burkette's involvement and how the sheriff in Idaho City had been able to give some warning of the thieves' plans. Enough that the posse could recover the gold. Enough so that Matthew's life was spared.

His expression softened. "I never expected it to be you who came looking for me."

"I had to find you. I had to tell you that . . . that I love you."

"So I wasn't dreaming that?"

"No. No, it wasn't a dream." She leaned in and kissed his cheek. "I was such a fool. To get so angry. To not give you a chance to explain. To be so quick to judge. To let my stupid pride be wounded."

Another twinge of pain tightened his features. When it had passed, he said, "I loved you before I knew I did. But Alice knew." He released a sound that was part laugh, part grunt. "My sister was always smarter than me."

"She was smarter than me too."

"Will you marry me, Shannon? Not for Todd's sake. For mine."

Although her heart leapt at his words, she said, "We can talk about that when you're better."

"I'll get better faster if you say yes."

"Then yes."

He smiled, already looking stronger. "You didn't say that as my nurse, did you? Just to make me well?"

"No." She returned the smile. "I said it because I love you."

He released a breath, his eyes drifting closed. "Good."

Words from the Bible whispered in her heart: *"Ask, and it shall be given you; seek, and ye shall find; knock, and it shall be opened unto you: For every one that asketh receiveth; and he that seeketh findeth; and to him that knocketh it shall be opened."*

Oh, she knew those words of the Savior had far deeper meaning than giving her the desire of her heart. But she had asked for Matthew's life, and it had been given her. Even before she'd asked, God had seen and known and designed it all so that she would find herself in this place, in this moment, loving him.

"Every good gift and every perfect gift is from above, and cometh down from the Father of lights."

"Thank You," she whispered before leaning back in her chair, closing her eyes, and resting in Him.

EPILOGUE

AUGUST 1864

Look at her, Adelyn. Have you ever seen a more beautiful bride than our Shannon?

Delaney smiled as his daughter walked down the aisle toward him.

Yes, Shannon was beautiful. But Delaney saw something much more wonderful about his daughter than mere physical perfection. He saw a young woman at peace, a young woman whose faith had been deepened and refined through testing. A young woman willing to risk love and receive love.

His prayers for his daughter had been answered, were still being answered.

He looked away from her. In the pews were their friends—friends he hadn't known they would make when he'd prayed about coming to Idaho Territory last winter. Many were members of his congregation. Some were people without faith in Christ, Jack Dickson among them. And a few knew the Lord but were of another race—Wu Lok and Sun Jie and Sun Ling. How gratified he was that they had come. How he prayed for a world where the color of a person's skin made them beautiful in the eyes of others. Different and yet loved the same by God.

We will make a difference here, Adelyn. Shannon and her husband even more than I because they still have their whole lives before them. We will put down roots and take care of our neighbors and speak peace into troubled circumstances. We will most likely never again be wealthy in the things of this earth, but we will be rich in all ways that matter. We will be rich in those things that matter to God's kingdom.

Delaney watched as Matthew Dubois reached out and took hold of Shannon's hand.

He was a fine man, his almost son-in-law. Matthew loved the Lord. He loved Shannon. He loved his nephew. Wherever life took this couple from today forward, they would lean into God for strength and guidance. They would trust the Lord to work all things for good in their lives. Knowing that made it much easier for Delaney to release his daughter into Matthew's care.

Life is ever changing, Adelyn. You understood that far better than I. It's exciting. Looking into the future, wondering what God shall accomplish.

Delaney smiled at the couple before him. "Dearly beloved, we are gathered together here in the sight of God and in the face of this company . . ."

Nevertheless, Lord, may Thy will be done.

A NOTE TO READERS

DEAR FRIENDS:

If there is anything I've learned through the years, it's that life has a way of interrupting my carefully laid plans. When I came up with the idea for the novel that would eventually become *Heart of Gold,* I didn't realize how difficult it would be to get it written. Not because the story would be hard to write (well, no more so than any of my previous books), but because I was in for a series of trials—shattering three bones in my ankle, an injury that would remain non-weight-bearing for several months; the death of my beloved mother at the age of ninety-six; and finally a cancer diagnosis followed by surgery and treatment. All of which laid waste to my writing schedule. To say that I learned over the course of those months to lean into God and to trust Him in a whole new way is a gross understatement.

I have long been a person who knows how to worry like a dog over a bone. I can chew and stew and fret and fuss with the best of them. But something happened to me in the aforementioned life storms—I was at peace.

Oh, it wasn't fun to go through the broken ankle, and I certainly had moments when I wondered how I was going to pay the mounting medical bills. But even when my brain asked, "How will I manage?" my heart answered, "Trust God." I wasn't afraid. I pressed in and pressed on (which, not surprisingly, were the words God had given to me at the start of 2010). I pressed into Jesus and pressed on in faith.

Of course I deeply grieved the passing of my mom. She was always there for me, every moment, every step, every day of my life. She was the best example of what it means to be a woman of faith. She was also my greatest fan and cheerleader. Even in those last months of her life when she was so frail and her mind was no longer sharp, she always introduced me to others like this: "This is my daughter Robin. She's an author. She writes wonderful books." Yes, I will always miss my mom. And yet I had peace with her passing, for I knew without a doubt that she was and is with her Savior, free of pain and the restrictions of a physical body grown old and tired.

But the complete and utter peace that blanketed me from that first moment I heard the doctor say, "It's cancer"—and the peace that stayed with me every moment after that—was unmistakably an act of a merciful God. So much so that there was no room left for worry and doubt to push their way in. The Comforter had come, and I could be at rest.

Well, finally and at last—and with the help and guidance of my wonderful and very patient editors—*Heart of Gold* did get written. I don't know if it is different than the book it might have been had I not passed through those life storms in 2010 and 2011. However, I imagine it must be somewhat different since *I* am somewhat different. I hope it's a story that you've enjoyed reading.

I have a couple of historical notes to share with you:

First, I took creative license in regard to the telegraph being present in the Boise Basin in 1864. Although telegraphy may have existed between towns in the territory (the Civil War was the first war where the commanders in chief received quick updates on battles, thanks to the telegraph), I was unable to rule it in or out. However, research tells me the first telegraph wires from outside the territory didn't arrive into Idaho until 1866.

Second, I also took creative license with Confederate Captain Rufus Henry Ingram, the Red Fox. There is no historical data that I found saying he was ever in Idaho Territory. The "gentlemanly robber" did escape capture in California in the late spring of 1864 and he did reportedly make it back to Missouri. I saw no reason for him not to continue his efforts to steal treasure that was being shipped out of the gold camps in Idaho before going back to the South.

In closing, I would like to tell you how much the e-mails and Facebook messages and comments on my blog meant to me during the above-mentioned life storms. I will forever be grateful for the prayers of so many readers, especially those who make up my prayer team. You have shared wisdom and comfort and laughter with me over and over and over again. You're still sharing all of that with me today, and I am filled with thanksgiving to God for each one of you. How very amazing that the Lord has given me an abundance of friends, most of whom I shall not meet this side of heaven.

At the end of my cancer treatments, I told some family and friends that I was looking forward to life returning to normal and that I wouldn't even mind a period of boring. My brother told me I shouldn't ask for boring because that would mean I wasn't living. He's right. Better to embrace it all as an adventure, especially since I know that God has plans for my life, plans for my future, plans that give me hope. He has wonderful and unique plans for you as well.

So now it's time to get back to work on my next book. I must see what sort of mischief I can stir up for a particular hero and heroine. Because, after all, they need to embrace the adventure right along with you and me.

In the grip of His grace,
Robin
www.robinleehatcher.com

READING GROUP GUIDE

1. In the beginning of the story, Shannon finds herself in a place she despises. Have you ever been somewhere that you'd rather not be? How did you handle your emotions? Did you ask God to help change your attitude?
2. A lifelong bachelor, Matthew struggles with the unexpected situation of taking in his sister and nephew. Have you ever encountered such an unplanned responsibility? Have family obligations ever required you to drastically alter your plans? If so, how did you deal with the changes?
3. Even in the face of death, Alice maintains incredible amounts of faith and courage. Have you ever known someone like Alice? When you encounter something frightening, how does God come to your aid?
4. According to Reverend Adair, every person is loved equally by God, no matter that person's race or politics; and he hopes that one day the divided town of Grand Coeur can be united under his church's roof. How do we let such differences get in the way

of bringing people together? How can Christians work against the divisive forces of prejudice?

5. When Matthew discovers how sick his sister really is, he feels guilt for not being a better brother to her in the past. Have you ever regretted neglecting a friend or family member during their time of need? Is it possible to make up for lost time?
6. Though Shannon arrives in Grand Coeur as a Confederate sympathizer, she soon becomes close to people whose politics could not be more different from hers. Have you ever become friends with people with whom you completely disagree on some things? What do you think it means to "live peaceably with all men" (Romans 12:18)?
7. Reverend Adair is an example of one who prays without ceasing. How does his constant prayer impact his own life, as well as the lives of others in the story? How can we learn from such a model of faithfulness?
8. Upon first meeting Matthew and Alice, Shannon judges them harshly. Have you ever made a judgment about someone, only to befriend that person later? How does it feel to discover you've been wrong about that person all along?
9. Though Alice is at peace with her diagnosis, Matthew wanted to "argue with God" about it. Have you ever had difficulty finding peace with something you can't understand? Why does God ask us to trust Him, especially when we can't comprehend His will?
10. After Shannon and Matthew have broken off their engagement, Reverend Adair tells Shannon that "pride is cold comfort." What does he mean by this? How does pride get in the way of healing broken relationships?

ABOUT THE AUTHOR

Best-selling novelist Robin Lee Hatcher is known for her heartwarming and emotionally charged stories of faith, courage, and love. She discovered her vocation after many years of reading everything she could put her hands on, including the backs of cereal boxes and ketchup bottles. The winner of the Christy Award for Excellence in Christian Fiction (*Whispers from Yesterday*), the RITA Award for Best Inspirational Romance (*Patterns of Love* and *The Shepherd's Voice*), two RT Career Achievement Awards (Americana Romance and Inspirational Fiction), and the RWA Lifetime Achievement Award, Robin is the author of more than sixty novels.

Robin enjoys being with her family, spending time in the beautiful Idaho outdoors, reading books that make her cry, and watching romantic movies. She is passionate about the theater, and several nights every summer, she can be found at the outdoor amphitheater of the Idaho Shakespeare Festival, enjoying plays under the stars. She makes her home on the outskirts of Boise, sharing it with Poppet, the high-maintenance papillon, and Princess Pinky, the kitten who currently terrorizes the household.